SCREAM QUEEN

AND OTHER TALES OF MENACE

Books by Ed Gorman

SCREAM QUEEN

CAGE OF NIGHT

NOIR 13

from Perfect Crime Books

SCREAM QUEEN

AND OTHER TALES OF MENACE

ED GORMAN

With an Introduction by Tom Piccirilli

PERFECT CRIME BOOKS

Printed in the United States of America.
Perfect Crime Books™ is a registered Trademark.

Cover design by J.T. Lindroos

This book is a work of fiction. The characters, entities and institutions are products of the Author's imagination and do not refer to actual persons, entities, or institutions.

Library of Congress Cataloging-in-Publication Data
Gorman, Ed
Scream Queen & Other Tales of Menace / Ed Gorman
ISBN: 978-1-935797-54-8

First Edition: April 2014

To John McHugh

whose front porch was the center of the universe for a bunch
of scruffy Catholic School boys

CONTENTS

Introduction by Tom Piccirilli

Angie   1

The Order of Things Unknown   15

Mother Darkness   30

Scream Queen   38

Cages   58

En Famille   71

Beauty   78

Famous Blue Raincoat   85

Render Unto Caesar   96

Stalker   108

Duty   122

Out There in the Darkness   131

The Brasher Girl   166

Calculated Risk   198

An Afterword, of Sorts   216

Introduction

Back in the early '90s, at the start of my writing career, I was lucky enough to have two incredible men become my mentors. The first was the late fantasist Jack Cady, a teacher and perfectionist in his work. Jack wrote about extraordinary people in extraordinary circumstances. His novels included *The Well*, about a family who for generations build booby traps in their huge home to catch the devil, and *The Man Who Could Make Things Vanish*, about a guy who happens to tumble onto the secret of, well, making things vanish.

The other guy was the amazing Ed Gorman, another perfectionist who wrote from an everyman perspective. You really couldn't put yourself in the shoes of most of Jack's protagonists, but with Ed, he wrote things that you felt and understood, about people who were just like you. That's no easy feat.

His new collection, like all the collections before it, is full of atmospheric, dark tales of folks pushed too far, haunted characters trying to clear their heads or their guilt-laden souls, or who are fast approaching the end of their lives and need that last shot at redemption. Here you'll find several classic pieces, including the heart-shattering "En Famille," the novella "The Brasher Girl," which was later expanded into one of my favorite novels, *Cage of Night*, and "Out There in the Darkness," which became the popular *The Poker Club*.

In those early days I always looked forward to letters from Jack and phone calls from Ed. Ed and I would talk for hours, mostly about noir and hardboiled writers from the '40s and '50s, and thanks to him co-starting the magazine *Mystery Scene*, he'd actually met many of these guys, interviewed them, even become buddies with them. I can remember hunkering down in the dark of my living room in New York, at his bended knee so to speak, as he held court from Iowa and spoke of men and women who made the crime field what it would eventually become: a place of literate, action-packed, honest work that drew in millions of readers. Charles Willeford, Charles Williams, Donald Westlake. In short, Ed blew my mind. But he was always doing that. Blowing my mind. Like with his novel *The Autumn Dead*, which is an annual reread for me. Great fiction draws you in, it puts you in the pages, spins the tale around your ears, makes you see yourself in the clothing of the protagonists, or even the antagonists. Ed's also one of the rare breed who writes short fiction as well he does long fiction. And he does novellas perhaps best of all. To wit, the novellas I've already mentioned as well as the title piece "Scream Queen." Long enough to really pull you in but short enough to speed you along to killer conclusions.

If you know Ed, in life or through his work, then you know why I count myself among the very lucky.

If you don't, then meet him here, on page one. I can guarantee it won't be the last time.

TOM PICCIRILLI
Tom Piccirilli is the author of *The Last Kind Words*.

Angie

Roy said, "He heard us last night."

Angie said, "Heard what?"

"Heard us talking about Gina."

"No, he didn't. He was asleep."

"That's what I thought. But I went back to the can one time and I saw his door was open and I looked in there and he was sittin' up in bed, wide awake. Listenin'."

"He probably'd just woken up."

"He heard us talkin'."

"How do you know?"

"I asked him," Roy said.

"Yeah? And what did he say?"

"He said he didn't."

"See, I told ya."

"Well, he was lyin'."

"How do you know?" she said.

"He's my son, ain't he? That's how I know. I could tell by his face."

"So what if he did hear?"

Roy looked at her, astonished. "So what if he did? He'll go to the cops."

"The cops? Roy, you're crazy. He's nine years old and he's your son."

"That little bastard don't give two turds about me, Angie. He was strictly a mama's boy. And now that he knows . . ."

He didn't need to say it. Angie had been waitressing at a truck stop when she'd met Roy. He was living in a trailer with his son, Jason, and his wife, Gina. He went for Angie immediately. On her nights off, he'd take her to Cedar Rapids, where they'd go to a couple of dance clubs. They always had a great time except when Roy got real drunk and started trouble with black guys who were dating white girls. Roy had some friends who were always talking about blowing up places with blacks and Jews and gays in them. Roy always gave them a certain percentage of his robbery money. That's what Roy did. He robbed banks, usually small-town ones that were located on the edge of town. Roy was a pro. He figured everything out carefully in advance. He knew the exit routes and where the banks kept the video surveillance cameras, and he checked out the teller windows in advance to see which clerk looked most vulnerable. He'd served six years in Fort Madison for sticking up a gas station when he was nineteen. He was thirty-six now and vowed never to be caught again. What she liked about him was that he had a goal in life. There was this one bank in Des Moines where he said he could get half a million on a payroll Friday. They'd go to Vegas and then they'd go see this whites-only compound up in the Utah mountains. That was the only part that Angie didn't like. She didn't understand politics and Roy and his buddies always carrying on about Jews and gays and colored people bored her. She had a way of looking awake when she was really not awake. She did that practically every time Roy and his buddies started talking about some militia deal they had heard about and intended to join. The wife got wind of the courtship between Roy and Angie, though, and raised hell. She wouldn't give him a divorce, and she threatened to tell the cops about all his robberies all over the Midwest. So one rainy night he killed her.

Shoved a knife into her right breast, which silenced her, and then cut her throat. He loaded her into a body bag and packed a hundred pounds of hand weights in there with her and then drove his two-year-old Ford out to the river that very moonglow night and threw her in just below the dam. The only trouble Roy had was his son, Jason. The kid just kept wailin' and carryin' on about where's my mom, where's my mom? He hadn't wanted the kid in the first place, had beat the shit out of her, but she still wouldn't get an abortion. Even back then he'd had the dream of this big Des Moines bank on payroll Friday, and who wanted a kid along when you had all the cash with you? But Gina had her way and Roy was stuck with the little prick. And now Jason had overheard him talkin' about killin' his mother. Roy knew that somehow, some way, the little prick would turn him in.

Roy said, "Don't worry, I'll handle it."

She watched him carefully. "Sometimes you scare the shit out of me, Roy. You really do. He's your own flesh and blood."

"I didn't want him. Gina wanted him."

"And you killed Gina."

"For you," he said. "I killed her for you." Then, "Shit, honey, here we go again. Arguin'. This ain't what I want and it ain't what you want, either. You c'mere now." Then, "A kid like that, he's a ball and chain."

He liked it when she sat in his lap. He liked to feel her up to the point that his erection got so big and bulgy it was downright painful. She'd wriggle on it and make him even crazier. Then, as now, they'd go in on their big mussed sleepwarm bed and do the trick.

Afterward, today, he said, "I better get into town. I want to be there at noontime. See what the place is like around then."

He was scoping out a bank. He was planning to rob it day after tomorrow. Their cash supply was way way down. The trailer park manager was on Roy's ass for back rent. Roy said, "Don't say nothin' to him when he gets home from school."

"All right."

"You just let me handle everything."

"All right."

"It'll be better for us," Roy said, trying to make her feel better. "Haulin' that kid everywhere we go, that isn't the kind of life we want. We want to be free, babe. That's just the kind of people we are. Free."

Roy had killed people before and it had never bothered her. But never a kid before, that she knew of. And his own kid to boot.

He kissed her breasts a final time and then said, "I'll figure out what to do about Jason and then you'n me'll go dancin' tonight. Okay?"

"Okay, Roy."

Roy was gonna kill him for sure.

One day, when Angie was thirteen, her grandmother said, "That body of hers is gonna get her in trouble someday." The irony being that Grandmother herself had had a body just like it—killer breasts and hips that made young men weep in public—when she'd been young. And so had Angie's mother, the person Grandmother was talking to. The thing being that the worst trouble Grandmother had ever gotten in was getting knocked up by a soldier home on leave from WW2, a pregnancy that had brought Angie's mother, Suzie, into the world. The worst Suzie had ever gotten into, in turn, was getting knocked up by a Vietnam soldier home on leave, a pregnancy that had brought Angie into the world.

Angie, however, got into a lot more trouble than just spreading her sweet young thighs. She saw a TV show one night where this beautiful girl was referred to as a "kept woman," a woman who lounged about an expensive apartment all day, looking just great, while this older man paid her rent, gave her endless numbers of gifts, and practically groveled every time the kept woman was even faintly displeased. An Iowa girl with a wondrous body like Angie's, was it any wonder she'd want to be a kept woman, too?

When she was fifteen, she ran away from home in the company of a thirty-two-year-old woman from Omaha who took her to a hotel in Des Moines. Angie slept with ten men in three years and made just over a thousand dollars. One of the men had been black, and that gave her some pause. She could just hear her dad if he ever found out about her (A) screwing men for money or (B) screwing a black man for money.

She went back home. Her dad, who worked as an appliance service repair man for Al's American Appliances, didn't have the money for a private shrink so they sent her to the county Human Services Department, where she saw this counselor for free. She spent two hours filling out the Minnesota Multiphasic Personality Test, which just about bored her ass off. He kept peeking in the room and asking her if she was about done. That's what he pretended to do, anyway. What he was really doing was staring at her breasts. He'd fallen in love with them the moment they walked in the door. She ended up screwing him on the side. He had a wife who worked at Wal-Mart in Cedar Rapids and two little girls, one of whom was lame in some way and whom he got all sad about sometimes. He was thirty-eight and bald and felt guilty about screwing her and cheating on his wife and all but he said that her tits just made him dizzy when he touched them, just dizzy. He kept her in rap CDs. She loved rap. The way the gangsters in the rap videos took care of their girlfriends.

That's what she wanted. She wanted to meet some guy who'd give her a life of ease. A kept woman. No work. No hassle. No sweat. Just sit around some fancy apartment and read comic books and watch MTV and porno movies. She loved porno movies. The thing was, she didn't like sex very much, except for masturbating, but if sex was the price she had to pay for a life of ease, so be it.

She dropped the counselor as soon as she managed to get through high school. She got a job in Cedar Rapids as a clerk in a Target store. She lasted three weeks. She took her paycheck and bought a very sexy dress and then she started hanging out in the lawyer bars downtown. Her first couple of months, things went pretty good. She hadn't found a guy who'd make her an official kept woman, but she'd found several guys who'd give her a little money now and then, enough money for a nice little apartment and a six-year-old Oldsmobile.

But things did not go well after a time. She caught the clap and profoundly displeased a couple of the men who gave her money. Then she ran into two men who were long of tongue but short of wallet, a car salesman who drove them around in sleek new Caddies, and a supper club owner who wore her like a pinkie ring. They were full of promises but had no real money. The Caddie man had two wives and two alimonies; and the supper club man owed the IRS boys so much in back taxes, he could barely afford a pack of gum. He'd had a supper club over in Rock Island several years back, and he'd been charged with tax evasion, later dropped to a simple (if overwhelming) tax debt.

Then, the worst thing of all happened. On the night of her twenty-sixth birthday, Angie got busted for prostitution. She was in a downtown bar sitting with a couple of hookers she knew getting birthday party drunk, when one of the lawyers suggested they all go out to his houseboat. Well, they did, and the cops followed them. Angie insisted that she accepted gifts but never cash for sex per se but it was a distinction apparently too subtle for the minds of the gendarmes. They hated these two particular lawyers and were gleeful about arresting them. Cedar Rapids had a new police station and Angie was impressed with it. She saw a couple of cute young cops, too, and thought she wouldn't mind dating a cop. It was probably fun. She was booked and fingerprinted and charged. It all, like much of Angie's life, had a dream-like quality. She was just walking through it—as if her life was a TV show and she was simply watching it—the reality of her trouble not hitting her until the next day when her name appeared in the paper. The Cedar Rapids paper was read by everybody in her hometown. Angie called home and tried to explain. Her mother was in tears, her father enraged. They told her not, definitely not, to attend the family reunion two weekends hence.

Now it was two years later and Angie was living with Roy, who robbed banks and killed people when he thought it was necessary. She saw plainly now that he was never going to have the kind of money it took to make her a kept woman. Hell, he'd even hinted a few times that she should get another waitress job to help out with the rent and the food. Plus, there were the people he'd killed, three that she knew of for sure. The only one that really bothered her was his wife. Killing his wife was a real personal thing, and it scared Angie. Killing his own son scared her even more.

She spent the afternoon getting depressed about her bikinis. School would be out in a week. Swimming pools would be opening up. Time to flaunt her body. But this year there was too much of her body to flaunt. She'd put on twenty pounds. Ripples of cellulite could be seen on the back of her thighs. She wished now Roy hadn't talked her into getting his name tattooed on both her boobs.

At three-thirty, Jason came home. He was a skinny, sandy-haired kid with a lot of freckles and eyeglasses so thick they made you feel sorry for him. Kids like Jason always got picked on by other kids.

Something was wrong. He usually went to the refrigerator and got himself some milk and a piece of the pie Angie always kept on hand for both of them. Roy had a whiskey tooth, not a sweet tooth. Then Jason usually sat at the dining room table and watched Batman. But not today. He just muttered a greeting and went back to his little room and closed the door.

Something really was wrong and she figured she knew what it was. She slipped a robe on over her bikini—you shouldn't be around him, your tits hangin' out that way, Roy said whenever she wore a bikini around the trailer—and went back to his room and knocked gently. She could never figure out what he thought of her. He was almost always polite but never more than that.

"I'm asleep," he said.

She giggled. "If you were asleep, you couldn't say I'm asleep.'"

"I just don't feel like talkin', Angie."

She decided to risk it. "You heard us talkin' last night, didn't you, Jason?"

There was a long silence. "No."

"About your mom."

"No."

"About what happened to her."

There was another long silence. "He killed her. I heard him say so."

So Roy was right. The kid had heard.

She opened the door and went in. He lay on the bed. He still had his sneakers on. A Spawn comic book lay across his chest. Sunlight angled in through the dirty window on the west wall and picked out the blond highlights in his hair.

She went over and sat down next to him. The springs made a noise. She tried not to think about her weight, or how her bikinis fit her. She was definitely going on a diet. She was going to be a kept woman, and one thing a kept woman had to do was keep her body good.

She said, "I just wanted you to know that I didn't have nothin' to do with it, what he did, I mean."

"Yeah," he said. "I know."

"And I also wanted you to know that your daddy isn't a bad man."

"Yes, he is."

"Sometimes he is. But not all the time."

"He broke your rib, didn't he?"

"He didn't mean to hit me that hard. He was just drunk was all. If he'd been sober, he wouldn't have hit me that hard."

"They say in school that a man shouldn't hit a woman at all."

"Well," she said, "you know what your daddy says about schools. That they're run by Jews and gays and colored people."

He stared at her. "I'm gonna turn him in."

She got scared. "Oh, honey, don't you ever say that to your daddy." She knew that Roy was looking for an excuse, any excuse, to kill Jason. "Promise me you won't. He'd get so mad he'd—"

She didn't need to finish her sentence. She sensed that the kid knew what she was talking about.

She said, "Is that a good comic book?"

"Not as good as Batman."

"Then how come you don't get Batman?"

"I already read it for this month."

"Oh."

She leaned forward and kissed him on the forehead. She'd never done that before. He was a nice kid. "You remember what I said now. You never say anything in front of your daddy about turnin' him in. You hear me?"

"Yeah, I guess so."

"You take a nap now."

She stood up.

Her mother had once said, "You give a man plenty of starch and a good piece of meat, he'll never complain about you or your cookin'." Angie had told this to Roy once and he'd grinned at her and pawed one of her breasts and said, "All depends on what kind of meat you're talkin' about." At the time, Angie had found his remark hilarious. There was nothing to smile about as she made the Kraft cheese and macaroni while the pork chops sizzled in the oven.

He was going to kill his own son. She couldn't get over it. His own son.

Forty-five minutes later, the three of them ate dinner. As always, Jason said grace to himself the way his mom had taught him. While he did this, Roy made a face and rolled his eyes. Little sissy son-of-a-bitch, he'd drunkenly said to Jason one night, sayin' grace like that.

Roy said, "Guess what I found today?"

Angie said, "What?"

"I was talkin' to the boy."

"Oh," Angie said, irritated with his tone of voice. "Pardon me for living."

She got up from the table and carried her dishes to the sink.

"Guess what I found today?" Roy said to Jason.

"What?"

"A real great spot for fishin'."

"Oh."

"For you and me. I always wanted to teach you how to fish."

"I thought you hated to fish," Jason said.

"Not anymore. I love fishin', don't I, babe?"

"Yeah," Angie said from the sink, where she was cleaning off her plate. "He loves fishin'."

Angie knew immediately that Roy had figured out how to kill the kid. He hated fishing, and even more he hated to do anything with the kid.

After supper, Jason went into his room. Most kids would be out playing in the warm spring night. Not Jason. He had a little twelve-inch TV in there and he had a lot of X-Files novels, too. He was well set up.

While she was doing the dishes, and Roy was sitting at the table nursing a Hamms from the bottle and watching some skin on the Playboy Channel, she said, "You're gonna do it."

"Yes, I am."

"He's your own flesh and blood."

He came over and pressed against her. He had a hard-on. Seems he always had a hard-on. She didn't have no complaints in that department. He groped her and kissed her neck and said, "We're free kind of people, Angie. Free. And with the kid along, we'll never be free. Especially with what he knows about us. One phone call from him and we'll be in the slammer."

"But he's your own son."

Jason's door opened. He went to the john. Roy said, "You let me take care of it."

Twenty minutes later, Roy and Jason left. She couldn't think of any way to stop them without coming right out and warning Jason about what was going on.

She paced. She paced and gunned whiskey from a Smurfs glass. She was so agitated her heart felt like thunder in her chest and every few minutes her right arm jerked grotesquely.

And then she remembered the gun. She didn't even know what kind of gun it was. One of her lawyer friends had given it to her once when one of her old boyfriends was hassling her. She'd shot it a few times. She knew how to use it. She kept it in the bureau underneath the crotchless panties Roy had bought her, his joke always being that he'd personally eaten the crotch out of them.

She got the gun and she went after them. Her only thought was the river. About half a mile on the other side of some hardwoods was a cliff and below it fast water that ran to a dam near Cedar Rapids. One time they'd been walking and Roy said it was a perfect place to throw a body. His cellmate, a lifer Roy had a lot of respect for, had said that while bodies did occasionally wash up right away, there was a better chance they'd give you a five-, six-day head start from the law.

The dying day was indigo in the sky, indigo and salmon pink and mauve spreading like a stain beneath a few northeasterly thunderheads and a biting wind that tasted of rain. Rainstorms always scared her. When she was little, she'd always hidden in the closet, her two older sisters laughing at her, scaredy-pants, scaredy-pants. But she didn't care. She'd hidden anyway.

The way she found them, they were sitting on a picnic table near the cliff, father and son, just talking. Darkness was slowly making them grainy, and soon would make them invisible.

Roy said, "What the hell you doing here?"

"She can be here if she wants to," Jason said.

She smiled. The kid liked her and that made her feel good.

"I guess I need to go to the bathroom," Jason said.

He walked over to the hardwoods and disappeared.

"I was afraid you already did something to him," Angie said.

He looked at her. Shrugged. "It's harder than I thought it would be."

"He's your own flesh and blood."

"Yeah, yeah, I guess that's it. I started to do it a couple times but I couldn't go through with it. I mean, it's not like shootin' a stranger or anything."

"Let's go back."

He shook his head. "Oh, no. You go back alone."

"But if you can't do it, why you want to stay out here?"

"I didn't say I can't do it. I just said it's harder than I thought it was. It's just gonna take me a little time is all. Now, you get that sweet ass of yours back home and wait for me. We'll be pullin' out tonight."

"Pullin' out?"

They could see Jason coming back toward them.

"Yeah," Roy said in a whispering voice, "school'll be askin' questions, him not around anymore. Better off pullin' out tonight."

Jason walked up. "Dad tell you there's twenty-pound fish in that river?"

"Yeah," she said, "that's what he said."

"Angle's got to get back home. She's makin' us a surprise."

"A surprise?" Jason said, excited. "What kinda surprise?"

"Well, if she tells ya, it won't be much of a surprise, will it?"

Jason grinned. "No, I guess not."

"You head home, babe," Roy said. "We'll be up'n a while."

She wanted to argue but you didn't argue with Roy. You didn't argue and win, anyway. And you got bruises and bumps and breaks for not winning.

"Guess I better go," she said.

"I can't wait to see the surprise," Jason said.

She went back but she didn't go home. She stood inside the hardwoods, inside the shadows, inside the night, and watched them.

He couldn't do it. That's what she was hoping. That when it came right down to it, he just couldn't do it. She said a couple of prayers.

But he did it. Pulled the gun out, grabbed Jason by the shoulder and started dragging him across the grassy space between picnic table and cliff.

All this was instinct: her running, her screaming. Roy looked real pissed when he saw her. He got distracted from the kid and the kid tried wrestling himself away, swinging his arms wild, trying to kick, trying to bite.

Roy didn't have any warning about her gun. She got up close to him and jerked it out of the back pocket of her Levi's and killed him point-blank. Three bullets in the side of the head.

He went over on his side and shit his pants before he hit the ground. The smell was awful.

The weird thing was how the kid reacted. You'd think he'd be grateful that she'd killed the son-of-a-bitch. But he knelt next to Roy and wailed and rocked back and forth and held a dead cold white hand in his hand and then wailed some more.

Maybe, she thought, maybe it was because his mom was dead, too. Maybe losin' both your folks, maybe it was too much to handle, even if your own flesh-and-blood dad had tried to kill you.

She dragged Roy over and pushed him off the cliff into the river. The stars were on the water tonight and the choppy waves glistened.

She dragged the boy away. He fought at first, biting, kicking, wrestling, and all. She let him have a good hard slap, though, and that settled him down. He kept cryin' but he did what she told him.

"How you doin'?"

"All right."

"You hungry?"

"Sort of, I guess."

"You'll like Colorado. Wait till you see the mountains."

"You didn't have to kill him."

"He was gonna kill you."

He didn't say anything for a long time. They were nearing the Nebraska border. The land was getting flatter. Cows, crying with prairie sorrow, tossed in their earthen beds, while night birds collected chorus-like in the trees, making the leafy branches thrum with their song. It was nice with the windows rolled down and all the summery Midwest roaring in your ears.

Sixty-three miles before they hit the border, just after ten o'clock, they found the Empire Motel, one of those 1950s jobs with the office in the middle and eight stucco-sided rooms fanned out on either side.

Angle rented a room and bought a bunch of candy and potato chips from the vending machine. She rented a sci-fi video from the manager for Jason.

She got him into the shower and then into bed and played the movie for him. He didn't last long. He was asleep in no time. She turned out the lights and got into bed herself. She was tired. Or thought she was, anyway. But she couldn't sleep. She lay there and thought about Roy and about when she was a little girl and about being a kept woman. It had to happen for her someday. It just had to. Then she remembered what she'd looked like in those bikinis. God, she really had to go on a diet.

She lay like this for an hour. Then she heard car doors opening and male laughter. She decided to go peek out the window. Two nice-looking, nicely dressed guys were carrying a suitcase each into a room two doors away. They were driving this just-huge new Lincoln. Sight of them made her agitated. She wanted a drink and to hear some music. Maybe dance a little. And laugh. She needed a good laugh.

Fifteen minutes later, she was fixed up pretty good, white tank top and red short-shorts, the ones where her cheeks were exposed to erotic perfection, her hair all done up nice, and enough perfume so that she smelled really good. The kid wouldn't miss her. He'd be fine. He'd be sleeping and the door would be locked and he'd be just fine.

Their names were Jim Durbin and Mike Brady. They were from Cedar Rapids and they owned a couple of computer stores and they were going to open a big new one in Denver.

Ordinarily, Jim would fly but Mike was scared to fly. And ordinarily, they would stay in a nicer motel than this but they couldn't find anything else on the road. Her excuse for knocking on their door this late was the front office didn't have a cigarette machine and she was out and she heard them still up and she wondered if either of them had a few cigarettes they'd loan her. Jim said he didn't smoke but Mike did.

Jim said he'd been trying for years to get Mike to quit. How do you like that? Jim said. Guy doesn't mind risking lung cancer every day of his life but he won't get on an airplane?

They had a nice bottle of I. W. Harper and invited her in.

It was obvious Mike was interested in her. Jim was married. Mike was just going through a divorce he called "painful." He said his wife ended up running off with this doctor she was on this charity committee with. Jim said Mike needed a good woman to rebuild Mike's self-esteem. That was a word Angie heard a lot. She liked the daytime talk shows and they talked a lot about self-esteem. There was a transvestite prostitute on just last week, as a matter of fact, and Angie felt sorry for the poor thing. He/she said that's all he/she was looking for, self-esteem.

Angie got sort of drunk and spent her time talking to Mike while Jim took a shower and got ready for bed. Angie could tell he was taking a real long time to give Mike and her a chance to be alone. And then they were making out and his hands were all over her and then she was down on her knees next to his bed and doing him and he was gasping and groaning and bucking and just going crazy and it made her feel powerful and wonderful to make a man this happy, especially a broken-hearted one.

When Jim came back, wearing a red terry-cloth robe and rubbing his crew cut with a white towel, Angie and Mike were sitting in chairs and having another drink.

"So, what's going on?" Jim said.

"Well," Mike said, and he looked like a teenager, excited and nervous at the same time, "I was going to ask Angie if she'd like to come to Denver with me. Spend a couple of weeks while we get the grand opening all set up and everything."

Jim said, still rubbing his crew cut with the white towel, "This is a guy who does everything first-class, Angie, let me tell you. You should see his condo. The view of the city. Unbelievable."

"You like Jet Skiing?" Mike said.

"Sure," Angie said, though she wasn't exactly sure what it was.

"Well, I've got two Jet Skis and they're a ball. Believe me, we could have a lot of fun. You could stay at my condo and do what you like during the day—shop or whatever—and then at night, we'll get together again."

Jim said, "God, Angie, you're a miracle worker. This sounds like my old buddy Mike Brady. I haven't heard him sound this happy in three or four years."

Mike grinned. "Maybe I'm in love." And he leaned over and slid his arm around Angie's neck and gave her a big whiskey kiss on the mouth.

All she could think of was how strange it was. Maybe she'd met the man who was going to make her into a kept woman. And this one wasn't married, either. He could marry her somewhere down the line.

She said, "Wait till I tell Jason."

Mike gave her a funny look. "Jason? Who's Jason?"

Jim came over, too. "Yeah, who's Jason?"

"Oh, sort of my stepson, I guess you'd say."

"You're traveling with a kid?" Mike said.

"Yeah."

Mike didn't have to say anything. It was all in his face.

He'd been outlining an orgy of activities and she went and ruined it all with reality. A kid. A fucking kid.

"Oh," Mike said, finally.

"He's a real nice kid," Angie said. "Real quiet and everything."

"I'm sure he's a nice kid, Angie," Jim said. "But I don't think that's what Mike had in mind. Nothing against kids, you understand. I've got two of my own and Mike's got three."

"I love kids," Mike said, as if somebody had accused him otherwise.

"He wouldn't be any trouble," Angie said. "He really wouldn't."

Mike and Jim looked at each other and Jim said, looking at Angie now, "You know what we should do? Why don't we take your phone number, you know where you're staying in Omaha and everything, and then Mike can give you a call when he gets settled into his condo?"

Mike didn't have nerve enough to say goodbye so Jim was doing it for him.

A ball and chain, she remembered Roy said about Jason. Mike wasn't going to call. Jim was just saying that. And she'd be somewhere in Omaha, maybe with a waitress job or something. And pretty soon school would roll around and she'd have to worry about school clothes and getting him enrolled in a new school and everything. While somebody else would be living with Mike in his Denver condo, and Jet Skiing, whatever that was, and using Mike's American Express to buy new clothes and stuff.

She said, "You know if there's a river around here somewhere?"

"A river?" Jim said.

"Yes," she said. "A river."

❋ ❋ ❋

Next morning at seven A.M. she knocked on the door. A sleepy pajamaed Jim opened it. "Hey," he said. "How's it goin'?" He sounded a little leery of seeing her. He'd obviously hoped they'd put the Denver matter to rest last night.

"Guess what?" she said.

"What?"

"I said I was sort of Jason's stepmother? Well, actually, I'm his aunt. My sister lives about ten miles from here and has troubles with depression. She wanted me to take him for a while but she stopped by the room here real early this morning and picked him up. Said she was feeling a lot better."

Mike could be seen over Jim's shoulder now. He said, excited, "So you don't have the kid anymore?"

"Free, white and twenty-one," she said.

"You're going to Denver!" he said.

Jim said, "I'm going to get some breakfast down the road. I'll be back in an hour or so."

He got dressed quick and left.

They did it their first time right in Mike's mussed bed. Only once or twice did she think of the kid, and how she'd smothered him in the room. She hadn't had any trouble finding the river. She had to give it to Roy. The ball-and-chain business. She had liked the kid but he really was a ball and chain.

A few hours later, they left for Denver. That night, they had spare ribs for supper at a roadside place. They drank a lot of wine, or vino, as Jim kept calling it, and Mike as a joke licked some of the rib sauce off her fingers. She was scared about later, when she went to sleep. Maybe she'd have nightmares about the kid. But she snuggled up to Mike real good and after they made love, they lay in the darkness sharing his cigarette and talking about Denver and she ended up not having any dreams at all.

The Order of Things Unknown

"I experience the horror of everything that is, to the point of longing for death." —Guy de Maupassant

1

In memory, the street was a perfect image from a song by Elvis early on, or Chuck Berry, or Little Richard—a street where chopped and channeled '51 Mercs and '53 Oldsmobiles ferried dazzling pony-tailed girls and carefully duck-tailed boys up and down the avenue, wlere corner boys dangled Lucky Strikes from their lips and kept copies of *The Amboy Dukes* in the back pocket of Levi's from which the belt loops had been cut away with razor blades. The sounds: glas-pak mufflers rumbling, jukeboxes thundering Fats Domino's "Ain't That a Shame," police sirens cutting the night and sounding somehow cool and threatening at the same time (like a sound effect from one of the juvenile delinquent movies that always played on the double bill at the State); Italian babies screaming from the tiny apartments above the various storefronts; Irish babies screaming; black babies screaming; an argument ending "Fuck you!", "Well, fuck you, too!" as one corner boy walks away from another not really wanting to get into it (unlike movie pain, real pain can hurt); and talk talk talk, wives and husbands, lovers, little kids having just glutted themselves on "Captain Video" and imitating the Cap'n now, and old lonely ladies saying prayers for somebody in the parish, heart attack or cancer suddenly striking. And the smells: "Evening in Paris" on the girls and Wildroot Hair Oil on the boys and cigarette smoke and Doublemint gum and bus exhaust and smoky autumn and cheeseburgers and night itself, the neon of it, the Indian summer heat of it, and the vast harrowing potential of it (a guy could get laid; a guy could get knifed; it was great giddy fun and it was spooky as hell).

This then was Hanlon's memory of the street and it was completely fictitious, or so it seemed the only time he came back here, twenty-seven years after leaving.

Richard Hanlon gave the package of Luckies to the Oriental man behind the counter of the reeking little grocery store and the man smiled at him with rotten teeth and spoke in a language Hanlon understood not at all.

"How much?" Hanlon asked.

The man, leathery-skinned and ancient in a way almost sinister, punched up the price on the aged cash register and pointed to the amount showing in the machine's oblong window up top.

Hanlon pulled two singles from his pocket and handed the money across. The man gave something like a bow, smiling again with his bad teeth, and rang up the purchase. Hanlon got eight cents in change back.

As he left the store, Hanlon recalled the days when a flush-faced mick named Sullivan owned this little store. It didn't stink of dead meat and rotting produce in those days and Sullivan—despite the fact that he wouldn't sell you cigarettes until you were eighteen and could prove it—Sullivan at least spoke English.

Hanlon went out and stood on the pavement, thinking of all the times he used to do this in the old days. He'd been a corner boy for sure. Man, the hours he'd spent here, after school till dinner and then after dinner till nine or ten at night, eleven or twelve in the summers. Talking about who was cooler, James Dean or Robert Mitchum (he'd always opted for Mitch), talking about screwing Doris Cosgrove (hell, he would have been happy just to get a quick little kiss from her), talking about how he was going to be a writer someday (always toting a James T. Farrell book in his back pocket) and live in New York, the old man's union having a college fund which would insure all these dreams.

But now; now.

In the dirty street light, in the dirty night, the rusted and battered cars of the underclass dragged by like creatures without the wit or luck to simply die. On the sidewalk hookers leaned against paint-peeling storefronts and comic-book pimps manicured their nails with switchblades. Two cops parked in a squad car ate hamburgers and two men holding hands walked down the street. And always there was the language—Vietnamese, he supposed—

crackling through the dirty air. He knew he was being racist and he tried not to be. But he had come back to a world he had always considered his and found it no longer his at all.

He smoked two Luckies, all the time staring up at the apartment over the Laundromat across the street. In the old days, the blind man with the gnarled hands and the garlic breath had always sat in his rocking chair at the window and looked out on the street below. As if he could see.

The blind man sat there now, staring, staring. Hanlon could make out his shape in the shadows.

Hanlon dropped his cigarette to the pavement and put it out with the toe of his black oxford.

So the blind man was expecting him.

Hanlon wasn't sure how he knew this; only that it was true. Taking a deep breath, he crossed the street.

2

Hanlon was blessed with one of those boyish, handsome faces that even people who should know better trust immediately. This was why he had no trouble luring women into his car and killing them.

He killed his first woman on the night of August 14, 1964. He had just left a local Democratic rally for President Lyndon Baines Johnson—who was running against the devil himself, Barry Morris Goldwater—when he saw a somewhat plump but very pretty woman in a pink waitress uniform standing in front of a somewhat battered 1956 Ford Fairlane, the hood up, steam pouring out of the radiator. She seemed so helpless and disconsolate that she looked positively fetching. The image of a helpless woman appealed to him enormously.

He pulled in behind where she'd parked just off the road, got out and went over to her.

"Pretty hot night for car trouble," he said, smiling sympathetically.

"It sure is." She rolled a slender wrist to her face, reading a tiny cheap watch. "I'm supposed to be at a party in twenty minutes. Bridal shower."

"Why don't we take a look?" he said, sounding like a doctor about to peek in at a sore throat.

He saw the problem immediately. A hole in her radiator. A rock could have put it there or kids sabotaging cars in a parking lot.

He leaned back from inside the hood. "Tell you what. Why don't I give you a ride? There's a Standard station down the way. They can come back and tow your car in and if it's not too far out of my way, I can give you a ride to your party."

"Jeeze, it's gonna need towing?"

He smiled again. "Afraid so."

She didn't say thanks for the offer of a ride; thanks for looking at my car. She was as cheap as her watch. "So what's wrong with it?"

"Hole in your radiator."

"Jeeze, why does this crap always happen to me?"

"My name's O'Rourke," he said. The odd thing was, the false name surprised him. He had no idea why he'd used it. No idea yet what he really had in mind. He put out a slender hand (he'd always hated his hands, tiny as a fourteen-year-old girl's, the wrists reedy no matter how long he lifted weights) and she took it.

"Paula. Stufflebeam."

"Now there's a sturdy name for you."

"Hah. Sturdy. Shitty is what you mean."

They got in the car and started driving. The radio played. When "Oh, Pretty Woman" by Roy Orbison came on she started sort of finger-popping and bopping with her hips and asked if he could maybe turn it up a little.

He smiled and complied.

When the song was finished, she said, "I like this car. What kind of monthly payments you have to make on it, anyway?"

"It was a gift."

"Huh?"

"My uncle gave it to me." He actually had a rich uncle.

"Jeeze, it must be nice."

The night was busy with traffic. Mosquitos slapped against the windshield. Mary Wells sang "My Guy." Two blocks from the Standard station, he suddenly veered right, still not knowing why. A sign said WARNER PARK, TWO BLOCKS EAST.

"Hey," she said.

"Pardon me?"

"This ain't the way to that gas station!'

"No?"

"No."

He increased his speed. He was going forty miles per hour. He had to be careful. He could get stopped by a cop.

"Don't get no ideas," she said. "About me, I mean."

"Wouldn't you like to look over the city? Just sort of take a break?"

"I don't even know you."

He turned toward her. He had an altar boy innocence.

"I'm not going to put the make on you, if that's what you're afraid of." He frowned. "I'll be honest with you."

"Oh, yeah?"

"Yeah. My girlfriend—" He sighed and then steeled himself, as if saying the words were painful beyond belief. "My fiancée, to be precise, told me last night that she's in love with somebody else."

"Jeeze," Paula Stufflebeam said, "and you was going to be married and everything?"

"And everything."

"Jeeze."

"So right now I could use some company, you know? Just—a friend. A friend and nothing more."

"Jeeze."

"So I just thought it'd be nice if we could go up to Steep Rock and look out over the city."

"Nothin' more?"

"Nothing."

"You promise?"

"I promise."

She sighed. "Yeah, why not? I guess I'm late already, what's another hour anyway?"

Steep Rock was a red clay promontory that looked out over the city below. Over the hundred years the city had been here, Steep Rock had been used variously for seduction, bird watching and suicide.

After he parked the car, they got out and went to the edge. The night air was slow and hot, filled with fireflies and mosquitos. Below the city lay like a vast marijuana dream, unreal in the way it sprawled shimmering over the landscape and then ended abruptly, giving way to the plains and the forests again. Next to him, Paula Stufflebeam smelled of sweat and faded perfume and sexual juices. She had a run in her stockings so bad he could see it even in the moonlit darkness and oddly it made him feel sorry for her. She wasn't cheap, she was poor and uneducated and there was a difference.

"So who'd she dump you for?" Paula said after they'd looked at the city for a time.

"Somebody named Steve."

Where was this stuff coming from (and so fluidly)? He had no girlfriend, let alone a fiancée, let alone one who'd dumped him for somebody named Steve.

"She give you the ring back?"

"The ring?"

"Engagement ring. Didn't you give her one?"

"Oh. The ring. Yes. She gave it back."

"Well at least she did that much for you."

He knew then he'd have to lure her. In the clearing where they stood ringed by the dark shapes of oaks and elms and pines, he put his head down abruptly, as if somebody had just stabbed him.

"You all right?" Paula Stufflebeam asked.

"Just—lonely, I guess. I'm sorry." He looked at her. "Maybe I'd better take you back."

"Jeeze, you're really strung out, aren't ya?"

"I'm afraid I am. I—"

And she accepted. He put his arms out wide and she came into them. And he held her tightly, feeling the shift of her breasts beneath the cotton of her uniform, smelling her bubble-gum-colored lipstick and the faint wisp of hairspray. They didn't kiss, merely embraced, one friend comforting another.

And he knew, then. Knew why he'd stopped for her. Knew why he'd brought her here.

Easing his hands from around her back, he quickly found her throat.

"Oh, God!" she shouted.

But before she could say anything else, his hands found their true place, and she squirmed against him almost carnally, and tried to get her arms up to push him away but he was too fast and strong, and then she sagged against him, spent, and then he lowered her to the ground and smelled the way she'd fouled herself.

Oh my God.

Oh. My. God.

What had he done?

And my God, why?

Why had he done this?

Why?

He stood in the clearing, moonlight-glazed, the city lights below so alien.

He looked at his hands. They seemed to be strange tools that belonged to someone else.

Her uniform skirt was up over her thighs. He could see the tops of her stockings and her garters. She was as lurid as a cover of a true detective magazine. He could smell her sex and smell her bowels, one sweet, the other sour. He thought of how it would all look in the paper, the details.

Why? My God, why?

The darkness came then and it was chilling—literally, goosebumps and hackles standing on end—a darkness different from night, different from unconsciousness, a darkness in which voices in the unfathomable gloom whispered words he heard only teasingly. It was inward-turning, this darkness; it was pleasure-denying, this darkness; and it would be forever more.

He stood as if naked in the moonlight and looked up and saw the moon and the stars and sensed for the first time that beyond them, somehow, there was another reality, one few ever glimpsed, one that filled early graves and asylums alike.

When he put the girl in the trunk, he was careful to set her on the tarpaulin. She had begun to leak.

Richard Christopher Hanlon graduated from Illinois State University two years later with a degree in business administration. At that time he got a job working as a salesman for General Mills out of Minneapolis and he married a fellow graduate named Susan Anne Todd. At the time of their wedding Susan was four months pregnant, a fact that displeased both of their parents greatly. Only on August 6, 1966 did the parents smile. This was not just the day of the wedding but the day Susan miscarried. Now there would be no baby to embarrass them. The dignity of both families would be intact. Susan and Richard tried again, of course, and a year later the first of three daughters was born to them.

Richard was these things: an amiable and compliant worker for the great corporation, an attentive husband and doting father, a good Democrat despite the fact that he had begun to see that the lower classes weren't always interested in helping themselves even when they had the chance, a tireless watcher of Cubs and Bears games, a tender and inventive lover when his wife was not unduly pregnant and then a champion masturbator, a golfer who would never be any good, a tireless reader of political biographies, and a troubled Catholic who felt that the Church had lost all sense of Jesus. At thirty-one, he had prostate problems. At thirty-three, he began to bald. At thirty-five, he developed this little tumor of a pot belly that no amount of exercise could quite quell. At thirty-six, he saw his eldest daughter win a national essay contest and go on the CBS Evening News and talk to Dan Rather. At thirty-nine, he was promoted to a divisional sales manager and his salary, with perks and bonuses, exceeded one hundred and fifty thousand per annum, which wasn't bad for a former corner boy. At forty-one he had a brief cancer scare that turned out to be an eminently treatable throat problem. His hair continued to fall out and by his mid-forties he tended to identify himself as bald. During all these years he was unfaithful only once (with a stewardess from Peoria), was threatening to his wife only once (he'd had a head cold and his irritability from the cold caused him to erupt when she made some minor grousing remark), and embarrassed his children only once (he insisted that he could do a good impersonation of a certain rock star and did so at Katie's ninth birthday party; Katie, ashamed, blushed so deeply it seemed a rash had broken out on her face).

Of course he continued murdering women, too.

In all, from the night with the waitress to the time he returned to his old neighborhood, he killed seventeen women. Some were strangled, some shot, some slashed very, very badly. The murders took place in Minnesota, Iowa, Illinois and Missouri and always when he was on the road for Mother corporation. He scarcely remembered them, actually. They always took place during a merciful fog, a blood frenzy that left few details to be recalled later on. He would see a bloody breast, a bloody thigh, a bloody buttock, but then the image would recede, recede and be forgotten utterly. If he'd recalled in any detail what he'd done, he would have gone crazy, literally, and been put in an institution.

In his mid-forties, the dreams began, and it was the dreams that brought him back to the old neighborhood this night.

3

At the top of the long dusty staircase was a fire door. The moon was framed perfectly in it as Hanlon ascended the worn and tilting steps. The narrow passage upward smelled of heat and garbage left too long and of time itself, that taint of dust and decay.

When Hanlon reached the top of the stairs, he stopped. Three dark doors stood to his right, each opening on a sleeping room not much bigger than a prison cell and every bit as drab. He remembered the blind man's room. Hanlon and some of the other corner boys used to come up here sometimes when they heard the blind man playing his accordion. In those days his music—which ran to polkas rather than popular tunes—gave the boys great pleasure. How he tapped his foot, the blind man, when the tune quickened and swelled; how he rolled his dead milk-of-magnesia eyes when the tune turned somber. As if in lament; as if in lament. But soon enough the blind man became just another joke to me boys, one of those half-hateful, half-pitiful figures who were fun to tell huge lies about when lights went out and tales were told. As he passed beneath the window on his way to this girl's or that girl's, Hanlon often heard the blind man playing and even once or twice was tempted to go up in the room and watch the blind man strap on the dazzling cumbersome Excelsior and play the "Too Fat Polka" or "The Blue Danube Waltz," the room smelling of Kool cigarettes and Vicks and rubbing alcohol.

Now Hanlon sneezed. The dusty stairway had incited his sinuses. The noise he made was as sharp as a gunshot in the dusty gloom.

He took two steps forward to the middle door, raised a hand, and let it fall loud and sharp—one rap only—against the dying wood.

No response.

Hanlon sneezed again.

Sonofabitch. What a time to stir his allergies up.

This time he knocked three times, quickly, and with a certain air of irritation.

A cane tapped the floor in the silence.

The door opened faster than he imagined it would and the blind man leaned over the threshold. "Yes, Richard, what is it?"

The blind man's skull seemed to be a shrunken head on top of which wild strands of white hair had been affixed. In the moonlight, his dead eyes rolled white and his slack mouth ran with silver spittle. He smelled unclean, like an animal that has been sick for a long time. The ragged white shirt he wore on his bony frame was stained as if from wounds that excreted not only blood but pus. He kept his knobby hands on top of the same knobby black cane he'd had when Hanlon was a boy. When he breathed in Hanlon's direction, Hanlon had to hold his breath. The stink of it literally made him nauseous.

"Come in," the blind man said.

And so Hanlon followed.

He noticed the window first, the framed portrait of the street below inside the window frame, streetlights and neon. To the right of the window the early American style rocking chair sat faintly squeaking, as if waiting impatiently for the old man to return.

"How do you know who I am?" Hanlon asked.

Something like a grin played at the old man's mouth. "Oh, Richard, I've known about you since the first day you came up here with the other little boys."

He moved then through the filth and shadows of the tiny room, the old man, back to his place in the rocking chair, back to his place at the window. From a stand next to the chair he rummaged in a half-eaten bag of Oreos, lifting a cookie with the reverence of a priest lifting a communion wafer. The old man sniffed the cookie before he tossed it into his mouth and began to crunch with loud enjoyment, smacking his lips every few moments.

When he had completely swallowed the cookie, he wiped the back of his mouth with his hand and said, "Forgive an old man his only pleasure." He tapped the cookie package. It rattled like tin in a hailstorm.

Then he farted.

"That's the only trouble with 'em," the old man said. "They give me gas, believe it or not."

The old man seemed amused with his farting and Hanlon wondered if he hadn't done it on purpose.

Hanlon went to the window and looked down at the street. He could almost see the ghost of his boyhood on the street below. Hear his own summer shouting.

Hanlon turned back from the window to the old man. "You know about me, don't you?"

The old man began to rock. The chair sounded like rusty metal that needed oil. "Yes."

"About the killings."

"Ummm-hmmm."

"And the dreams?"

The old man stopped rocking.

The room was dust and silence.

"The dreams?" Hanlon repeated. "You know about them?"

The old man resumed his rocking. After a time he said, "Yes, I know about the dreams."

"What do they mean?"

"That you have been selected."

"Selected?"

"By the god that inspires the dream. I can't even pronounce its name. It is a vile god. A very vile god."

The old man rattled the Oreo package again. Brought a cookie to his lips. Chomped down on it. Quit rocking.

This time he talked as he ate, gesturing with the cookie the way some people gesture with a cocktail glass.

"The first time you ever came here, I had this sense about you. I recognized myself in you. You see, forty years ago, I wasn't blind and I did what you're doing now."

"Killing?"

"Yes, oh my God; yes. I think there were thirty of them in fact." He finished the cookie and wiped his mouth again. He resumed his rocking. Loudly.

Hanlon went back to the window, sighed. "I didn't start having the dreams until after I'd killed several of the women. And then I realized that I wasn't killing the women at all—that it was this god I saw and heard in my dreams—who was killing them. It just used me as a human instrument. Then I wondered if I was insane."

"Just as it used me," the old man said.

Hanlon looked back at the old man. "I don't want to kill anymore. I won't."

The old man snorted. "That's very noble, Richard, and I made the same statement many times back when I—when I was doing its bidding. But I'm afraid you don't have much choice."

Hanlon said, "Where did it come from?"

The old man rocked for a long time, his head down. "Several centuries ago, a Druid cult made human sacrifices here, where the neighborhood is now. They buried bones in satanic formations and prayed to this god. Ever since then, the god has selected people from here as its tools. That's what you're doing to those women, Richard. You're offering sacrifice."

"Not anymore."

"That's what I said."

"But obviously you stopped."

The old man sighed again. "Yes, I stopped."

"How?"

The old man rocked some more, reached over after a time and snatched a cookie, and began eating noisily again. "I quit taking my medicine."

"What medicine?"

"For my eyes. Blindness is often hereditary, I knew that given my family history, I needed to take a certain medicine as I got into my thirties. But I stopped." He paused. "I went blind in six months."

"My God, on purpose?"

"Of course. What good would a blind man be as a killer?"

Hanlon listened to the old man rock. "Did you ever write their families letters?"

"Indeed."

"I even started sending some of them money—to try and make up for what I'd done. I never identified myself, of course. I've tried to turn myself in."

The old man snorted again. "No, I'm afraid that doesn't work, does it? The one time I tried to walk into a police station and hand myself over, I had a heart attack and was rushed to the hospital. For a year and a half I was unable to move or speak and was comatose most of the time. That was when I plotted my idea for blindness."

"There's one woman, I even visit her grave. She was very young. Seventeen."

"It's not your fault, Richard. Knowing what you know now, you can't blame yourself. It uses us till it's done with us."

Hanlon said nothing. Turned back to the window. To the boy of him in the streets below. So innocent, then. But as always thoughts of blood intruded and he saw their faces, their eyes so shocked and afraid, and knew that even if he was only an instrument, still he was guilty.

"I appreciate your talking with me," Hanlon said, pushing away from the window.

"Where are you going?"

"I'm not sure," Hanlon said, though of course he was sure. Quite sure.

Rocking, reaching again for an Oreo, the blind man with his milk-of-magnesia eyes stared out the window. "The neighborhood has changed, hasn't it?"

"Too much."

"Even the smells are different now."

Hanlon was at the door.

The old man starting chewing again.

Hanlon opened the door.

"Don't run away, Richard," the old man said. "There's no place to run to."

Hanlon closed the door softly behind him and started down the stairs again. By the time he was halfway down, he began sneezing.

❉ ❉ ❉

"Hi, hon."

"Hi. You about ready to come home?"

"Soon as I finish with that paperwork."

"Sara was disappointed you weren't able to be at her recital tonight"

"It's just all this damn paperwork," Hanlon said to his wife.

"I know, honey. I know."

Hanlon stood inside a lighted phone booth. The phonebook had been torn from its protective cover and the shelf beneath the phone was covered with four-letter-word graffiti.

"I just wanted to tell you how much I love you and the girls," Hanlon said.

There was a pause on the other end. "Richard?"

"What?"

"Are you all right?"

"Sure. Why?"

"You just sound—funny, I guess."

"I'm fine. I just wanted to tell you that."

"You're probably just feeling guilty that you missed Sara's recital. You know how guilty you Catholics get." She laughed.

"I'm sure that's it."

"I made a chocolate cake for the girls. If you're nice to me, I'll cut you a slice when you get home." She paused again. This time there was a certain urgency in her tone, as if she was still troubled by something in his voice. "Why don't you come home right now, hon?"

"Soon as I can." Pause. "Be sure and tell the girls how much I love them."

"See you soon," she said.

"Soon," he whispered, and hung up.

He had parked his car three blocks from the blind man's. After hanging up, he went straight there.

Because he was parked in a fairly well-lighted area, he drove awhile until he found an area that was mostly rubble, and lay completely in gloom.

He pulled up to the curb, shut off the engine, leaned over to the glove compartment and took the gun out.

He had planned this so mamny times that he was able to accomplish it without any reluctance or hesitation.

He lay his head back against the seat rest.

He opened his mouth wide, the way he used to for communion.

He thought of the death and grief he'd brought to this world.

And then he thought purely and lovingly of his family, the girls and his wife.

I love you.

I love you.

The finger he used had a hangnail. But that didn't slow it from its course, pulling the trigger back, firing the bullet that would excise a small ragged circle from the rear of his skull.

4

At least twice a day, different people—a friend, a nurse, a doctor—would lean into his vision and tell him how lucky he was.

His wife, sensing that this sentiment displeased him in some way, said it only once and then quit.

On the sixth afternoon, his wife brought him a box of chocolates—he'd always had a sweet tooth—and the latest Tom Clancy novel. He thanked her for them.

Afterwards, they sat in the sunny white room, her hand on his. They didn't speak. There was nothing to say. Their hands were eloquent enough.

Around four, the phone next to his bed rang. She started to pick it up but he waved her away and got it himself

He recognized the blind man immediately. "I admire you for trying, Richard."

"Is that one of the girls?" his wife smiled. "They said they'd call after school."

Hanlon shook his head, which was wrapped in startling white gauze.

"But it's not through with you, Richard. It's not through with you. Not yet. That's why you didn't die." He paused. "I'm sorry, Richard."

The blind man hung up.

After a time, their hands still touching, the sunny white room darkening with wintry dusk, he began crying, huge silver difficult tears and knowing better than to ask why, his wife simply kissed his tear-hot cheeks and held his hand the tighter.

5

In the spring, Hanlon was in Buffalo, New York at a sales conference. It was here he met a hotel hostess named Sally Wedmore. They had a few drinks and some conversation and he offered to give her a ride back to her apartment.

In the morning, she was found strangled with her own pantyhose, her stomach ripped away with a knife.

When Hanlon spoke to his wife long distance that evening, she assumed he sounded depressed because he was tired and when she mentioned this he agreed.

"Yes," Hanlon said, sighing. "I wish I could tell you just how tired I am."

Afterword

I first read Lovecraft seriously when I was in my mid-thirties. Till then he'd struck me as overly ornate and too quaint by half. But when I read "The Colour Out of Space" again I heard those particular resonances and echoes so many other people find in his stories. He was the great paranoid and it was his paranoia that gave him his concept of the universe, all those gears and levers, all that machinery of fate, operating in the cold shadows that keep hidden the real truths. In that respect, Lovecraft will be a modem no matter what age he's read in because we'll never be sure exactly what existence means—if it means anything at all—and old H.P.'s guess is a lot more fun than any other I've come by.

Mother Darkness

The man surprised her. He was black.

Alison had been watching the small filthy house for six mornings now and this was the first time she'd seen him. She hadn't been able to catch him at seven-thirty or even six-thirty. She'd had to try six o'clock. She brought her camera up and began snapping.

She took four pictures of him just to be sure.

Then she put the car in gear and went to get breakfast.

An hour-and-a-half later, in the restaurant where social workers often met, Peter said, "Oh, he's balling her all right."

"God," Alison Cage said. "Can't we talk about something else? Please."

"I know it upsets you. It upsets me. That's why I'm telling you about it."

"Can't you tell somebody else?"

"I've tried and nobody'll listen. Here's a forty-three year old man and he's screwing his seven-year-old daughter and nobody'll listen. Jesus."

Peter Forbes loved dramatic moments and incest was about as dramatic as you could get. Peter was a hold-over hippie. He wore defiantly wrinkled khaki shirts and defiantly torn Lee Jeans. He wore his brown hair in a ponytail. In his cubicle back at social services was a faded poster of Robert Kennedy. He still smoked a lot of dope. After six glasses of cheap wine at an office party, he'd once told Alison that he thought she was beautiful. He was forty-one years old and something of a joke and Alison both liked and disliked him.

"Talk to Coughlin," Alison said.

"I've talked to Coughlin."

"Then talk to Friedman."

"I've talked to Friedman, too."

"And what did they say?"

Peter sneered. "He reminded me about the Skeritt case."

"Oh."

"Said I got everybody in the department all bent out of shape about Richard Skeritt and then I couldn't prove anything about him and his little adopted son."

"Maybe Skeritt wasn't molesting him."

"Yeah. Right."

Alison sighed and looked out the winter window. A veil of steam covered most of the glass. Beyond it she could see the parking lot filled with men and women scraping their windows and giving each other pushes. A minor ice storm was in progress. It was seven thirty-five and people were hurrying to work. Everybody looked bundled up, like children trundling to school.

Inside the restaurant the air smelled of cooking grease and cigarettes. Cold wind gusted through the front door when somebody opened it, and people stamped snow from their feet as soon as they reached the tile floor. Because this was several blocks north of the black area, the juke box ran to Hank Williams, Jr. and the Judds. Alison despised country western music.

"So how's it going with you?" Peter said, daubs of egg yolk on his graying bandito mustache.

"Oh. You know." Blonde Alison shrugged. "Still trying to find a better apartment for less money. Still trying to lose five pounds. Still trying to convince myself that there's really a God."

"Sounds like you need a Valium."

The remark was so—Peter. Alison smiled. "You think Valium would do it, huh?"

"It picks me up when I get down where you are."

"When you get to be thirty-six and you're alone the way I am, Peter, I think you need more than Valium."

"I'm alone."

"But you're alone in your way. I'm alone in my way."

"What's the difference?"

Suddenly she was tired of him and tired of herself, too. "Oh, I don't know. No difference, I suppose. I was being silly I guess."

"You look tired."

"Haven't been sleeping well."

"That doctor from the medical examiner's office been keeping you out late?"

"Doctor?"

"Oh, come on," Peter said. Sometimes he got possessive in a strange way. Testy. "I know you've been seeing him."

"Doctor Connery, you mean?"

Peter smiled, the egg yolk still on his mustache. "The one with the blue blue eyes, yes."

"It was strictly business. He just wanted to find out about those infants."

"The ones who smothered last year?"

"Yes."

"What's the big deal? Crib death happens all the time."

"Yes, but it still needs to be studied."

Peter smiled his superior smile. "I suppose but—"

"Crib death means that the pathologist couldn't find anything. No reason that the infant should have stopped breathing—no malfunction or anything, I mean. They just die mysteriously. Doctors want to know why."

"So what did your new boyfriend have to say about these deaths? I mean, what's his theory?"

"I'm not going to let you sneak that in there," she said, laughing despite herself. "He's not my boyfriend."

"All right. Then why would he be interested in two deaths that happened a year ago?"

She shrugged and sipped the last of her coffee. "He's exchanging information with other medical data banks. Seeing if they can't find a trend in these deaths."

"Sounds like an excuse to me."

"An excuse for what?" Alison said.

"To take beautiful blondes out to dinner and have them fall under his sway." He bared yellow teeth a dentist could work on for hours. He made claws of his hands. "Dracula; Dracula. That's who Connery really is."

Alison got pregnant her junior year of college. She got an abortion of course but only after spending a month in the elegant home of her rich parents, "moping" as her father characterized that particular period of time. She did not go back to finish school. She went to California. This was in the late seventies just as discos were dying and AIDS was rising. She spent two celibate years working as a secretary in a record company. James Taylor, who'd stopped in to see a friend of his, asked Alison to go have coffee. She was quite silly during their half hour together, juvenile and giggly, and even years later her face would burn when she thought of how foolish she'd been that day. When she returned home, she lived with her parents, a fact that seemed to embarrass all her high school friends. They were busy and noisy with growing families of their own and here was beautiful quiet Alison inexplicably alone and, worse, celebrating her thirty-first birthday while still living at home.

There was so much sorrow in the world and she could tell no one about it. That's why so many handsome and eligible men floated in and out of her life. Because they didn't understand. They weren't worth knowing, let alone giving herself to in any respect.

She worked for a year-and-a-half in an art gallery. It was what passed for sophisticated in a Midwestern city of this size. Very rich but dull people crowded it constantly, and men both with and without wedding rings pressed her for an hour or two alone.

She would never have known about the income maintenance job if she hadn't been watching a local talk show one day. Here sat two earnest women about her own age, one white, one black, talking about how they acted as liaisons between poor people and the Social Services agency. Alison knew immediately that she would like a job like this. She'd spent her whole life so spoiled and pampered and useless. And the art gallery—minor traveling art shows and local ad agency artists puffing themselves up as artistes—was simply an extension of this life.

These women, Alison could tell, knew well the sorrow of the world and the sorrow in her heart.

She went down the next morning to the Social Services agency and applied. The black woman who took her application weighed at least three-hundred-and-fifty pounds which she'd packed into lime green stretch pants and a flowered polyester blouse with white sweat rings under the arms. She smoked Kool filters at a rate Alison hated to see. Hadn't this woman heard of lung cancer?

Four people interviewed Alison that day. The last was a prim but handsome white man in a shabby three-piece suit who had on the wall behind him a photo of himself and his wife and a small child who was in some obvious but undefined way retarded. Alison recognized two things about this man immediately: that here was a man who knew the same sorrow as she; and that here was a man painfully smitten with her already. It took him five-and-a-half months but the man eventually found her a job at the agency.

Not until her third week did she realize that maintenance workers were the lowest of the low in social work, looked down upon by bosses and clients alike. What you did was this: you went out to people—usually women—who received various kinds of assistance from various government agencies and you attempted to prove that they were liars and cheats and scoundrels. The more benefits you could deny the people who made up your case load, the more your bosses liked you. The people in the state house and the people in Washington, D.C. wanted you to allow your people as little as possible. That was the one and only way to keep taxpayers happy. Of course, your clients had a different version of all this. They needed help. And if you wouldn't give them help, or you tried to take away help you were already giving them, they became vocal. Income maintenance workers were frequently threatened and sometimes punched, stabbed, and shot, men and women alike. The curious thing was that not many of them quit. The pay was slightly better than you got in a factory and the job didn't require a college degree and you could pretty much set your own hours if you wanted to. So, even given the occasional violence, it was still a pretty good job.

Alison had been an income maintenance worker for nearly three years now.

She sincerely wanted to help.

An hour after leaving Peter in the restaurant, Alison pulled her gray Honda Civic up to the small house where earlier this morning she'd snapped photos of the black man. Her father kept trying to buy her a nicer car but she argued that her clients would just resent her nicer car and that she wouldn't blame them.

The name of this particular client was Doreen Hayden. Alison had been trying to do a profile of her but Doreen hadn't exactly cooperated. This was Alison's second appointment with the woman. She hoped it went better than the first.

After getting out of her car, Alison stood for a time in the middle of the cold, slushy street. Snow sometimes had a way of making even rundown things look beautiful. But somehow it only made this block of tiny, aged houses look worse. Brown frozen dog feces covered the sidewalk. Smashed front windows bore masking tape. Rusted-out cars squatted on small front lawns like obscene animals. And factory soot touched everything, everything. It was nineteen days before Christmas—Alison had just heard this on the radio this morning—but this was a neighborhood where Christmas never came.

Doreen answered the door. Through the screen drifted the oppressive odors of breakfast and cigarettes and dirty diapers. In her stained white sweater and tight red skirt, Doreen still showed signs of the attractive woman she'd been a few years ago until bad food and lack of exercise had added thirty pounds to her fine-boned frame.

The infant in her arms was perhaps four months old. She had a sweet little pink face. Her pink blanket was filthy.

"I got all the kids here," Doreen said. "You all comin' in? Gettin' cold with this door open."

All the kids, Alison thought. My God, Doreen was actually going to try that scam.

Inside, the hot odors of food and feces were even more oppressive. Alison sat on the edge of a discount-store couch and looked around the room. Not much had changed since her last visit. The old Zenith color TV set—now blaring Bugs Bunny cartoons—still needed some kind of tube. The floor was still an obstacle course of newspapers and empty Pepsi bottles and dirty baby clothes. There was a crucifix on one wall with a piece of faded, drooping palm stuck behind it. Next to it a photo of Bruce Springsteen had been taped to the soiled wallpaper.

"These kids was off visitin' last time you was here," Doreen said. She referred to the two small boys standing to the right of the armchair where she sat holding her infant.

"Off visiting where?" Alison said, keeping her voice calm.

"Grandmother's."

"I see."

"They was stayin' there for a while but now they're back with me so I'm goin' to need more money from the agency. You know."

"Maybe the man you have staying here could help you out."

There. She'd said it quickly. With no malice. A plain simple fact.

"Ain't no man livin' here."

"I took a picture of him this morning."

"No way."

Alison sighed. "You know you can't get full payments if you have an adult male staying with you, Doreen."

"He musta been the garbage man or somethin'. No adult male stayin' here. None at all."

Alison had her clipboard out. She noted on the proper lines of the form that a man was staying here. She said, "You borrowed those two boys."

"What?"

"These two boys here, Doreen. You borrowed them. They're not yours."

"No way."

Alison looked at one of the ragged little boys and said, "Is Doreen your mother?"

The little boy, nervous, glanced over at Doreen and then put his head down.

Alison didn't want to embarrass or frighten him anymore.

"If I put these two boys down on the claim form and they send out an investigator, it'll be a lot worse for you, Doreen. They'll try and get you for fraud."

"God damn you."

"I'll write them down here if you want me to. But if they get you for fraud—"

"Shit," Doreen said. She shook her head and then she looked at the boys. "You two run on home now, all right?"

"Can we take some cookies, Aunt Doreen?"

She grinned at Alison. "They don't let their Aunt Doreen forget no promises, I'll tell you that." She nodded to the kitchen. "You boys go get your cookies and then go out the back door, all right? Oh, but first say goodbye to Alison here."

Both boys, cute and dear to Alison, smiled at her and then grinned at each other and then ran with heavy feet across the faded linoleum to the kitchen.

"I need more money," Doreen said. "This little one's breakin' me."

"I'm afraid I got you all I could, Doreen."

"You gonna tell them about Ernie?"

"Ernie's the man staying here?"

"Yeah."

"No. Not since you told me the truth."

"He's the father."

"Of your little girl?"

"Yeah."

"You think he'll actually marry you?"

She laughed her cigarette laugh. "Yeah, in about fifty or sixty years."

The house began to become even smaller to Alison then. This sometimes happened when she was interviewing people. She felt entombed in the anger and despair of the place.

She stared at Doreen and Doreen's beautiful little girl.

"Could I hold her?" Alison said.

"You serious?"

"Yes."

"She maybe needs a change. She poops a lot."

"I don't mind."

Doreen shrugged. "Be my guest."

She got up and brought the infant across to Alison.

Alison perched carefully on the very edge of the couch and received the infant like some sort of divine gift. After a moment the smells of the little girl drifted away and Alison was left holding a very beautiful little child.

Doreen went back and sat in the chair and looked at Alison. "You got any kids?"

"No."

"Wish you did though, huh?"

"Yes."

"You married?"

"Not so far."

"Hell, bet you got guys fallin' all over themselves for you. You're beautiful."

But Alison rarely listened to flattery. Instead she was watching the infant's sweet white face. "Have you ever looked at her eyes, Doreen?"

" 'Course I looked at her eyes. She's my daughter, ain't she?"

"No. I mean looked really deeply."

" 'Course I have."

"She's so sad."

Doreen sighed. "She's got a reason to be sad. Wouldn't you be sad growin' up in a place like this?"

Alison leaned down to the little girl's face and kissed her tenderly on the forehead. They were like sisters, the little girl and Alison. They knew how sad the world was. They knew how sad their hearts were.

When the time came, when the opportunity appeared, Alison would do the same favor for this little girl she'd done for the two other little girls.

Not even the handsome Doctor Connery had suspected anything. He'd just assumed that the other two girls had died from crib death.

On another visit, someday soon, Alison would make sure that she was alone with the little girl for a few minutes. Then it would be done and the little girl would not have to grow up and know the even greater sadness that awaited her.

"You really ain't gonna tell them about Ernie livin' here?"

"I've got a picture of him that I can turn in any time as evidence. But I'll tell you what, Doreen; you start taking better care of your daughter—changing her diapers more often and feeding her the menu I gave you—and I'll keep Ernie our secret."

"Can't afford to have no more money taken from me," Doreen said.

"Then you take better care of your daughter," Alison said, holding the infant out for Doreen to take now. "Because she's very sad, Doreen. Very very sad."

Alison kissed the little girl on the forehead once more and then gave her up to her mother.

Soon, little one, Alison thought; soon you won't be so sad. I promise.

Scream Queen

Allow me to introduce myself. My name's Jason Fanning. Not that I probably need an introduction. Not to be immodest but I did, after all, win last year's Academy Award for Best Screenplay.

Same with my two friends, Bill Leigh the Academy Award-winning actor. And Spence Spencer, who won the Academy Award two years ago for Best Director. People with our credentials don't *need* any introductions, right?

Well . . .

That's the kind of thing we talked about nights, after Vic's Video closed down for the night and we sat around Bill's grubby apartment drinking the cheapest beer we could find and watching schlock DVDs on his old clunker of a TV set. Someday we were going to win the Academy Award for our respective talents and everybody who laughed at us and called us geeks and joked that we were probably gay . . . well, when we were standing on the stage with Cameron Diaz hanging all over us . . .

We had special tastes in videos, the sort of action films and horror films that were the staples of a place like Vic's Video.

If it's straight-to-video, we probably saw it. And liked it. All three of us were on Internet blogs devoted to what the unknowledgeable (read: unhip) thought of as shitty movies. But we knew better. Didn't Nicholson, Scorcese, DeNiro and so forth all get their start doing low-ball movies for Roger Corman?

That's how we were going to win our Academy Awards when we finally got off our assess and piled into Spence's eight-year-old Dodge Dart and headed for the land of gold and silicone. We knew it would be a little while before the money and the fame started rolling in. First we'd have to pay our dues doing direct-to-video. We were going to pitch ourselves as a team. My script, Bill's acting, Spence name-above-the-title directing.

In the meantime, we had to put up with working minimum wage jobs.

Mine was at Vic's Video, a grimy little store resting on the river's edge of a grimy little Midwestern city that hadn't been the same since the glory days of the steamboats Mark Twain wrote so much about.

Even though we worked different gigs, we all managed to go hang at Bill's, even though from time to time Bill and I almost got into fistfights. He never let us forget that he was the normal one, what with his good looks and his Yamaha motorcycle and all his ladies. We were three years out of high school. We'd all tried the community college route but since they didn't offer any courses in the films of Mario Bava or Brian DePalma, none of us made it past the first year.

I guess—from the outside, anyway—we were pretty geeky. I had the complexion problem and Spence was always trying to make pharmaceutical peace with his bi-polarity and Bill—well, Bill wasn't exactly a geek. Not so obviously, anyway. He was good-looking, smooth with girls and he got laid a lot. But he was only good-looking on the outside . . . inside he was just as much an outcast as the seldom-laid Spence and I . . .

Do I have to tell you that people we went to high school smirked whenever they saw us together? Do I have to tell you that a lot of people considered us immature and worthless? Do I have to tell you that a big night out was at GameLand where we competed with ten- and twelve-year-olds on the video games? If Spence was off his medication and he lost to some smart-ass little kid, he'd get pretty angry and bitter. A lot of the little kids were scared of us. And you know what? That felt kinda good, having somebody scared of us. It was the only time we felt important in any way.

And then Michele Danforth came into our lives and changed everything. Everything.

Spence was the first one to recognize her. Not that we believed him at first. He kept saying, That little blonde chick that comes in here every other night or so—that's Michele Danforth. But we didn't believe it, not even when he set three of her video boxes up on the counter and said, You really don't recognize her?

Michele Danforth, in case you don't happen to be into cult videos, was the most popular scream queen of all a couple of years ago. A scream queen? That's the sexy young lady who gets dragged off by the monster/ax-murderer in direct-to-video horror movies. She screams a lot and she almost always gets her blouse and bra ripped off so you can see her breasts. Acting ability doesn't matter so much. But scream ability is vital. And breast ability is absolutely mandatory.

The funny thing is with most scream queens, you never see them completely naked. Not even their bottoms. It's as if all the seventeen-year-old masturbation champions who rent their videos want their scream queens to be pretty virginal. Showing breasts doesn't violate the moral code here. But anything else—well, part of the equation is that you want your scream queen to be the kind of girl you'd marry. The marrying kind never expose their beavers except in doctors' offices.

Couple quick things here about Michele Danforth. She was very pretty. Not cute, not beautiful, not glamorous. Pretty. Soft. A bit on the melancholy side. The kind you fall in love with so uselessly. Uselessly, anyway, if your life's work is watching direct-to-video movies. And those sweet breasts of hers. Not those big plastic monsters. Perfectly shaped medium sized good-girl breasts. And she could actually act. All the blog boys predicted she'd move into mainstream. And who could disagree?

Then she vanished. Became a big media story for a couple weeks and then some other H-wood story came along and everybody forgot her. Vanished. The assumption became that some stalker had grabbed her and killed her. Even though she always said she couldn't afford it—scream queens don't usually make much more than executive secretaries—she had to hire a personal bodyguard because of all the strange and disturbing mail she got.

Vanished.

And now, according to Spence, she resurfaced 1500 miles and three years later. Except that instead of dark-haired, brown-eyed and slender, she was now blonde, blue-eyed and maybe twenty-five pounds heavier. With very earnest brown-rimmed glasses sliding down her nose.

We had to admit that there was a similarity. But it was vague. And it was a similarity that probably belonged to a couple of million young women.

The night the question of her identity got resolved, I was starting the check-out process when the door opened up and she came in. She went right to the Drama section. I'd never seen her go to any of the other sections. Her choices were always serious flicks with serious actors in them. Bill and Spence had taken off to get some beer at the supermarket, the cost of it being way too much at convenience stores.

I'd agreed to the little game they'd come up with. I thought it was kind of stupid but who knew, maybe it would resolve the whole thing.

It was a windy, chill March night. She wore a white turtleneck beneath a cheap, shapeless thigh-length brown velour jacket. She was just one more Midwestern working girl. Nothing remarkable about her at all. She always paid cash from a worn pea-green imitation-leather wallet. Tonight was no different. She never said much, though tonight, as I took her money, she said, Windy. She went under the name Heather Simpson.

Yeah. Where's that warm weather they promised?

She nodded and smiled.

I rang up the transaction and then as I handed her the slip to sign, I nudged the video box sitting next to the cash register out in front of me. *Night of the Depraved* was the title. It showed a huge, blood-dripping butcher knife about to stab into the white-bloused form of a very pretty girl. Who was screaming. The girl was Michele Danforth. The quote along the top of the box read: *Depraved* to the Max . . . and scream queen Danforth is good enuf to eat . . . if you know what I mean! —Dr. Autopsy.com

Oops, I said, hoping she'd think this was all accidental. You don't want that one. I picked up the box and looked at it. I wonder what ever happened to her.

She just shrugged. I wouldn't know. I never watch those kind of movies. She took her change and said, I'm in kind of a hurry.

I handed her the right movie and just as I did so she turned toward me, showing me an angle of her face I'd never seen before. And I said, It's you! Spence was right! You're Michele Danforth!

And just then the door opened up, the bell above it announcing customers, and in came Bill and Spence. They'd left the beer in the car. Video Vic would've kicked my ass all the way over into Missouri if he ever caught us with brew on the premises.

She turned and started away in a hurry, so fast that she brushed up against Spence. The video she carried fell to the floor.

Bill picked it up. He must have assumed that I had played the little game with her—bringing up Michele Danforth and all—because after he bent to pick up the video and handed it to her with a mock-flourish, he said, I'm pleased to present my favorite scream queen with this award from your three biggest fans.

She made a sound that could have been a sob or a curse and then she stalked to the door, throwing it open wide and disappearing into the night. My mind was filled with the image of her face—the fear, the sorrow.

She'll never be back, I said.

I told you it was her, Spence said. She wouldn't have acted that way if it wasn't.

I wanna fuck her, Bill said, and I'm going to.

Spence said, Man, she's nobody now. She's even sort of fat.

Yeah, but how many dudes can say they bopped Michele Danforth?

Wait'll we get to La-La Land, Spence said, we'll be boppin' movie stars every night. And they won't be overweight.

Our collective fantasy had never sounded more juvenile and impossible than it did right then. In that instant I saw what a sad sham my life was. Shoulda gone to college; shoulda done somethin' with my life. Instead I was just as creepy and just as pathetic as all the other direct-to-video freaks who came in here and who we all laughed at when they left. Video Vic's. Pathetic.

Hey, man, hurry up, Bill said to me. I'll get the lights. You bag up the money and the receipts. We'll drop it off at the bank and then tap the beer.

But I was still back there a few scenes. The terror and grief of her face. And the humiliating moment when Spence had spoken our collective fantasy out loud. Something had changed in me in those moments. Good or bad, I couldn't tell yet. I got this sore throat.

Yeah, Bill said, it's such a bad sore throat you can't even swallow beer, huh?

Spence laughed. Yeah, that sounds like a bad one, all right. Can't even swallow beer.

I could tell Bill was looking at me. He was the only one of us who could really intimidate people. So what the hell's really goin' on here, Jason?

I sounded whiny, resentful. I got a sore throat, Lord and Master. If that's all right with you.

It's when I said I'm gonna fuck her, wasn't it? He laughed. In your mind she's still this scream queen, isn't she? Some fucking virgin. She's nobody now.

Then why you want to screw her so bad? I said.

Because then I can say it, asshole. I can say I bopped Michele Danforth. He looked at both me and Spence. I'll have actually accomplished something. Something real. Not just all these fantasies we have about going to Hollywood.

I shouldn't have done it to her, I said. We shouldn't have said anything to her at all. She had her own reasons for vanishing like that.

Yeah, because she was getting fat between movies and they probably didn't want her any more. He laughed.

Hard to tell which rang in his voice the clearest—his cruelty or his craziness. Bill was climbing out on the ledge again. Sometimes he lived there for days. Times like these, we'd get into shoving matches and near-fights.

Spence's attitude had changed. You could see it in his dark eyes. He'd thought it was pretty funny and pretty cool, Bill screwing a scream queen like this. But now I could tell that he thought it was just as twisted as I did. Bill always got intense when he went after something. But this went beyond intensity. He actually looked sort of crazy when he talked about it.

Maybe Jason's right, Bill, Spence said gently. Maybe we should just leave her alone.

The look of contempt was so perfectly conjured up, it was almost like a mask. So was the smirk that came a few seconds later. The Wuss brothers. All these fantasies about what great talents you are. And all the big times you're gonna have in Hollywood. And then when you get a chance to have a little fun, you chicken out and run away. We could all screw her, you know. All three of us. A gang-bang.

Yeah, I said, now there's a great idea, Bill. We could kill her, too. You ever thought of that?

Now who's crazy? All I was talking about was the three of us—

I was as sick of myself just then as I was of Bill. I was already making plans to go call the community college again. See when I needed to enroll for the next semester. I knew that maybe I wouldn't go through with it. But right then with Bill's mind lurching from a one-man seduction to a three-man rape . . . Prisons were filled with guys who'd had ideas like that. And then carried them out.

I got to finish up here, I said, working on the cash register again.

Yeah, c'mon, Spence, let's leave the Reverend here to pray for our souls. We'll go get drunk.

Spence and I had never been very good about standing up to Bill. So I knew what courage it took for Spence to say, I guess not, Bill. I'm not feeling all that well myself.

He called us all the usual names that denote a male who is less than masculine. Then he went over to a stand-up display of the new direct-to-video Julia Roberts movie and started picking up one at a time and firing them around the store. They made a lot of noise and every time one of them smashed into something—a wall, a line of tapes, even a window—both Spence and I felt a nervous spasm going through us. It was like when you're little and you hear your folks having a violent argument and you're afraid your dad's going to kill your mom and you hide upstairs under the covers. That kind of tension and terror.

I came fast around the counter and shouted at him. Then I started running at him. But he beat me to the door.

Good night, ladies. He stood there. Every time I see you from now on, I'm gonna punch your ugly faces in. You two pussies've got an enemy now. And a bad one. He'd never sounded scarier or crazier.

And with that, he was gone.

※ ※ ※

It was misting by the time I got back to my room-and-a-bathroom above a vacuum cleaner repair store. I had enjoyed the walk home.

The mist was dirty gold and swirling in the chilly night. And behind it in doorways and alleyways and dirty windows the eyes of old people and scared people and drug people and queer people and insane people stared out at me, eyes bright in dirty faces. This was an old part of town, the buildings small and fading, glimpses of ancient Pepsi-Cola and Camel cigarette and Black-Jack gum signs on their sides every other block or so, TV repair shops that still had tiny screens inside of big consoles in the windows for nostalgia's sake, and railroad tracks no longer used and stretching into some kind of Twilight Zone miles and miles of gleaming metal down the endless road. There was even a dusty used bookstore that had a few copies of pulps like *The Shadow* and *Doc Savage* and *Dime Detective* in the cracked window and you could stand here sometimes and pretend it was 1938 and the world wasn't so hostile and lonely even though there was a terrible war on the way. It was a form of being stoned, traveling back in time this way, and a perfect head trip to push away loneliness.

To get to my room you took this rotting wooden staircase up the side of the two-story stucco-peeling shop. I was halfway up them before I looked up and saw her sitting there. The scream queen. If the misting bothered her, she didn't seem to mind it.

She smoked a cigarette and watched me. She looked pretty sitting there, not as pretty as when she'd been in the movies, but pretty nonetheless.

How'd you find me?

Asked the guy at the 7-11 if he knew where you lived.

Oh, yeah. Dev. He lives about three down. I smiled. In our gated community.

Sorry I got so hysterical.

I shrugged. We're video store geeks. We can get pretty hysterical ourselves. You should've seen us at our first Trekkie convention in Spock ears and shit. If you had any pictures of us from back then, you could blackmail us.

She smiled. That's assuming you had any money to make it worthwhile.

I laughed. I take it you know how much video store geeks make.

I must've done three hundred signings in video stores. The smile again. It was a good clean one. It erased a lot of years. Most of you are harmless.

We could always go inside, I said.

❋ ❋ ❋

After I handed her a cheap beer, she said, I didn't come up here for sex.

I didn't figure you did.

She glanced around. You could fix this up a little and it wouldn't be so bad. And those *Terminator* posters are a little out of date.

Yeah. But they're signed.

Arnold signed them?

I grinned. Nah, some dude at a comic book convention I went to. He had some real small part in it.

She had a sweet laugh. Played a tree or a car or something like that?

Yeah, you know, along those lines.

She'd taken off her brown velour jacket. Her white sweater showed off those scream queen breasts real real good. It was unsettling, sitting so near a girl whose videos had driven me to rapturous self-abuse so many times. And I had the hairy palms to prove it. Even with the added weight, she looked good in jeans. I'll make you a deal, Jason.

Yeah? What kind of deal. I mean, since we ruled out sex. Much to my dismay.

Oh, c'mon, Jason. You don't really think I just go around sleeping with people do you? That's in the movies. This is straight business, what I'm proposing. I'll clean your apartment here and fix it up if you'll convince your two friends not to let anybody know who I am or where I am.

Spence won't be any trouble.

Is he the good-looking one?

That's Bill.

He looks like trouble.

He is.

She sank back on the couch—one night Spence and I managed to get a couple of girls up here and we all played a game of Guess the Stain with the couch—and covered her face with her hands. I thought she was going to cry. But no sounds came. The only thing you could hear was Churchill, my cat, yowling at cars passing in what was now a downpour.

You OK?

She shrugged. Said nothing. Hands still covering her face. When she took them down, she said, I left LA for my own reasons. And I want to keep them my reasons. And that means making a life for myself somewhere out here. I'm from Chicago. I like the Midwest. But I don't want some tabloid to find out about me.

Well, like I say, Spence won't be any trouble. But Bill—

Where's he live?

I was thinking about what Bill had said about screwing a scream queen. Even if she wasn't a scream queen anymore. It didn't make much sense to me but it sure seemed to make a lot of sense to him.

Why don't I talk to him first?

She looked relieved. Good. I'd appreciate that. I'm supposed to start this job next week. A good job. Decent bennies and from what everybody says, some real opportunities there. I want to start my life all over.

I'll talk to him.

She was all business. Grabbing her coat. Sliding into it. Standing up. Looking around at the stained and peeling wallpaper and all the posters, including the latest scream queen Linda Sanders. She's a nice kid. Had a real shitty childhood. I hope she can beat the rap—you know, go on and do some real acting. I saw her at a small playhouse right before I left LA. She was really good.

I liked that. How charitable she was about her successor. A decent woman.

Churchill came out and rubbed his head against her ankle. She held him up and gave him that smile of hers. We both need to go to Weight Watchers, my friend.

He stays up late at night and watches TV and orders from Domino's when I'm asleep.

She gave him a kiss. I believe it.

She set him down, put out her hand and shook, that formal forced way people do in banking commercials right after the married couple agrees to pay the exorbitant interest rates. I really appreciate this, Jason. I'll start figuring out how I'm going to fix up your apartment. I live in this tiny trailer. I've got it fixed up very nicely.

You didn't screw her, did you? Bill said when he came into the store.

He'd been hustling around the place, getting the displays just so, setting up the 50% OFF bin of VHS and DVD films we hadn't been able to move, snapping Mr. Coffee to burbling attention. When I told him she'd come over to my place last night, he stopped, frozen in place and asked if I'd screwed her.

Yeah. Right on the front lawn. In the rain. Just humping our brains out.

You'd better not have, you bastard. I'm the one who gets to nail her.

At any given time Bill is always about seven minutes away from the violent ward but I couldn't ever recall seeing him this agitated about something.

She isn't going to screw anybody, Bill. Now shut up and listen.

Oh, sure, he said, now you're her press agent? All the official word comes from you?

She's scared, asshole.

Listen, Jason. Spare me the heartbreak, all right? She's been around. She doesn't need some video geek hovering over her. Then: That's how you're gonna get in her panties, isn't it? Be her best friend. One of those wussy deals. Well, it's not gonna work because she'll never screw a pus-face like you. You checked out your blackheads lately, Jason?

I swung on him, then. When my fist collided with his cheek, he gaped at me in disbelief, then sort of disintegrated, started screaming at me real high-pitched and all, as he stumbled backwards into a display of a new Disney family movie. Most surprisingly of all, he didn't come after me. Maybe I'd just stunned him. He'd always seen Spence and I as his inferiors—we were the geeks, according to him; he wasn't a geek; he was a cool dude who pitied us enough to hang out with us—and so maybe he was just in shock. His slave had revolted and he hadn't had time to deal with it mentally yet.

She's afraid you'll tell somebody who she is, I said. And if you do, you're going to be damned sorry.

And then I couldn't believe what I did. I hit him again. This time he might have responded but just then the front door opened, the bell tinkled, the first customer of the day, a soccer-mom with a curly-haired little girl in tow, walked in with an armload of overdue DVDs. Mrs. Preston. Her stuff was always overdue.

I had just enough time to see that a pimple of blood hung from Bill's right nostril. I took an unholy amount of satisfaction in that.

Michele didn't want to see me. She was nice about it. She said she really appreciated me talking to Bill about her and that she really appreciated me stopping by like this but she was just in a place where she wanted to be alone, sort of actually needed to be alone and she was sure I understood. Because that was obviously the kind of guy I was, the understanding kind.

In other words, it was the sort of thing I'd been hearing from girls all my life. How nice I was and how understanding I was and how they were sure, me being so understanding and all, that it was cool if we just kind of left things as they were, you know being just friends and all. Which is what she ended up saying.

As usual, I'd gotten ahead of myself. By this time, I had this crush on her and whenever I get a crush of this particular magnitude I start dreaming the big dream. You know, not only having sex but maybe her really falling in love with me and maybe moving in together and maybe me getting a better job and maybe us—it could happen—getting married and settling down just as the couples always do in the screwball comedies of the Thirties and Forties Bill and Spence always rag on me for liking so much.

Over a three-day period I must have called Spence eight or nine times, always leaving a message on his machine. He never called back. I finally went over there after work one night. He had a two-room apartment on a block where half the houses had been torn down. I was just walking up to the front door when Spence and Bill came out.

They were laughing until they saw me. Beery laughter. They'd both been gunning brew.

Bill was the one I watched. His hands formed fists instantly and he dropped back a foot and went into a kind of boxer's crouch. You got lucky the other day, Jason.

I don't think so, Bill. I think you got lucky because Mrs. Preston came in.

Spence's face reflected the disbelief all three of us were probably feeling. I couldn't believe it, either. I'd stood up to Bill the other day but I think both of us thought it was kind of a fluke. But it wasn't. I was ready to hit him again.

The only difference between the other morning and now was that he was half-drunk. Brew makes most of us feel tougher and handsomer and smarter and wittier than we really are. Prisons are packed with guys who let brew addle their perception of themselves. Or dope. Doesn't matter.

He came at me throwing a roundhouse so vast in scope it couldn't possibly have landed on me. All I had to do was take a single step backward.

I don't want to fight you, Bill. Spence, pull him back.

Whatever Bill said was lost in his second lunge. This punch connected. He got me on my right cheek and pain exploded across my entire face. He followed up with a punch to my stomach that doubled me over. Kick his ass, Bill, Spence said.

Even though I was in pain, even though I should have been focused on the fight I was in, his words, the betrayal of them, him choosing Bill over me when it should have been Spence and I against Bill—that hurt a lot more than the punches. He'd been my friend since third grade. He was my friend no longer.

Bill hit me with enough force to knock me flat on the sidewalk, butt first. If this had been the other night, I would've jumped to my feet and started swinging. But I was still hearing Spence say to kick my ass and I guess I didn't have enough pride or anger left to stand up and hit back. I just felt drained.

You all right? Spence said to me. I could hear his confusion. Better to stick with Bill. But still, we'd been friends a long time and to see me knocked down—

He's just a pussy, Bill said. C'mon.

I didn't stand up till they were gone. Then I walked home slowly. I took the long way so that I'd go past Michele's place. The light was on. I turned off the sidewalk and started moving toward the house but then I stopped. I wasn't up for another disappointment tonight.

Video Vic's real name wasn't Vic it was Reed, Reed Patrick, and when I called him next morning and gave him my week's notice, he said, You don't sound so good, kiddo. You all right?

I just need to be movin' on, Reed. I enjoyed working for you, though.

You ever want to use me for a reference, that'll be fine with me.

Thanks, Reed.

That night, I surprised my folks by showing up for dinner. Mom had made meat loaf and mashed potatoes and peas. I figured that was about the best meal I'd ever had. They were surprised that I'd quit my job but my Dad said, Now you can start looking for something with a future, Jason. You could start taking classes again out to the college. Get trained for some kind of computer job or something.

Computers, honey, my Mom said, patting my hand. Jobs like that pay good money.

And they've got a future.

That's right, Mom said, computers aren't going anywhere. They're here for good.

You should call out there tomorrow, Dad said. And my buddy Mike can get you on at the supermarket he runs.

I pretended to be interested in what he was saying. I'd never seemed interested before. He looked happy about me, the way he had when I was a little kid. I hadn't seen him look this happy in a long time. He also looked old. I guess I hadn't really, you know, just looked at him for a real long time. The same with Mom. The lines in their faces. The bags under their eyes. The way both my folks seemed kind of worn out through the whole meal. When I left I hugged them harder than I had in years. And all the way back to my little room, I felt this sadness I just couldn't shake.

Over the next week, the sadness stayed with me. I'd realized by then that it wasn't just about Mom and Dad, it was about me and everything that had happened in the past couple of weeks. I tried Michelle a couple more times. The second times she was real cold. You know how girls are when they aren't happy to hear from you and just want to get you off the phone. After I hung up, I sat there in the silence with Churchill weighing a ton on my lap. I felt my cheeks burn. It was pretty embarrassing, the way she'd maneuvered me off the phone so fast.

The next night, no longer gainfully employed, I walked over town to the library. I was reading the whole run of George R.R. Martin fantasy novels. He was one of the best writers around.

Even though they'd bought six copies of his new hardcover, they were all checked out. I picked up a collection of his short stories. He was good at those, too.

On the walk back home, I saw them coming out of a Hardees. He had his arm around her. They were laughing. I was ready to fight now. Just walk right up to him and punch him in the fucking chops. He'd be the one sitting down on his butt this time, not me. And I'd remind her that she still owed me an apartment cleaning.

Good ole Michele and good ole Bill. That's the thing I've never understood about girls. Hard to imagine a guy more full of himself than Bill. But she thought obviously he was just fine and dandy. Otherwise she wouldn't let him have his arm around her. He was going to sleep with her and then he was going to tell everybody. I wondered how she'd react if I told her.

But I couldn't. Much as I wanted to go over there and tell her what was really going on, I couldn't make my legs move in that direction. Because I could live with my self-image as a geek, a loser, a boy-man but I could never live with myself as a snitch.

A few days later I signed up for computer classes at the community college. I gave up my room on the rent-due day and moved back home. The folks were glad to have me. I was being responsible. Dad said his buddy Mike could get me on at his supermarket and so he had.

What I did for the next few nights, after bagging groceries till nine o'clock, was glut myself on the past. I still had boxes of old *Fangorias* and *Filmfaxes* in my old closet and I hauled them out and spread them on the bed and just disappeared into my yesterdays, back to the time when there was no doubt that I was going to Hollywood, no doubt that I'd be working for Roger Corman, no doubt that someday I'd be doing my own films and no doubt they'd be damned good ones.

But my time machine sprung a leak. I'd get all caught up in being sixteen again and grooving on *Star Wars* and *Planet of the Apes* and *Alien* but then the poison gas of now would seep in through those leaks. And I'd start thinking about Michele and Bill and Spence and how my future seemed settled now—computer courses and a lifelong job in some dusty little computer store in a strip mall somewhere— and then I'd be back to the here and now. And not liking it at all.

On a rainy Friday night, my Mom knocked on my door and said, Spence is downstairs for you, honey.

I hadn't told my folks about the falling out Spence and I had had.

I just said OK and went down to see him. He was talking to my Dad. Dad was telling him how happy they were about my taking those computer courses.

I grabbed my jacket and we went out. I hadn't so much as nodded at Spence. In fact, we didn't say a word until we were in his old Dodge Dart and heading down the street.

How you been? he said.

Pretty good.

Your Dad seems real happy about you being in computer classes.

Yeah.

You don't sound so happy, though.

What's this all about, Spence?

What's what all about?

What's what all about? What do you think it's all about? You took Bill's side on this whole thing. Now you come over to my house.

He didn't say anything for a while. We just drove. Headlights and neon lights and street lights glowed like water-colors in the rain. Girls looked sweet and young and strong running into cafes and theaters to get out of the downpour. His radio faded in and out. Every couple minutes he'd slam a fist on the dash and the radio would be all right again for a few minutes. The car smelled of gasoline and mildewed car seats.

He's getting really weird.

Who is?

Who is? Who do you think is, Jason? Bill is.

Weird about what?

About her. Michele.

Weird how?

He's really hung up with Michele. He won't tell me what it is but somethin's really buggin' him.

I'm supposed to feel bad about it?

I'm just telling you is all.

Why? Why would I give a shit?

He glanced over at me. I shoulda stuck up for you with Bill. The night he knocked you down, I mean. I'm sorry.

You really pissed me off.

Yeah, I know. And I'm sorry. I really am. I—I just can't handle being around Bill anymore. This whole thing with Michele. She's all he talks about and she won't let him do nothin'. He says it's like bein' in sixth grade again.

I wasn't up for just driving around. I'd done enough cruising in my high school years. I said, You seen that new Wes Craven flick?

Huh-uh.

There'll be a late show. We could still make it.

So you're not still pissed?

Sure I'm still pissed. But I want to see the Wes Craven and you're the only person I know who's got a car.

I don't blame you for still bein' pissed.

I don't blame me for still bein' pissed, either.

I didn't hear from Spence till nearly a week later. After the Craven flick, which was damned good, he started talking about other things we could do but I just told him I was busy. Sometimes, friendships, even long ones, just end. One thing happens and you realize that the friendship was never as strong as you'd thought. Or maybe you just realize that you're one cold, unforgiving prick. Whichever it was, I wasn't up for seeing Spence or Bill or Michele for a long time. Maybe never.

I went my glum way to computer classes and my even glummer way to the supermarket.

※　※　※

He was in the supermarket parking lot waiting for me when I got off work. I walked over to his car. It was a warm, smoky October night. Big ass harvest moon. I wanted to be a kid again in my Halloween costume. I could barely—just quite—remember what it had been like to go trick or treating before the days when perverts and sadists hid stick pins and razor blades in candy apples.

I walked over to the driver's side of his car. I wanted to walk home. October nights like this were my favorites.

Hey, he said.

Hey.

You doin' anything special?

Yeah. Nicole Kidman called. She wants to go get a pizza with me. She said she'll pay for it. And the motel room afterward.

Remember to bring a condom.

She's got me covered there, too. She bought a big box of them.

We just looked at each other across an unbreachable chasm of time and pain. He'd been a part of my boyhood. But I wasn't a boy anymore. Not a man yet, to be sure. But not a boy, either.

He's pretty fucked up.

We talking about Bill?

Yeah. Had the day off. Drinking beers with whiskey chasers.

Good. We need to drink more. Make sure we're winos before we hit twenty-five.

I think maybe we should go over to Michele's place.

Why?

He stared at the passing cars. When he looked back at me, he said, You better get in, Jason. This shit could be real bad.

It was one of the little Silverstream trailers that are about as big as an SUV. Except, given its condition, this one should have been called Ruststream. It sat between two large oak trees on a corner where a huge two-story house had been torn down the summer before. The rest of the neighborhood blazed with laughter and throbbing car engines and rap music and folks of both the black and white persuasion filling porches and sidewalks, most of them trying to look and sound like bad asses. Her trailer was a good quarter block from its nearest neighbor.

Bill's motorcycle leaned against one of the trees. No lights, no sound coming from the trailer.

Maybe he's getting the job done, Spence said.

Maybe, I said.

The door was open half an inch. I opened it wide and stuck my head in.

What the fuck you think you're doin'?

I couldn't see him at first, couldn't see anything except vague furniture shapes. Smells of whiskey and cigarettes. A cat in the gloom, crying now.

Get out of here, Jason.

Where's Michele?

Where you think she is, asshole?

I wanna talk to her.

I told you once, Jason. Get out of here. I knocked you on your ass once. And I can do it again.

No, you can't.

Two steps led up to the trailer floor. I was about to set my right foot on the second step when he came at me. My mind had time to register that he was wearing jeans, no shirt, no socks, and he had a whiskey bottle in his hand.

He tackled me and drove me all the way to the ground. He meant to hit me with the whiskey bottle but I had the advantage of being sober. He smelled of puke and booze and sex and greasy food, maybe a hamburger.

As the bottle arced downward, I rolled to the right, moving slowly enough to slam my fist hard into the side of Bill's head. The punch dazed him but not enough to keep him from trying to get me again with the bottle. This time I didn't have time to move away from it. All I could do was grab the wrist and slow the bottle as it descended. It connected but not hard enough to knock me out. Or to stop me from landing another punch on the same side of his head as before. This one knocked him loose from me. His straddling legs loosened enough to let me buck him off. He went over backwards. He was drunk enough to be confused by all this happening so quickly. Now it was my turn to straddle him. I just wanted to make his face bloody. I hit him until my hands started to hurt and then I stood up, grabbed him by an arm and started dragging him to his motorcycle.

Go get his stuff from inside, OK? I said to Spence.

He nodded and ran over to the trailer. He didn't need to go inside. Michele was in the doorway, dropping Bill's shoes, socks, shirt and wallet one by one into Spence's hands. She wore a white terrycloth robe. She had a cigarette going. You stay with me for a while, Jason? she said.

Sure.

By now, Bill was on his motorcycle, roaring it to raucous life. Spence handed him his belongings.

Spence said, Looks like her nose is busted, man. You do that?

Shut the fuck up, Spence, Bill said. Then he made his bike louder than I'd ever heard it before. Bill glared at Spence for a long time and said, I don't know what I ever saw in a pussy like you, Spence. Don't call me anymore.

You beat her up, man. You don't have to worry about me callin' you.

He roared away, grass and dirt churning from beneath his back wheel. He got all the way down the block before I said anything. I'll just walk home later.

Wait'll you see her, Jason. He beat the shit out of her.

He walked back to the street and drove away.

The light was on in the front part of the trailer now. She was gone from the door. When I sat down at the small table across from her, she pushed a cold can of Bud my way. I thanked her and gunned an ounce or two. My head hurt from where he got me with the bottle. She'd fixed up her trailer just the right way—so that you forgot you were in a trailer.

Her delicate nose didn't look broken, as Spence had said, but it was badly bruised. She had a black eye, a bloody, swollen mouth and her left cheek was bruised.

Maybe you should go to an ER, I said.

I'll survive. She made an effort to laugh. I let him sleep with me but that wasn't enough for him.

What the hell else did he want?

Well, he slept with me but I wouldn't take my bra or my blouse off. I said I had my reasons and I wanted him to respect them. In some weird way, I'd started to like him. Maybe I was just lonely. I never could pick men for shit. You should've seen some of the losers I went out with in LA. My girl friends always used to laugh and say that if there was a serial killer on the dance floor, he'd be the one I end up with for the night.

So you made love and—

We made love. I mean, it wasn't the first time. The last couple weeks, we'd been sleeping together. And he tried real hard to deal with me not taking my top off. I wouldn't let him touch my breasts. She smiled with bloody teeth. My scream queen breasts. She shook her head. Or tried. She was halfway through turning her head to the left when she stopped. She had a bad headache, too, apparently. It was building up. His thing about my breasts. And tonight, afterwards, he just went crazy. Said if I really loved him I'd be completely nude for him. I liked him. But not enough to trust him. You know, with my secret.

She lighted a cigarette with a red plastic lighter. I'd never seen her smoke before. She looked around a bit and then back at me and said, It's why I left LA.

What is?

I don't have breasts any more. I had this really bad kind of breast cancer. I had to have both of them removed. She exhaled through bloody lips. So how would that be? A scream queen known for her breasts doesn't have any more? I went to Eugene, Oregon to get the diagnosis. I kind've suspected I had breast cancer. I didn't want anybody in LA to know. I paid cash, gave a fake name, they didn't have any idea who I was. I had the double mastectomy there, too. I had some money saved and I used it to disappear. I just couldn't've handled all the publicity. All the bullshit about how my breasts inspiring all these young boys—and then not having them anymore. You know how the tabloids are. And then do a couple weepy interviews on TV. So I've just been traveling around. And I'll be doing more traveling tomorrow. Because I know Bill will call some reporter or tabloid or somebody like that. I just don't want to face it.

She said, C'mere, OK?

I stood up and walked over to her. My knees trembled. I didn't know why.

She took my right hand and guided it to her chest and then slid it inside the terrycloth so that I could feel the scarring from the mastectomy. I wanted to jerk my hand away. I'd never felt anything like that before. But then a tenderness came over me and I let my hand linger and then she eased my hand out of her robe and kissed my fingers, as if she were grateful.

Then she started sobbing and it was pretty bad and I said everything I knew to say but it didn't do any good so I steered her into bed and just lay with her there in the darkness and we held hands and she talked about it all, everything from the day she first felt the tiny lump on the underside of her left breast to being so afraid she'd die from the anesthetic—she'd had an uncle who died while being put under, died right there on the table—and how she went through depression so bad she lost twenty-five pounds in three months and how that then turned around and become the opposite kind of eating disorder, this relentless urge to gorge, which she was battling now.

In the morning, I helped her load her car. She didn't have all that much. I told her I'd pay the rent off with the money she gave me and return the key. She kissed me then for the first and only time—the kind of kiss your sister would give you—and then she was gone.

The story hit one of the supermarket papers three weeks later. She'd been right. The whole thing dealt with the irony of a girl who'd been made into a scream queen at least partly because of her beautiful breasts—and then losing them to cancer. A minister somewhere said that it was God's wrath, exploiting your body for filthy Hollywood money, and then getting your just desserts. You know how God's people like to talk.

As for me . . . tomorrow I'm flying to LA. My Dad has a friend out there who owns a video company that produces training films for various companies. Not exactly Paramount pictures, or even Roger Corman. But a start. My folks even gave me five thousand dollars as seed money. They're pretty sure that in a year I'll be back here. And maybe they're right . . .

It's funny about Michele. I watch her old videos all the time. That's how I prefer to remember her. It's not because of her breasts. It's because of that lovely girly radiance that was in her eyes and her smile back in those days.

I still watch them and I'm sure Spence does, too. He got a job in Chicago and moved there a couple months back. Bill joined the Army. I wonder if he still watches them.

But most of all I wonder if Michele ever watches them. Probably not.

Not now, anyway. But maybe someday.

Cages

He knows the bad thing will happen, the way it always happens, his father coming home late and all dreamdusted up and his mother shrieking and screaming how he spent all the money on the dreamdust and then the—

He knows when to put the pillow over his head so he will not hear when his father slams his mother into the wall and starts hitting her.

Sometimes he tries to stop it but it never does any good. He is three-foot-six and has only the one arm and is no match at all for his father.

Then in the room next to his, in the darkness, after the hitting and the screaming, there are other sounds now on the bed, grunts and sighs and whimpers and then

Sleep.

A dream.

His mother and father and himself in a new car riding down the street. People pointing at them. Envious. Such a nice family. The envious people do not even seem to notice his bald head or his lone shriveled arm or the way the sticky stuff runs from his ear and

Awake.

Late night.

Sirens.

Laser blasts.

Coppers hunting down dreamduster gangs.

He wants to kill the man who invented dreamdust. All the misery it causes. Mrs. Caruso's daughter letting all those men stick themselves up the slit between her legs. Mr. Feinmann smashing his wife's head in with a bottle because she wouldn't give him the tips from her waitress job. Little Betty Malloy being killed by the dreamduster who put a broomhandle up her backside and then cut her up with a butcher knife.

Night.

Hot.

Goes out on the fire escape.

Tomorrow it will just start again. The argument about you fucking cunt where'd all the money go? and her shrieking you dreamdust fucker you dreamdust fucker!

Always: money money money.

And then he remembers the commercial on the vid. Seen that commercial a lot the last five six weeks. And always has the same thought,

$$$

flashing on the screen and this real loud guy telling you how you can collect them.

All you gotta do see is.

Be so easy.

So fucking easy.

And then they'd have plenty of $.

No more fights.

No more hitting.

He lies out on the fire escape thinking about tomorrow morning. His mother will be gone to work and so will he.

No trouble going in the closet where

And getting a sack

And

Going down to the place it says in the commercial

And

He can see all those fuckers who pick on him and hit him and call him faggot and mutant and all that shit.

He can see them standing enviously on the corner when he cruises by in the back seat of his parents' new car.

Fuck you.

You're the faggot.

You're the mutant.

Not me.

Fuckers.

And yes yes won't they be sorry and yes yes won't they be envious.

He wishes it was tomorrow morning already.

Bitch can't even fix me any fucking breakfast? You know how fuckin hard I work on that fuckin dock you cunt?

Early morning battle.

Father slamming out heading for the choppy dark waters on this muggy overcast day.

Mother not long behind him.

Coming in and leaning down to his bed and giving him this wet perfume kiss and still crying from the early morning battle and because she got clipped a good one on the right cheekbone even a little bruise there.

And him going fitfully back to sleep.

And dreaming the car dream again.

And dreaming about going to see this doctor who fixes him up so he looks just like the fuckers who pick on him all the time.

Hey Quasimodo they say sometimes.

Hey hunchbacka Notre Dame little faggot.

And is awake now.

And in the bathroom taking down the underwear his mother always washes out at night him only having the one pair but no amount of washing taking the brown stains from the back or the yellow from the front.

And then moving fast.

Afraid one of them might pop back in and see what he's doing and with his sack he hurries from the apartment.

Horns and exhaust fumes and perfume and farts and fat people and skinny people and people talking to themselves and dreamdusters and gangs and whores and faggots and

And he's hurrying fast as he can down his little street carrying his little sack and he makes it no more than half a block when he sees Ernie that fucking Ernie wouldn't you know.

And nigger Ernie steps in front of him and says, What shit you got there in that sack?

Is scared. Isn't sure what to say. Ernie is real real tall with gold teeth and knuckles that feel like sharp rocks when they hit your skull.

Takin back some popsies. You know get the refund.

Popsies shit. That ain't popsies in that sack, you little fuckin mutant.

Then Gil then Bob then Mike are there all friends of Ernie two of them be white but no matter they're every bit as mean as Ernie hisself.

And Mike grabs for the sack and says gimme it you little faggot.

Hunchbacka Notre Dame Bob says.

You heard him Ernie says give it to him.

Just a plain brown sack but you can see stains on the sides of it now damned thing leaking from inside.

Thinks he's gonna get a clear run for it starts to weave and wobble between them.

But then Gil and Mike grab him by the shoulders and throw him up against the building and

Ernie grabs the sack from him.

And smiles with his gold teeth.

And hold the sack teasing up real high.

And says you can have it faggot if you can jump this high.

And he starts to cry but stops himself knowing that will only make it worse.

Fuckin Ernie anyway.

Nigger Ernie.

Hey asshole Mike says look inside.

So Ernie does.

Turns away.

And holds the sack down.

And opens it up.

Holy shit.

What's wrong?

Man, you gotta see what's in this sack, man.

So Gil takes a look. And he makes the same kinda sick face that Ernie did. Aw God. I wanna puke.

He's afraid they'll do something to it. He keeps thinking of the place he saw on the commercial. He wants to be there now. Getting his money.

You just bring 'em right down here for more cash $$$$ than you ever seen in your life. You just ask for Smilin' Bob. That's me.

And reaches out to snatch the sack back.

And gets hit fullfist by Mike.

Please c'mon you guys please.

Doesn't want to start crying.

And then they start throwing the sack back and forth over their heads.

Fuckers you fuckers he cries running back and forth between them.

And then he sees the cop, an android, not a real person, android coppers being the only kind they'll send to a shithold like this one

And the android senses something wrong so he comes over.

And of course Ernie and the others split because androids always want to ask a lot of questions being programmed to just that and all, and people like

Ernie and Gil always having something to hide and never wanting to answer questions.

They drop his sack on the ground and take off running.

He bends and picks it up and then he starts running, too. He doesn't like androids any better than Ernie does.

He keeps his sack pulled tight.

By the time he gets to Smilin' Bob's, the rain has started, dirty hot city rain summer rain dirty summer rain, and he's drenched.

And there's a line all the way out the front door and all the way down the block.

People of all ages and descriptions holding boxes and sacks and bags. And the things inside them making all kinds of squeals and groans and moans and grunts and cries. And smelling so bad sometimes he thinks he's gonna puke or pass out.

And then this guy dressed all in yellow with this big-ass laser gun dangling down from the long line saying, If you got somethin' dangerous, you let us know in advance, folks, cause otherwise we'll just have to kill the thing right on the spot unless you warn us about it. He says this in both English and Spanish. And then just keeps walking up and down and down saying it over and over and over again.

All the time raining its ass off.

All the time getting bumped and pushed and kicked because he's so little.

All the time his sack wiggling and wiggling trying to get free.

There's a lot of talk in line:

How this one guy heard about this other guy who brought this little sack to Smilin' Bob's and two days later the fucker was a millionaire.

How this one guy heard about this other guy he's waitin' in line here just like now ('cept it ain't rainin' in this here particular story) and this fuckin' thing comes right up outta this other guy's sack and kills the first guy right on the spot, goes right for his throat and tears it right out.

How this one guy heard about this other guy said that he had two of them once that ate each other—just like cannibals you know what I'm sayin'—but then they'd puke each other back up whole and start all over again. No shit. I swear onna stack of Bibles and my pappy's grave. True facts. Puked each other up and started all over again . . .

Finally finally finally the rain still raining and the thing in his sack still crying, he reaches the head of the line and goes inside.

🕷 🕷 🕷

First one this fat girl, they say no.

What you do inside is stand in another line and when you're first up they take your sack or your box from you and carry it inside this room that's bright with a special kind of lighting and they half-close the door and they talk among themselves except Smilin' Bob himself who stands at the head of the line sayin', You folks jes relax we're getting to ya fast as we can. He's got up just like on TV big-ass ten-gallon hat and western-style shirt and string tie and downhome accent.

And when they're done with the fat girl's bag this tall pale guy comes out and shakes his head and says sorry ma'am just won't do us no good.

Fucker you fucker you know how bad I need this money? she shrieks.

But Smilin' Bob jes kinda leans back and says, No call for talkin' that way to Butch here' no call at all.

And the fat girl goes away

And a black kid steps up and they take his box and they go inside the blinding bright room and lights flash and male voices mutter and they come back out and hand him the box and the tall pale one is wiggling and waggling his hand sayin' that little fucker bit me you want me to I'll kill him for you kid. We got an easy way of doin' it kid won't hurt the little fucker at all.

But the kid snatches the box back and takes off all huffy and pissed because there's no money in it for him.

And next and next and next and next and finally

his turn.

Is scared.

Knows they're not going to take it.

Knows he won't get no money.

Knows that his dad'll beat the shit out of his mom tonight soon as they start arguin' about money and dreamdust and shit like that.

Smilin' Bob takes the sack and peeks inside and makes the same face Ernie did and says Well well well and my my my and I'll be jiggered I'll just be jiggered and then hands the sack over the tall pale assistant who takes it inside the bright room and starts all the usual stuff lights flashing meters clicking voices mumbling and muttering and

Holy shit.

That's what the guy inside says:

Holy shit. Lookit that friggin' meter.

Smilin' Bob he hears it too and he looks back over his shoulder and then back at him and winks.

Maybe you dun brung Smilin' Bob somethin' special.

I sure hope so Smilin' Bob somethin' special.

I sure hope so Smilin' Bob.

And Smilin' Bob smiles and says: I give you a lotta money, what y'all gonna do with it anyways?

Give it to my dad and mom.

Well ain't that sweet.

He's a dreamduster and they fight all the time and I'm scared some night he's gonna kill her and maybe if I get enough money and give it to my mom maybe they won't have to argue anymore and

The door opens.

Tall pale guy comes out.

Walks right over to Smilin' Bob and whispers something in his ear

And Smilin' Bob real solemn like nods and then comes over and puts his hand on his shoulder and leads him away from the line.

You know how much we're gonna give you? Smilin' Bob asks.

He's excited. How much?

$500

$$$$$$$$$

Just like on the commercial.

That's all he can think of.

$$$$$$$$$

Just like on the commercial.

That's all he can think of.

$$$$$$$$$

How happy his Mom will be.

How proud his Mom will be.

No more arguments

No more beatings for anybody

$$$$$$$$.

Oh thank you Smilin' Bob thank you.

One hour and twenty-eight minutes later he's on his way home. No sweat with Ernie and those fuckers. Rainin' too hard. They're inside.

Wants to beat Mom home.

Wants to be sittin' there this big grin on his face

And all this money sittin' right on the table

And wants to see her face

See her smile.

And say oh honey oh honey now me'n your dad we won't have to argue no more.

Oh honey.

Which is just where he is when she comes through the door.

Right at the table

And which is just what he's doing

Counting out the money so she's sure to see it.

$$$$$$

And at first she's so tired she don't even notice it.

Just comes in all weary and all sighs and says think I gotta lay down hon I'm just bushed

And starts draggin' herself past him into the little living room with all the smashed-up furniture from the last couple of fights.

And then she notices.

Out of the corner of her eye.

Says: Hey, what's that?

Money.

Aw shit honey them cops they'll beat you sure as shit they catch you stealin' like that.

Didn't steal it ma honest.

Comes closer to the table and sees just how much is there: Aw honey where'd you ever get this much money?

And he tells her.

And she says: You what?

Sold it.

Sold it! It ain't an "it" for one thing it's your sister.

Ain't my sister he says (but already he's feeling hot and panicky and kinda sick; not turnin' out the way he planned not at all) ain't nobody's sister she's just this little—

And she slaps him.

And he can't believe how terrible and rotten everything has turned out.

Where's her smile?

Where's her sayin they won't argue no more?

Where's her sayin what a good boy he is?

She fuckin' slaps him.

Slaps him the way the old man always slaps him

And after he did so good too

Gettin the money and all.

Slaps him!

Then she's really on him

Shakin him and slappin him even harder.

Where is she? Where is she?

Smilin' Bob's got her he says.

Who's Smilin' Bob.

He's this guy on TV Ma.

SHE'S YOUR SISTER YOU STUPID LITTLE BASTARD! CAN'T YOU UNDERSTAND THAT SHE'S YOUR OWN FLESH AND BLOOD! Now you take me to this Smilin' Bob.

Never seen her like this.

Not even when the old man beats her.

All crazy screamin' and fidgetin' and cryin'.

Grabs him and pulls him up from the chair and says: Take me to this Smilin' Bob and right now.

And so they stumble out into the early night

And

On the way she explains things again even though he can't seem to understand them: sixty years ago bad people put bad things into the river and ever since then some of the babies have been strange and sad and sometimes even frightening creatures, some babies (like his sister) being born so ugly that they had to hide them from the government, which is why they kept his little sister in the spare room because word would get around the neighborhood and government agents might find out and would kill the little girl.

But she isn't a little girl he says she don't even look like a little girl.

(His mother hurrying down the streets now, hurrying and jerking him along)

And these Smilin' Bob fuckers (she says) what they do is they take in these babies and the ones they think are telepathic (or something else worth study) they sell to the government or private labs to study. They wouldn'ta paid you no $500 unless they thought she was gonna bring 'em a lot back.

The rain has stopped. Night has come. A chill night. The neon streets shine blue and yellow and green with neons. The freaks and the geeks are back panhandling.

As she hurries hurries

And (she says) You was lucky and don't you ever forget it. You was lucky, the way you was born I mean, you wasn't normal but you wasn't like your sister. Nobody wouldn'ta taken you away like they woulda her.

And then she starts crying again

Which is the weird thing as they hurry along

How she keeps shifting in and out of sobbing and tears and curses

One minute she'll be all right talking to him and then she just goes crazy again

You shouldnt'a fuckin done it you shouldnt'a fuckin done it over and over and over again.

Without the long lines (and in the night) Smilin' Bob's looks very different, long shadows and soft street light hiding the worst of the graffiti

And

You show me the door you went in.

Right there ma.

And she goes up and peers inside

And then goes crazy again

Banging and kicking on the door

And screaming you gimme my little girl back you fuckers you gimme my little girl back

And is crying again of course

Sobbing screaming keening

And banging and kicking and banging and kicking and

Just the darkness inside

Just the silence

You gimme my little girl back

And then

She runs around the back and all he can do is follow

Alley very dark smelling awful as they pass a dumpster

She opens the dumpster lid and peeks inside and

Screams

Freaks and geeks of every kind inside the rejects that they thought they could sell but couldn't

half-cat half-baby things things with one cyclopean eye in the middle of their forehead things with a flipper-like little arm sticking out of their sternums things that are doll-like little replicas of human beings except in the open eyes (even dead) you can see their stone madness

And every one of them had been hidden by their mothers till some stupid family member decided to earn some extra money by coming down to Smilin' Bob's or some place just like it and sell off the family shame

And you didn't have to be legal age because the Smilin' Bobs all got together in Washington and had a bill passed sayin' any family member at all of any age could bring in these mutants and

They lay like fish piled high in a net these dumpster mutants moonlight glistening on their bloody faces and limbs and the stench.

Then she runs to the back door which doesn't even have a window to peer in and starts banging and kicking again

You fuckers you fuckers

And him going up to her now and sayin'

Ma I'm sorry Ma please don't be like this it scares me when you get like this.

And she turns on him and shrieks

She's your little sister! Can't you understand that!

And then she turns back to the doors and starts banging and kicking again

And then something startling happens

Door opens

And Smilin' Bob is standing there and

Evenin ma'am he says (in his Texas way) help you ma'am?

You bought my little girl today. You give my boy here $500. I wanna give it back to you and take my little girl home.

And Smilin' Bob takin off his white ten-gallon hat and scratchin' his head says Well now, lemme get a better look at this young 'un here

And he opens the door and looks down and says 'fraid not ma'am 'fraid I never did see this here kid before and I'd certainly remember if I had, givin' him $500 Yankee cash and all like you said.

Tell him (she says) tell him

And so he tells him

How he waited so long in line

How everybody ahead of him got turned down

How he got $500

But Smilin' Bob he just looks down at him and nods his head and says Oh yeah, now I remember you. You brung that teeny-tiny girl with three eyes.

She pushes the money at him.

Please take it.

'fraid I can't ma'am. Deal's a deal, least where I come from.

I just want her back.

'fraid she's gone ma'am.

Gone?

Lab guy, he just happened to pop by and we showed her to him and— well, he took her.

You liar.

No call for that kinda language, ma'am.

You fuckin' *fuckin'* liar is what you are. She's in there ain't she?

And suddenly hurls herself at Smilin' Bob and tries to get past him

And he flings himself at her tryin' to get her off Smilin' Bob but as he grabs out he feels Smilin' Bob's arm and

Smilin' Bob is an android!

But Smilin' Bob is also somethin' else besides—a very pissed off citizen hitting an alarm button to the right of the door.

She just keeps tryin' to get inside

Kickin' scratchin' hittin' even bitin' (but with android flesh bitin' don't matter much).

And then footfalls in the night

Jackboots

Two three four of them maybe

Comin' real fast

And then surrounding them there in the alley

Four android coppers, lasers pulled and ready to blast and

Two of the coppers go up and pull her off Smilin' Bob.

Sure glad you boys got here.

She hurt you Smilin' Bob?

Little lady like that? Not likely (Smilin' Bob smilin' about it all). But sure would appreciate it if you'd get her out of here so I could get some work done

You bet we will Smilin' Bob (and some kind of look exchanged some kind of murky android look that no human could ever understand) and the coppers pull her even further away from the door as Smilin' Bob goes back inside.

She your ma (one of the coppers says).

Un-huh.

Then we're gonna put her in your custody. You understand?

Yessir.

We're gonna give you a pill.

A pill?

(Android nods) She gets all crazy again, you give her this. You understand?

Yessir.

You think you can handle this?

Yessir.

We already gave her a little juice with a stun needle.

Yessir.

So she's calmer now. But if she should happen to get—
Yessir. This here pill.
The coppers nod and leave.

Halfway home the rain starts up again but this time it's just a mist and the black streets shine with blue neon and red neon and yellow neon and in the shabby little rooms and holes and hallways you can hear the human music of conversation and laughter and crying and sex.
His mother walks in silence
The stun needle having curbed her tongue
Her fingers touching her stomach
Remembering what it was like to have the little girl in her womb
And not until it is too late does he realize that as they've been walking
His mother has been letting the filthy useless money fly from her hands
And leave a trail of dollars behind them
In the long sad night
The long sad night.

Author's Note

"Cages" just happened. I'm not sure why or how. I'm not even exactly sure what it's about. But I do know that it's a metaphor for how I've felt most of my life. I submitted it to an editor I really admire and she really liked it and battled for months with the publisher to let her run it. But he said, "This story will cost us subscribers." And you know, I think he was probably right.

En Famille

By the time I was eight years old, I'd fallen disconsolately in love with any number of little girls who had absolutely no interest in me. These were little girls I'd met in all the usual places, school, playground, neighborhood.

Only the girl I met at the racetrack took any interest in me. Her name was Wendy and, like me, she was brought to the track three or four times a week by her father, after school in the autumn months, during working hours in the summer.

Ours was one of those impossibly romantic relationships that only a young boy can have (all those nights of kissing pillows while pretending it was her—this accompanied by one of those swelling romantic songs you hear in movies with Ingrid Bergman and Cary Grant—how vulnerable and true and beautiful she always was in my mind's perfect eye). I first saw her the spring of my tenth year, though we saw each other at least three times a week. But she was always with me, this girl I thought about constantly, and dreamed of nightly, the melancholy little blonde with the slow sad blue eyes and the quick sad smile.

I knew all about the sadness I saw in her. It was my sadness, too. Our fathers brought us to the track in order to make their gambling more palatable to our mothers. How much of a vice could it be if you took the little one along? The money lost at the track meant rent going unpaid, grocery store credit cut off, the telephone frequently disconnected. It also meant arguing. No matter how deeply I hid in the closet, no matter how many pillows I put over my head, I could still hear them shrieking at each other. Sometimes he hit her. Once he even pushed her down the stairs and she broke her leg. Despite all this, I wanted them to stay together. I was terrified they would split up. I loved them both beyond imagining. Don't ask me why I loved him so much. I have no idea.

The day we first spoke, the little girl and I, that warm May afternoon in my fifteenth year, a black eye spoiled her very pretty, very pale little face. So he'd finally gotten around to hitting her. My father had gotten around to hitting me years ago. They got so frustrated over their gambling, their inability to *stop* their gambling, that they grabbed the first person they found and visited all their despair on him.

She was coming up from the seats in the bottom tier where she and her father always sat. I saw her and stepped out into the aisle.

"Hi," I said after more than five years of us watching each other from afar.

"Hi."

"I'm sorry about your eye."

"He was pretty drunk. He doesn't usually get violent. But it seems to be getting worse lately." She looked back at her seats. Her father was glaring at us. "I'd better hurry. He wants me to get him a hot dog."

"I'd like to see you sometime."

She smiled, sad and sweet with her black eye. "Yeah, me, too."

I saw her the rest of the summer but we never again got the chance to speak. Nor did we make the opportunity. She was my narcotic. I thought of no one else, wanted no one else. The girls at school had no idea what my home life was like, how old and worn my father's gambling had made my mother, how anxious and angry it had made me. Only Wendy understood.

Wendy Wendy Wendy. By now, my needs having evolved, she was no longer just the pure dream of a forlorn boy. I wanted her carnally, too. She'd become a beautiful young woman.

Near the end of that summer an unseasonable rainy grayness filled the skies. People at the track took to wearing winter coats. A few races had to be called off. Wendy and her father suddenly vanished.

I looked for them every day, and every night trudged home feeling betrayed and bereft. "Can't find your little girlfriend?" my father said. He thought it was funny.

Then one night, while I was in my bedroom reading a science fiction magazine, he shouted: "Hey! Get out here! Your girlfriend's on TV!"

And so she was.

"Police announce an arrest in the murder of Myles Larkin, who was found stabbed to death in his car last night. They have taken Larkin's only child, sixteen-year-old Wendy, into custody and formally charged her with the murder of her father."

I went twice to see her but they wouldn't let me in. Finally, I learned the name of her lawyer, lied that I was a shirttail cousin, and he took me up to the cold concrete visitors' room on the top floor of city jail.

Even in the drab uniform the prisoners wore, she looked lovely in her bruised and wan way.

"Did he start beating you up again?" I asked.

"No."

"Did he start beating up your mother?"

"No."

"Did he lose his job or get you evicted?"

She shook her head. "No. It was just that I couldn't take it anymore. I mean, he wasn't losing any more or any less money at the track, it was just I—I snapped. I don't know how else to explain it. It was like I saw what he'd done to our lives and I—I snapped. That's all—I just snapped."

She served seven years in a minimum-security women's prison upstate during which time my parents were killed in an automobile accident. I finished college, got married, had a child and took up the glamorous and adventurous life of a tax consultant. My wife, Donna, knew about my mental and spiritual ups and downs. Her father had been an abusive alcoholic.

I didn't see Wendy until twelve years later, when I was sitting at the track with my seven-year-old son. He didn't always like going to the track with me—my wife didn't like me going to the track at all—so I'd had to fortify him with the usual comic books, candy and a pair of "genuine" Dodgers sunglasses.

Between races, I happened to look down at the seats Wendy and her father usually took, and there she was. Something about the cock of her head told me it was her.

"Can we go, Dad?" my son, Rob, said. "It's so boring here."

Boring? I'd once tried to explain to his mother how good I felt when I was at the track. I was not the miserable, frightened, self-effacing owner of Advent Tax Systems (some system—me and my low-power Radio Shack computer and software). No . . . when I was at the track I felt strong and purposeful and optimistic, and frightened of nothing at all. I was pure potential—potential for winning the easy cash that was the mark of men who were successful with women, and with the competitors, and with their own swaggering dreams.

"Please, Dad. It's really boring here. Honest."

But all I could see, all I could think about, was Wendy. I hadn't seen her since my one visit to jail. Then I noticed that she, too, had a child with her, a very proper-looking little blonde girl whose head was cocked at the odd and fetching angle so favored by her mother.

We saw each other a dozen more times before we spoke.

Then: "I knew I'd see you again someday."

Wan smile. "All those years I was in prison, I wasn't so sure." Her daughter came up to her then and Wendy said: "This is Margaret."

"Hello, Margaret. Glad to meet you. This is my son, Rob."

With the great indifference only children can summon, they nodded hellos.

"We just moved back to the city," Wendy explained. "I thought I'd show Margaret where I used to come with my father." She mentioned her father so casually, one would never have guessed that she'd murdered the man.

Ten more times we saw each other, children in tow, before our affair began.

April 6 of that year was the first time we ever made love, this in a motel where the sunset was the color of blood in the window, and a woman two rooms away wept inconsolably. I had the brief fantasy that it was my wife in that room.

"Do you know how long I've loved you?" she said.

"Oh, God, you don't know how good it is to hear that."

"Since I was eight years old."

"For me, since I was nine."

"This would destroy my husband if he ever found out."

"The same with my wife."

"But I have to be honest."

"I want you to be honest."

"I don't care what it does to him. I just want to be with you."

In December of that year, my wife, Donna, discovered a lump in her right breast. Two weeks later she received a double mastectomy and began chemotherapy.

She lived nine years, and my affair with Wendy extended over the entire time. Early on, both our spouses knew about our relationship. Her husband, an older and primmer man than I might have expected, stopped by my office one day in his new BMW and threatened to destroy my business. He claimed to have great influence in the financial community.

My wife threatened to leave me but she was too weak. She had one of those cancers that did not kill her but that never left her alone, either. She was weak most of the time, staying for days in the bedroom that had become hers, as the guest room had become mine. Whenever she became particularly angry about Wendy, Rob would fling himself at me, screaming how much he hated me, pounding me with fists that became more powerful with each passing year. He hated me for many of the same reasons I'd hated my own father, my ineluctable passion for the track, and the way there was never any security in our lives, the family bank account wholly subject to the whims of the horses that ran that day.

Wendy's daughter likewise blamed her mother for the alcoholism that had stricken the husband. There was constant talk of divorce but their finances were such that neither of them could quite afford it. Margaret constantly called Wendy a whore, and only lately did Wendy realize that Margaret sincerely meant it.

Two things happened the next year. My wife was finally dragged off into the darkness, and Wendy's husband crashed his car into a retaining wall and was killed.

Even on the days of the respective funerals, we went to the track.

"He never understood."

"Neither did she," I said.

"I mean why I come here."

"I know."

"I mean how it makes me feel alive."

"I know."

"I mean how nothing else matters."

"I know."

"I should've been nicer to him, I suppose."

"I suppose. But we can't make a life out of blaming ourselves. What's happening. Happened. We have to go on from here."

"Do you think Rob hates you as much as Margaret hates me?"

"More, probably," I said. "The way he looks at me sometimes, I think he'll probably kill me someday."

But it wasn't me who was to die.

All during Wendy's funeral, I kept thinking of those words. Margaret had murdered her mother just as Wendy had killed her father. The press made a lot of this.

All the grief I should have visited upon my dead wife I visited upon my dead lover. I went through months of alcoholic stupor. Clients fell away; rent forced me to move from our nice suburban home to a small apartment in a section of the city that always seemed to be on fire. I didn't have to worry about Rob anymore. He got enough loans for college and wanted nothing to do with me.

Years and more years, the track the only constant in my life. Many times I tried to contact Rob through the alumni office of his school but it was no use. He'd left word not to give his current address to his father.

There was the hospital and, several times, the detox clinic. There was the church in which I asked for forgiveness, and the born-again rally at which I proclaimed my happiness in the Lord.

And then there was the shelter. Five years I lived there, keeping the place painted and clean for the other residents. The nuns seemed to like me.

My teeth went entirely, and I had to have dentures. The arthritis in my foot got so bad that I could not wear shoes for days at a time. And my eyesight, beyond even the magic of glasses, got so bad that when I watched the horse races on TV, I couldn't tell which horse was which.

Then one night I got sick and threw up blood and in the morning one of the sisters took me to the hospital where they kept me overnight. In the morning the doctor came in and told me that I had stomach cancer. He gave me five months to live.

There were days when I was happy about my death sentence. Looking back, my life seemed so long and sad, I was glad to have it over with. Then there were days when I sobbed about my death sentence, and hated the God the nuns told me to pray to. I wanted to live to go back to the track again and have a sweet, beautiful winner.

Four months after the doctor's diagnosis, the nuns put me in bed and I knew I'd never walk on my own again. I thought of Donna, and her death, and how I'd made it all the worse with the track and Wendy.

The weaker I got, the more I thought about Rob. I talked about him to the nuns. And then one day he was there.

He wasn't alone, either. With him was a very pretty dark-haired woman and a seven-year-old-boy who got the best features of both his mother and father.

"Dad, this is Mae and Stephen."

"Hello, Mae and Stephen. I'm very glad to meet you. I wish I was better company."

"Don't worry about that," Mae said. "We're just happy to meet you."

"I need to go to the bathroom," Stephen said.

"Why don't I take him, and give you a few minutes alone with your dad?" Mae said.

And so, after all these years, we were alone and he said, "I still can't forgive you, Dad."

"I don't blame you."

"I want to. But somehow I can't."

I took his hand. "I'm just glad you turned out so well, son. Like your mother and not your father."

"I loved her very much."

"I know you did."

"And you treated her very, very badly."

All his anger. All these years.

"That's a beautiful wife and son you've got."

"They're my whole life, everything that matters to me."

I started crying; I couldn't help it. Here at the end I was glad to know he'd done well for himself and his family.

"I love you, Rob."

"I love you, too, Dad."

And then he leaned down and kissed me on the cheek and I started crying harder and embarrassed both of us.

Mae and Stephen came back.

"My turn," Rob said. He patted me on the shoulder. "I'll be back soon."

I think he wanted to cry but wanted to go somewhere alone to do it.

"So," Mae said, "are you comfortable?"

"Oh, very."

"This seems like a nice place."

"It is."

"And the nuns seem very nice, too."

"Very nice." I smiled. "I'm just so glad I got to see you two."

"Same here. I've wanted to meet you for years."

"Well," I said, smiling. "I'm glad the time finally came."

Stephen, proper in his white shirt and blue trousers and neatly combed dark hair, said, "I just wish you could go to the track with us sometime, Grandpa."

She didn't have to say anything. I saw it all in the quick certain pain that appeared in her lovely gray eyes.

"The race track, you mean?" I said.

"Uh-huh. Dad takes me all the time, doesn't he, Mom?"

"Oh, yes," she said, her voice toneless. "All the time."

She started to say more but then the door opened up and Rob came in and there was no time to talk.

There was no time at all.

Beauty

Most of us use code words. I suppose that sounds a bit melodramatic, but how else are you going to separate the wheat from the chaff? Or, more specifically, the real client from the undercover FBI agent who wants to bust your ass and send you away for a long, long time.

The lady called me while I was on the Stairmaster in my hotel room. She'd guaranteed a nice sum to fly to her city. I was nice and winded from my workout while she went through this nervous little introduction without once giving me that one word that could put us in business.

"Oh, damn," she said. "The—what do you call it?—the code word. You want that, don't you?"

"Be nice to hear it."

"Associates."

"There you go."

"So how do we proceed from here? I suppose you can tell I'm sort of nervous."

"Where are you?"

She told me. I mentioned a nice little Chinese place two blocks from her hotel.

During my brief tenure in the loving arms of the fine folk who run Joliet state pen—bank robbery gone wrong; nothing to do with my present occupation—I spent a lot of time reading psychology books. I figured that psychology would be useful no matter what kind of work I took up when they gave me back my cheap suit and the free bus ticket.

I had a friend in high school that had spent every possible minute tending to this cherry 1957 red Ford Thunderbird his wealthy father had bought him at the start of our senior year. Ken had once been a fun guy. No more. After he got the T-Bird, he lost interest in girls, smoking dope, cruising our hangouts, and even the XXX videos that had just become available to the general public.

The woman who slid into the booth across from me also had an obsession. Her obsession wasn't with a thing. It was with herself.

I don't keep up on all the things women can do to keep themselves beautiful if they have the money. I know about plastic surgery, of course, and facials and bikini waxes and things like that. But I'm sure there are at least a dozen devious little tricks most men know nothing about. With her, it was probably two dozen devious little tricks.

She was stunning more than beautiful. A lot of her appeal was in the important way she carried herself. She was fighting forty and winning.

The smile disarmed you. One of those ridiculously outsize Hollywood smiles that mere mortals can't muster. And what the smile couldn't accomplish, the blue blue eyes did. Now you were not only disarmed, but raising your arms in surrender. The elegant suit looked to be Armani, the enormous tooled earrings looked to be real gold, and the long, calculatedly tousled golden hair finished you off.

But she irritated me immediately. "What if I change my mind?"

"I'm told that's a woman's prerogative."

"Do you have a kill fee?" The smile was genuine. "Oh, God, I used to work at a magazine and that's what we called it when we canceled an article but wanted to give the writer something for his work. A kill fee. In this case, I guess it's a bad choice of words."

I smiled. "Nothing to worry about. And a kill fee is already taken care of."

"It is?"

I nodded. "Remember what I said on the phone. First half is payable right here, right now. If I don't have the second half in cash by the end of the day, I keep the first half whether I do the job or not."

"What if I called the police?"

"Again, your prerogative. But you'd be implicated in hiring me to kill someone. Conspiracy to commit murder probably wouldn't go over too well with your friends at the country club."

"How do you know I belong to a country club?"

"Please."

She frowned. "What you're saying is that I'm a cliché."

Never accuse a narcissist of anything. Their egos move in for the kill.

"You have a manila envelope. Let's get to it, shall we?"

"I resent your remark."

I started to slide out of the booth.

She held up her perfectly manicured hand. "Oh, forget it. I am very country club and I may as well admit it. It's just that common people are so snobby about country clubs. They don't know about all the fine people you meet at them."

Like ladies who hire hit men, I thought. Not to mention robber barons that cheat their employees out of their pensions, and then go home to sleep on thousand-dollar silk sheets in their ten-bedroom mansions.

She opened the 8 X 10 manila envelope and slid out a small package wrapped in brown paper, accompanied by a newspaper story that included a full-color photo with the caption: *Beauty of Beauties*. The rest of the text listed the names of the three runners-up and the beauty pageant winner. The runners-up tried desperately to look happy. The queen didn't have that problem, flashing a Hollywood smile that made you reach for your sunglasses.

"You won this beauty contest."

"State winner. I went on to Miss U.S.A. I was eighteen, just a sophomore in college." When she mentioned her age, melancholy hushed her voice to a whisper. I wondered if she'd cry. She wasn't putting me on. She was lamenting her lost youth. I suppose we all do that, though lamenting all the county jail time I'd put in wasn't a whole lot of my youth I even wanted to remember, let alone lament. "I didn't win Miss U.S.A. I was the second runner-up." She mentioned the name of a prominent male singer popular at that time in the mid-80s. "He was one of the judges. He knew I should have won and he wanted to help me get through it. He took me dancing and other things."

I knew better than to inquire about those "other things."

"Now my daughter is in a beauty contest and I don't want the same thing to happen to her."

"What 'same thing'?"

"To be cheated out of it. The word I'm getting is that the advertising agency man who runs this particular pageant is actually the father of one of the contestants. He got a girl pregnant when he was already married and now the daughter is in his show. I think the mother is blackmailing him. He won't have any choice but to figure out some way for his daughter to win. This could be a very important stepping stone for my daughter. I don't want some dirty old man to ruin it for her."

"When's the pageant?"

"Tomorrow night." She named a convention hall. "Eight o'clock. My daughter's all ready to go. She's not only the most beautiful, she's also the most talented."

"If you do say so yourself."

Another genuine smile. "If I do say so myself. I'm sorry if I sound egotistical. It's just that I want my daughter to win this."

"So I address my skills to the advertising man?"

"Oh, no. The man might be dead, but his illegitimate daughter would still be alive and ready to compete again. I hate to admit this, but she's a very good looking girl. And not bad in the talent department."

"So I direct my attention to her."

She leaned forward. "Yes, but not the full thing."

"The full thing?"

She nodded. "Right." Her voice dropped even lower. "I don't want her killed. I just want her disfigured. Permanently."

I spent the rest of the day deploying all the things I'd need for a perfect strike. Access would be the first problem. While the girl would be in her hotel room at various times, her floor would be shared by other contestants. A whole lot of problems there. She would be at a banquet tonight. I could get the security uniform I'd need, but again, the contestants would be everywhere. A clean getaway was dicey. My client had given me an itinerary that the girl followed every day. Up early for a quick jog around the hotel pool and then fifteen minutes of swimming before showering, eating a light breakfast, and then her singing and ballet lessons. A star in the making. The only problem was that this star seemed to always be accompanied by another woman, an older one, perhaps her mother or aunt or someone. It didn't matter to me; she was an inconvenience, nothing more.

I disguised myself for a quick tour of all the hotel sites that were possibilities for the attack. Late in the day, I went downstairs to where the maids and the bellboys check in and check out. Each had its own small locker room. I always carry a few elementary burglary tools with me. In one locker I found a bellhop uniform still in its dry-cleaning plastic. It wouldn't fit perfectly, but it would fit well enough.

Tonight, coming back from the banquet, the girl and her escort would probably walk back to her room via a wandering garden-like area that led directly to her entrance. My client said that this was the route they had followed the last three nights. She also said that the two never joined the other contestants in staying out a little longer. They went right back to their room. They would be virtually alone on the garden walk. Neither one would be startled by seeing a bellhop.

❈ ❈ ❈

I don't pretend to be Superman. I don't even pretend to be Jimmy Olson. Over the years, I've found that my job-related anxiety is at its worst two or three hours before the gig itself. I've tried antidepressants, a few shots of whiskey, even a joint or two of pot. But they all left me logy. Maybe the worst danger of all to a man in my profession.

Then I discovered the Stairmaster. I now insist on hotel rooms with Stairmasters. Pricey, yes, but invaluable. An hour of hard exercise and then a cold shower leaves me not only wide awake but focused entirely on the task ahead.

I'd just stepped out of the shower when the call came that I'd been expecting.

"I guess I'm backing out."

"Figures."

"You don't have to be sarcastic."

"I'm ready to go. Guess I'll have to find some other amusement for tonight."

"I was just thinking to myself *I'm not this kind of woman*. I'm a Junior Leaguer, for God's sake."

"All right. I've got the money and I'm hanging up now."

"I feel foolish. You must think I'm an airhead."

"A Junior League airhead? A contradiction in terms."

"There's that f-ing sarcasm again."

"Good night, Madam."

I was just adjusting the clip-on necktie that fitted the white shirt I wore under the uniform jacket when the second call came.

"I've changed my mind."

"Who is this?"

"You know damn well who this is. Now quit playing around."

"Oh, yes, the Junior League lady."

"I ought to hang up on you, you bastard."

"Go ahead. It's your turn."

"I want you to do it."

"I've already made other plans."

"You prick. You've got my money and I want satisfaction. And don't get cute with that last word."

I checked my Rolex. If I was going to do it, I had to move fast.

"One thing," I said.

"What?"

"I never want to hear your voice again."

I hung up, grabbed my stun gun, and drove over to the hotel.

The banquet ran late. A minor celebrity sang some songs and an even more minor celebrity gave a speech about why beauty pageants were the best expression ever of true American values. If there'd been a vomitorium nearby, I would have gladly bought my ticket.

Someday when I tell this story again to a few friends of mine, I'll fill it with a lot of intrigue and suspense. The whole stalking sequence you see in all those noir films. Close cuts of me hiding in the front of the garden area. The beautiful contestant coming out the door that leads to the garden, her mother holding her hand. Her innocently looking around. My hand tightening around my weapon of choice for this evening. Her walking briskly toward her entrance door. And then me coming up behind her, devilishly disguised, and saying in a safe, sensible voice, "Excuse me."

And her turning around and—

I'd just poured myself a drink when the phone rang in my hotel room. I picked up and said, "I thought I told you I never wanted to hear your voice again." Nobody else it could be. Nobody else knew where I was.

"I just wanted to thank you."

"I did my job."

"You did a fine job. Of course, I feel terrible about it. It's not the sort of thing I'd normally do but my daughter—" Then, "But this Tiny Tiara contest is real important to her." I could feel rather than hear her smile on the other end of the phone. "Call me the ultimate stage mother, I guess."

"I'm hanging up now."

"Well, that's nice. All I wanted to do was thank you. I mean it must've been weird for you throwing acid in the face of a little five-year-old girl. I'm just glad you could get through it."

I hung up.

The local news was all over it of course. A beauty contest for five- to seven-year-old girls. A barbaric act unheard of in the history of these pageants. Police searching for a dark-haired man dressed as a bellhop. So stealing the uniform and spending the time to get just the right wig had been worth the trouble.

Sleep didn't come easy but when it finally arrived I had an unwanted dream about screwing the woman who'd hired me. She was a lot better than I would've thought.

Famous Blue Raincoat

I suppose Chad thought I'd forgive him, the time he slept with my wife Tish, I mean. He had a kind of innocent quality about him. You never quite held him responsible for things. He'd inherited two things—a huge fortune and guileless good looks. No wonder people were always forgiving him.

The spring it happened, I surprised him a little. I didn't forgive him.

It was much easier forgiving Tish. In the second year of our marriage, she'd forgiven me the nurse at the medical clinic where I work—the affair went on the better part of the winter—so I couldn't get too pious about her going to bed with Chad.

And the fact was, I almost couldn't blame her. Our lives were pretty drab and we both knew it. Four years after graduating from college, we found ourselves living in the kind of middle-class housing development that we'd once laughed about, and working at jobs that meant nothing to us. We needed the security and the insurance. We clung to our mediocrity, fearful as supplicants. Instead of my dream of med school, I was a physician's assistant; and instead of a TV anchorwoman, Tish settled for writing advertising copy for a small ad agency.

Tish once joked that Chad was our "human TV." And in a way, he was. We'd known him in college. We'd never been quite sure why he liked us. He spent his life working his way through half the pretty girls on campus. We used to sit with him in one of the student bars and listen to his travails with women. He fell in love easily. The trouble was, he never stayed in love. When a woman treated him badly, his love was almost suffocating. But once she was nice to him, he became bored. Sometimes he had two or three affairs a month. It really was like watching a TV saga with all the ups and downs that only lust can inspire.

Best of all, he asked our advice. It was sort of interactive. He'd come to us with this problem—"Susan's going to see her old boyfriend this weekend, and I'm not sure how to handle it—I mean, should I tell her I'm going to break up with her if she does?"—and we would give him suggestions, which he'd almost always use.

That was the endearing thing about Chad: he had money and looks and poise but he had absolutely no self-confidence. That was our part of the bargain, giving him our wisdom. His part was to keep the great soap opera going—this one needing an abortion, that one starting to bore him, this one (this brand-new one) exciting him so much he just knew she was the woman he'd waited for all his life. So it went, and we could vanquish our griefs and disappointments in it all. No time for fretting over mediocrity when Chad was out there bedding every beauty in sight.

He had his breakdown the summer of our graduation. We went to see him constantly. His parents were both dead and he was not fond of his sister, so we became his stand-in family. Or at least that was how his shrink treated us, anyway. Told us all about Chad's depression, his electroshock treatments, his almost total dependence on how we told him to conduct his life. He spent nine weeks in the sanitarium, lost fifteen pounds, and practically leapt on us every time we went up to see him. Since I had gotten a job that summer, I couldn't visit him as often as Tish could. She went every day. When he got out of the hospital, he rented an apartment next door to ours and had dinner with us every night. He spent more time at our place than his, even during the day, with Tish.

Then he decided to see the world. We got letters and faxes from China, Samoa, Paris, Zurich and London asking our advice on how he should handle this or that woman. Chad Atwater had taken the show on the road, as it were. Tish seemed curiously despondent, and no matter what I did or said, she didn't seem to have much interest.

That was when I drifted into my two affairs. I've had some men tell me that cheating on their wives only makes their own bed all the more exciting. Not me. I didn't want to touch Tish. There were days I didn't even want to see her.

Then, five years later, Chad came back to our little Midwestern city, bought himself a condo out along the river, and settled back into our lives.

Human TV was once again on the air.

The first two women that spring didn't represent any particular obstacles for Chad, and as such were pretty dull. What I'm saying is that Chad knew how to handle them without much advice from us.

Andrea, our favorite of the two, was a high school English teacher with a fetching smile and the somewhat aggravating habit of apologizing for practically every word she said. It was a month before they went to bed—I think she probably sensed that once they began having sex regularly, he'd start looking around for the next one—and ultimately she began using us to plead with him on her behalf. She would make him the perfect wife, she asked us to tell him. She was a nurturer, she said; a nurturer; and that's what he needed, nurturing. We advised against her, of course, when we were alone with him, I mean. Nice as she was, she wasn't any fun, not for him, not for us. Human TV required better story lines than hers.

Heather was a bitch but she was entertaining. She was faithless as our Chad himself, at least at first, and it was she who first played the Leonard Cohen song, "Famous Blue Raincoat," for us. Cohen tells a story of a somewhat mysterious man who enters the life of a husband and wife and proceeds to tie them up in psychic knots. The narrator of the song, who obviously suspects that his wife had an affair with the man, asks him to come back, along with his famous blue raincoat, because their lives, despite all the pain, just aren't the same without him.

Heather cunningly saw that the song was a reasonable parallel of our situation with Chad. She thought it was funny. After playing it for us in our living room, she laughed and said, "'Chad told me all about 'Human TV.' I think it's great. I'll try to be as interesting as I can for you people." She was gorgeous and ruthless and we had a lot of hope for her. Unfortunately . . .

Unfortunately, our advice to Chad was a little too sage. Just when it looked as if she'd never be faithful to him, we suggested that he seduce her best friend, who Chad felt had some interest in him. Heather herself had told us that she and her best friend, Jane, had an agreement—they would never sleep with any man the other friend was going out with.

The night the deed was to be done, Tish came up with a diabolical twist: Chad had the key to Heather's apartment, right? Why not really add insult to injury and make love to Jane in Heather's bed?

Which was exactly what he did.

Heather came over two nights later and wept in our kitchen. Chad had humiliated and debased her and now she realized that she really, truly did love him after all.

Chad slept with her a few more times and then, on our advice, said goodbye.

A month later Chad slept with Tish.

I came home one rainy afternoon and found Tish curled up on the couch, looking despondent.

"Famous Blue Raincoat" was playing on the CD player.

She had her moods and this seemed to be one of them. I sat down on the floor next to the couch and put my hand on hers. Her hand was cold and made no effort to respond to my touch. Thunder rumbled. Rain hissed.

"You all right?" I said.

"I slept with him."

I didn't have to ask who "him" was. For years I'd been dreading this moment, and it had come now, and in an odd way I was curious about how I'd react now that it had finally happened.

"This afternoon?"

"Uh-huh."

"That was the only time?"

"Uh-huh."

"Are you sorry?"

"Sorry for me. I don't want to be just one more of his conquests."

"But not sorry for me?"

"You had your little nurse."

"Ah."

"But that wasn't why I slept with him."

"Oh? Then why *did* you sleep with him?"

"Because it was raining."

The thing was, I knew my wife well enough to know that for her this was a complete answer. Rain had a terribly melancholic effect on her, and sometimes lovemaking is the only defense you can put up against the vagaries of the universe.

"You think it'll happen again?" I said.

"No."

"Are you in love with him?"

"I hope not."

"That's not an answer."

"I could be."

"That's not an answer, either."

"I'm afraid I might be."

"That's an answer."

"I wish I was suicidal."

"I'm very angry," I said.

"You don't sound very angry."

'You want me to slap you around or something like that?"

"No."

I stood up. "What I really want to do is slap Chad around."

"That won't change anything. It will still have happened."

"Right now, I don't give a shit if it will change things or not," I said, and drove over to Chad's.

As soon as I saw his face in his doorway, I drove my fist into his nose and watched as blood bloomed in both nostrils.

When he'd gotten a cool washcloth for his nose, and a scotch for both of us, and when he took the chair and I took the couch, he said, "I'm sorry I hurt you."

"No, you're not."

"I didn't want it to happen."

"You've been wanting it to happen for a long time. One of the few women you've never taken to bed."

"I'll do anything you want."

"I don't want you to call us or phone us or write us ever again."

He took the washcloth from his nose. "Are you serious?"

"Very."

"But we're sort of a trio."

"Not anymore."

"There's this new woman I met. I wanted to tell you about her. See what you and Tish thought I should do."

"You heard what I said, Chad. No more contact of any kind."

I left.

I was impotent for the next three months. Every time I tried to touch my wife, all I could think of was her in bed with Chad. She reminded me that this was how she'd felt after learning about my nurse.

The worst thing was, of course, that she was in love with him. I'd catch her staring at the phone, or looking out the window, or losing attention while we watched TV, and I knew who she was thinking of. One day I came home early and found her sitting in the kitchen, her eyes red from crying. It was raining. They were alike about rain, how it made them so melancholy.

One night, after coming home from the Cineplex, we made love in the car, her climbing on top of me in the front seat as we'd done back in our college days. And then we started making love again a few times a week. I just hoped she didn't close her eyes and imagine I was Chad.

Summer came, and then autumn, and the emptiness was still there. Somehow, we'd never found a life rhythm again after Chad disappeared.

There were too many silences, too many nights when we went to bed and lay there silent and isolate, her dreaming of Chad, I supposed, me dreaming of the wife she'd once been.

We heard about Chad's car accident through a mutual friend. Three weeks in the hospital, we were told, and a decided limp for the rest of his life. And depression. Chad had gone back to psychotherapy.

I saw him first. This was on a winter morning, all the downtown display windows rimed with frost, and he was just leaving the medical arcade. He had a limp, all right, and he had the pallor of a sick man.

Before I could turn and hurry away, he saw me and waved. I didn't have a hell of a lot of choice.

"God, it's good to see you," he said.

"I heard about your car accident."

"You know the worst thing about running into that tree?" he said, trying to make it a joke. "I was sober." Then: "I really miss you people. I shouldn't ever have—done what I did. I'm really sorry, and I hope you believe me."

"I accept your apology, Chad. But I still don't want you in my house."

"Not in your house, then."

"What?"

"We'll see each other, the three of us, but not in your house. We'll go out. I've got a new woman and I really want you to meet her. I know you won't believe this but I think she's the one."

"That means you haven't broken her heart yet. As soon as you do—"

"No," he said. "While I was healing up, I thought about a lot of things. It's time I settle down. It really is. Her name is Anne."

That was how it started up again, having dinner, the four of us, in a restaurant. Within a few weeks Chad and Anne were dropping by our house, and within a few weeks after that Tish and Anne were having the occasional lunch and the Saturday shopping afternoon. Just as they did "girl" things, Chad got me to do a few "boy" things, like helping him pick out a new boat for impending summer, or helping him decide which riverside cabin was best to buy.

Human TV didn't start again until he began coming over a night or two a week by himself. He was careful to make sure I was there when he came.

At first, I wasn't sure I wanted to hear any of it, but gradually the soap operatics of it all started to draw me in. Anne, quite a stylish if not exactly beautiful, woman, had been dumped three times in the past and wasn't sure that she ever wanted to get serious with anybody again. While Chad was wildly serious, she was cautious. She wanted her own life—nights out with her female friends, taking a night school course in fine arts, and keeping separate houses.

Tish's theory was that Anne knew Chad was a heartbreaker and was therefore wary of getting any closer to him. My theory was that she was just what she seemed—a very bright and independent woman who didn't want to move in with Chad. Or marry him.

I didn't realize how serious any of this was until I came home one night to hear Tish screaming from inside.

I ran in the back door to find Chad slumped over the kitchen table. He'd slashed his left wrist with my safety razor. Blood was pooled around his arm.

"You can't let him die," she said. "You can't let him die."

I'd been wondering if Tish had gotten over Chad and now I had my answer. In her hysteria, I saw how much she loved him, how sacred he was to her.

I wrapped a towel around his wrist and carried him to the car and drove through several red lights to reach the nearest hospital.

They stitched him up and gave him three different kinds of white pills.

That night, at Tish's insistence, Chad moved into our guest room. Given his psychiatric history, I supposed it was a humane idea. But I also knew that now I'd never get my wife back again.

Anne changed. His suicide attempt softened her. She no longer seemed quite so sharp-edged or independent. This made me assume that she was going to give in to Chad and marry him. But no, she wasn't.

"She's all I can think of," Chad said night after night at our dinner table. It was like having a badly depressed son around the house. "I won't ever be able to love anybody else again."

She watched him, Tish did, constantly, love-sick as he was himself. As long as Anne was around, Chad would never love her. I'm sure she realized that.

"What do you think I should do?" he said to me one night as we were having dessert.

"I think you have to break if off," I said.

"That's easy for you to say."

"You asked for my advice, Chad," I said. "So I'm giving it to you."

In the old days, Human TV had been such fun.

"What he means," Tish said, "is that you should be with somebody who understands you and loves you and wants to be with you the rest of your life."

She couldn't help herself. She got so emotional during her little speech that she put her hand on his.

Chad looked first at her hand and then at me. He looked afraid that I'd punch him again.

I just sat there.

It became quite a saga, the thing with Anne. They even went to see a counselor together. But Anne wouldn't change her mind. There would be no moving in, no marriage.

He took to sobbing late at night, and Tish took to going in and comforting him. I tried not to think about what was happening in our guest room as the moon waned near dawn, and their voices fell to whispers.

But one night they weren't whispering at all. They were shouting at each other.

I ran in in my pajama bottoms to see what was wrong.

"I won't do it," he said. "That's crazy."

"It's the only way you'll ever be free," she said. "I'm only saying this for your own sake. Look what your life's become because of her. You need to be with somebody who loves you, Chad. Who venerates you the way I do." Then: "Haven't I always given you good advice, Chad?"

I'm not even sure they saw me peek past the dark door I'd just opened, not sure they heard me at all.

I wondered what sort of advice she'd given him. Whatever it was, it had shaken him badly. Just as their shouting had shaken me. I was as hopelessly in love with Tish as Tish was with Chad.

Sixteen nights later, Anne's naked and badly mutilated body was found in a shallow woods. She'd been dead for two days.

Chad was the first and foremost suspect. A homicide detective named Haney was at our house the night following the discovery of the murder.

He took Chad out on the deck and they talked just as sweet spring winds came up from the woods.

Tish found me in the TV room.

"I was just talking with Detective Haney," she said.

I looked at her, leaned close so I could whisper. "He killed her, Tish. Our Chad killed her."

"I told him that Chad didn't leave the house the night she died."

When I heard about Anne's death, my first thought was selfish: Chad will be out of our lives for good now.

"But he did go out," I said. "And he did kill her."

"That doesn't matter."

"It doesn't?" I smiled sadly. "You got what you wanted, didn't you, Tish? Anne's dead, and Chad's all yours. All you had to do was convince him to kill her."

"If you want to stay my husband," she said, "you'll tell the police the same thing I did."

Which I did.

Haney must have dropped in on us ten times over the next few weeks. He didn't believe us; he was angry; he even hinted that he might charge us as accomplices. But he couldn't get us to change our story. By summer's end, they were making love again, Tish and Chad. At least they were sensitive enough to use the guest room, rather than our bedroom. My first impulse was to get angry, of course, and go to the police and tell them that our alibi had been false. But I would lose Tish forever. My second impulse was to confront Chad. But he was so psychologically beleaguered—he talked to himself; he had terrible nightmares; he was constantly asking Tish to check in the closets to make sure monsters weren't hiding in there—that I couldn't say anything without looking like a terrible bully, even to myself.

Not long after that, Chad had his little experience of running down our nice quiet residential street without any clothes on.

He was in the sanitarium for four months this time. He went into deep analysis, he received several experimental drugs for depression, and he took more than two dozen electroshock treatments. His psychiatrist kept the police at bay, allowing them only occasional visits. The detectives still wanted to prove that Chad had murdered Anne.

And then Chad had the sort of luck Chad always had. The police took into custody the serial killer they'd been looking for the past three years. His specialty was women in their mid-twenties. Beautiful women in their mid-twenties. Like Anne. They charged him with eleven homicides, so what was one more? They blamed him for Anne's death, too, and closed the case.

Two weeks before Chad left the sanitarium, he told us about Molly. She was a ballet dancer who'd had a complete breakdown and had been in the asylum for more than four years. He'd fallen in love with her. And she was in love with him. There would be no games this time, on either side. Within a few months, they'd be married. There would be children, and a nice normal life. He was sure of it. But for all he told us about her—that sense of candor he always had—I sensed that there was something about her past he was holding back. Why had she been put in the sanitarium, anyway? Chad never told us.

After his release, Chad moved back in with us. On that first Saturday night, Molly came to dinner at our place for the first time. She was lovely in a delicate, troubled way; she was all wonderful facial bones and tiny tics of eye and mouth, and she was so wrapped up in Chad it was almost painful to see. Because it was clear, at least to me, that Chad was already losing interest in her. I'd overheard him on the phone the other day, using his best seductive tones. He'd found somebody else to play with on the side.

Tish, too, must have sensed that Chad was already bored. She didn't resent Molly the way she had Anne. She was friendly to the woman in an almost sisterly way.

Molly came around many times, of course. She ate dinner at our place probably three or four times a week. The more she talked about their marriage, the less Chad even bothered to look at her. He'd taken to going out late at night. Obviously, he had another woman. And just as obviously, Tish was angry about this other woman. I was awakened one dawn by Tish and Chad arguing bitterly in the living room. When I came out to see what was going on, Tish fled from the room in tears. Chad sat up late in his room playing "Famous Blue Raincoat" again and again.

The next day, I started inquiring about Molly Stevenson. I did it very discreetly, of course, with the help of a friend I had at the credit bureau. They can find out virtually anything about you in a very short period of time.

Spring came, and so I thought it would be nice to have my first lunch with Molly outdoors, at an open-air café next to the river. She was startled when I called, and not really all that enthusiastic about going, but I hinted that there was something important about Chad we needed to discuss.

We liked each other, and I think she was surprised. I was able to make her laugh a lot and she seemed to appreciate that a great deal. I told her how much I liked her, and I also told her that I didn't want to see her get hurt. And I started giving her little warning hints about Chad. He hadn't, it seemed, mentioned most of the women in his background.

There were many more lunches filled with laughter and tics of eye and mouth. She took tranquilizers constantly and sometimes suffered little moments of shuddering, as if she were about to have a seizure of some kind.

A month into these lunches, I told her about Tish and Chad sleeping together. I also told her that I thought it was still going on, and that Chad couldn't even be faithful to Tish. He was also seeing another mystery woman on the side. I emphasized that I wouldn't be telling her any of these things if I didn't care for her so much.

She smashed her wineglass against the edge of the table and then picked up a jagged piece of glass and slashed it down her very lovely cheek. Then she put her head down on the table and wept.

☠ ☠ ☠

The call came two weeks later, late in the night.

Tish, who was still up waiting for Chad, no doubt, took the call and then let out a scream. I padded out to the living room and took her into my arms. I'd never heard her sob that way. She seemed to be having convulsions of some kind.

Chad's lawyer asked us to handle all the funeral arrangements and I was happy to.

The District Attorney put Molly back into the hospital, until he could decide if he was going to agree with her lawyer that she wasn't competent to stand trial.

Tish started sleeping with me again. Not making love, you understand. I assumed that was a ways off as yet. The memory of Chad would be too fresh and painful. But she did let me hold her, and I was grateful enough to let her use me as she wished, as father and brother and friend rather than husband and lover.

One night, when the past seemed to aggrieve her particularly, she lay next to me in the moonlight and said, "I just wish Chad had known about her background. God, he never would have gone out with her if he had. I mean, the way she killed her first husband when she found out he'd been unfaithful to her." Then she fell to sobbing again.

You really can find out an awful lot about people from the credit bureau.

I always think about this when I go to visit Molly in the sanitarium. This time, she's up on the third floor where the violent patients are.

The last time I saw her, she said, "I really want to thank you for telling me the truth about him. I really do want to thank you. I was making a fool of myself over him."

Some nights, Tish plays "Famous Blue Raincoat" again and again. Those are the hardest nights of all to take because the song is a measure of how distant she still is from me. And every time the song plays, the distance is just that much greater.

A few weeks ago, I had a couple of drinks after work with the nurse I had the affair with.

We ended up late that night out in her car, wrestling around like high schoolers on the back seat.

But when the moment came, I just sat there with my head hung low, and felt nothing. Absolutely nothing at all.

Render Unto Caesar

I never paid much attention to their arguments until the night he hit her.

The summer I was twenty-one I worked construction upstate. This was 1963. The money was good enough to float my final year-and-a-half at college. If I didn't blow it the way some of the other kids working construction did, that is, on too many nights at the tavern, and too many weekends trying to impress city girls.

The crew was three weeks in Cedar Rapids and so I looked for an inexpensive sleeping room. The one I found was in a neighborhood my middle-class parents wouldn't have approved of but I wasn't going to be here long enough for them to know exactly where I was living.

The house was a faded frail Victorian. Upstairs lived an old man named Murchison. He'd worked forty years on the Crandic as a brakeman and was retired now to sunny days out at Ellis Park watching the softball games, and nights on the front porch with his quarts of cheap Canadian Ace beer and the high sweet smell of his Prince Albert pipe tobacco and his memories of WW II. Oh, yes, and his cat Caesar. You never saw Murch without that hefty gray cat of his, usually sleeping in his lap when Murch sat in his front porch rocking chair.

And Murch's fondness for cats didn't stop there. But I'll tell you about that later.

Downstairs lived the Brineys. Peter Briney was in his early twenties, handsome in a roughneck kind of way. He sold new Mercurys for a living. He came home in a different car nearly every night, just at dusk, just at the time you could smell the dinner his wife Kelly had set out for him.

According to Murch, who seemed to know everything about them, Kelly had just turned nineteen and had already suffered two miscarriages. She was pretty in a sweet, already tired way. She seemed to spend most of her time cleaning the apartment and taking out the garbage and walking up to Dlask's grocery, two blocks away. One day a plump young woman came over to visit but this led to an argument later that night. Peter Briney did not want his wife to have friends. He seemed to feel that if Kelly had concentrated on her pregnancy, she would not have miscarried.

Briney did not look happy about me staying in the back room on the second floor. The usual tenants were retired men like Murch. I had a tan and was in good shape and while I wasn't handsome girls didn't find me repulsive, either. Murch laughed one day and said that Briney had come up and said, "How long is that guy going to be staying here, anyway?" Murch, who felt sorry for Kelly and liked Briney not at all, lied and said I'd probably be here a couple of years.

A few nights later Murch and I were on the front porch. All we had upstairs were two window fans that churned the ninety-three-degree air without cooling it at all. So, after walking up to Dlask's for a couple of quarts of Canadian Ace and two packs of Pall Malls, I sat down on the front porch and prepared myself to be dazzled by Murch's tales of WW II in the Pacific Theater. (And Murch knew lots of good ones, at least a few of which I strongly suspected were true.)

Between stories we watched the street. Around nine, dusk dying, mothers called their children in. There's something about the sound of working class mothers gathering their children—their voices weary, almost melancholy, at the end of another grinding day, the girls they used to be still alive somewhere in their voices, all that early hope and vitality vanishing like the faint echoes of tender music.

And there were the punks in their hot rods picking up the meaty young teenage girls who lived on the block. And the sad factory drunks weaving their way home late from the taverns to cold meals and broken-hearted children. And the furtive lonely single men getting off the huge glowing insect of the city bus, and going upstairs to sleeping rooms and hot plates and lonesome letters from girlfriends in far and distant cities.

And in the midst of all this came a brand new red Mercury convertible, one far too resplendent for the neighborhood. And it was pulling up to the curb and—

The radio was booming "Surf City" with Jan and Dean—and—

Before the car even stopped, Kelly jerked open her door and jumped out, nearly stumbling in the process.

Briney slammed on the brakes, killed the headlights and then bolted from the car.

Before he reached the curb, he was running.

"You whore!" he screamed.

He was too fast for her. He tackled her even before she reached the sidewalk.

Tackled her and turned her over. And started smashing his fists into her face, holding her down on the ground with his knees on her slender arms, and smashing and smashing and smashing her face—

By then I was off the porch. I was next to him in moments. Given that his victim was a woman, I wasted no time on fair play. I kicked him hard twice in the ribs and then I slammed two punches into the side of his head. She screamed and cried and tried rolling left to escape his punches, and then tried rolling right. I didn't seem to have fazed him. I slammed two more punches into the side of his head. I could feel these punches working. He pitched sideways, momentarily unconscious, off his wife.

He slumped over on the sidewalk next to Kelly. I got her up right away and held her and let her sob and twist and moan and jerk in my arms. All I could think of were those times when I'd seen my otherwise respectable accountant father beat up my mother, and how I'd cry and run between them terrified and try to stop him with my own small and useless fists . . .

Murch saw to Briney. "Sonofabitch's alive, anyways," he said looking up at me from the sidewalk. "More than he deserves."

By that time, a small crowd stood on the sidewalk, gawkers in equal parts thrilled and sickened by what they'd just seen Briney do to Kelly . . .

I got her upstairs to Murch's apartment and started taking care of her cuts and bruises . . .

I mentioned that Murch's affection for cats wasn't limited to Caesar. I also mentioned that Murch was retired, which meant that he had plenty of time for his chosen calling.

The first Saturday I had off, a week before the incident with Peter and Kelly Briney, I sat on the front porch reading a John D. MacDonald paperback and drinking a Pepsi and smoking Pall Malls. I was glad for a respite from the baking, bone-cracking work of summer road construction.

Around three that afternoon, I saw Murch coming down the sidewalk carrying a shoebox. He walked toward the porch, nodded hello, then walked to the backyard. I wondered if something was wrong. He was a talker, Murch was, and to see him so quiet bothered me.

I put down my Pepsi and put down my book and followed him, a seventy-one-year-old man with a stooped back and liver-spotted hands and white hair that almost glowed in the sunlight and that ineluctable dignity that comes to people who've spent a life at hard honorable work others consider menial.

He went into the age-worn garage and came out with a garden spade. The wide backyard was burned stubby grass and a line of rusted silver garbage cans. The picket fence sagged with age and the walk was all busted and jagged. To the right of white flapping sheets drying on the clothesline was a small plot of earth that looked like a garden.

He set the shoebox down on the ground and went to work with the shovel. He was finished in three or four minutes. A nice fresh hole had been dug in the dark rich earth.

He bent down and took the lid from the shoebox. From inside he lifted something with great and reverent care. At first I couldn't see what it was. I moved closer. Lying across his palms was the dead body of a small calico cat. The blood on the scruffy white fur indicated that death had been violent, probably by car.

He knelt down and lowered the cat into the freshly dug earth. He remained kneeling and then closed his eyes and made the sign of the cross.

And then he scooped the earth in his hands and filled in the grave.

I walked over to him just as he was standing up.

"You're some guy, Murch," I said.

He looked startled. "Where the hell did you come from?"

"I was watching." I nodded to the ground. "The cat, I mean."

"They been damn good friends to me—cats have—figure it's the least I can do for them."

I felt I'd intruded; embarrassed him. He picked up the spade and started over to the garage.

"Nobody gives a damn about cats," he said. "A lot of people even hate 'em. That's why I walk around every few days with my shoebox and if I see a dead one, I pick it up and bring it back here and bury it. They're nice little animals." He grinned. "Especially Caesar. He's the only good friend I've made since my wife died ten years ago."

Murch put the shovel in the garage. When he came back out, he said, "You in any kind of mood for a game of checkers?"

I grinned. "I hate to pick on old farts like you."

He grinned back. "We'll see who's the old fart here."

When I got home the night following the incident with Kelly and Briney, several people along the block stopped to ask me about the beating. They'd heard this and they'd heard that but since I lived in the house, they figured I could set them right. I couldn't, or at least I said I couldn't, because I didn't like the quiet glee in their eyes, and the subtle thrill in their voices.

Murch was on the porch. I went up and sat down and he put Caesar in my lap the way he usually did. I petted the big fellow till he purred so hard he sounded like a plane about to take off. Too bad most humans weren't as appreciative of kindness as good old Caesar.

When I spoke, I sort of whispered. I didn't want the Brineys to hear.

"You don't have to whisper, Todd," Murch said, sucking on his pipe. "They're both gone. Don't know where he is, and don't care. She left about three this afternoon. Carrying a suitcase."

"You really think she's leaving him?"

"Way he treats her, I hope so. Nobody should be treated like that, especially a nice young woman like her." He reached over and petted Caesar who was sleeping in my lap. Then he sat back and drew on his pipe again and said, "I told her to go. Told her what happens to women who let their men beat them. It keeps on getting worse and worse until—" He shook his head. "The missus and I knew a woman whose husband beat her to death one night. Right in front of her two little girls."

"Briney isn't going to like it, you telling her to leave him."

"To hell with Briney. I'm not afraid of him." He smiled. "I've got Caesar here to protect me."

Briney didn't get home till late. By that time we were up off the porch and in our respective beds. Around nine a cool rain had started falling. I was getting some good sleep when I heard him down there.

The way he yelled and the way he smashed things, I knew he was drunk. He'd obviously discovered that his compliant little wife had left him. Then there was an abrupt and anxious silence. And then there was his crying. He wasn't any better at it than I was, didn't really know how, and so his tears came out in violent bursts that resembled throwing up. But even though I was tempted to feel sorry for him, he soon enough made me hate him again. Between bursts of tears he'd start calling his wife names, terrible names that should never have been put to a woman like Kelly.

I wasn't sure of the time when he finally gave it all up and went to bed. Late, with just the sounds of the trains rushing through the night in the hills, and the hoot of a barn owl lost somewhere in leafy midnight trees.

The next couple days I worked overtime. The road project had fallen behind. In the early weeks of the job there'd been an easy camaraderie on the work site. But that was gone for good now. The supervisors no longer took the time to joke, and looked you over skeptically every time you walked back to the wagon for a drink of water.

Kelly came back at dusk on Friday night. She stepped out of a brand new blue Mercury sedan, Pete Briney at the wheel. She carried a lone suitcase. When she reached the porch steps and saw Murch and me, she looked away and walked quickly toward the door. Briney was right behind her. Obviously he'd told her not to speak to us.

That night, Murch and I spoke in whispers, both of us naturally wondering what had happened. Briney had gone over to her mother's, where Murch had suggested she go, and somehow convinced Kelly to come back.

They kept the curtains closed, the TV low and if they spoke, it was so quietly we couldn't hear them.

I spent an hour with Caesar on my lap and Murch in my ear about politicians. He was a John Kennedy supporter and tried to convince me I should be, too.

For the next two days and nights, I didn't see or hear either of the Brineys. On Saturday afternoon, Murch returned from one of his patrols with his shoebox. He went in the back and buried a cat he'd found and then came out on the porch to smoke a pipe. "Poor little thing," he said. "Wasn't any bigger than this." With his hands, he indicated how tiny the kitten had been.

Kelly came out on the porch a few minutes later. She wore a white blouse and jeans and had her auburn hair swept back into a loose ponytail. She looked neat and clean. And nervous.

She muttered a hello and started down the stairs.

"Ain't you ever going to talk to us again, Kelly?" Murch said. There was no sarcasm in his voice, just an obvious sadness.

She stopped halfway toward the sidewalk. Her back was to us. For long moments she just stood there.

When she turned around and looked at us, she said, "Pete don't want me to talk to either of you." Then, gently, "I miss sitting out on the porch."

"He's your husband, honey. You shouldn't let him be your jailer," Murch said.

"He said he was sorry about the other night. About hitting me." She paused. "He came over to my mother's house and he told my whole family he was sorry. He even started crying."

Murch didn't say anything.

"I know you don't like him, Murch, but I'm his wife and like the priest said, I owe him another chance."

"You be careful of him, especially when he's drinking."

"He promised he wouldn't hit me no more, Murch. He gave his solemn word."

She looked first at him and then at me, and then was gone down the block to the grocery store. From a distance she looked fifteen years old.

He went two more nights, Briney did, before coming home drunk and loud.

I knew just how drunk he was because I was sitting on the porch around ten o'clock when a new pink Mercury came up and scraped the edge of its right bumper long and hard against the curbing.

The headlights died. Briney sat in the dark car smoking a cigarette. I could tell he was staring at us.

Murch just sat there with Caesar on his lap. I just sat there waiting for trouble. I could sense it coming and I wanted it over with.

Briney got out of the car and tried hard to walk straight up the walk to the porch. He wasn't a comic drunk, doing an alcoholic rhumba, but he certainly could not have passed a sobriety test.

He came upon the porch and stopped. His chest was heaving from anger. He smelled of whiskey and sweat and Old Spice.

"You think I don't fucking know the shit you're putting in my old lady's mind," he said to Murch. "Huh?"

Murch didn't say anything.

"I asked you a fucking question, old man."

Murch said, softly, "Why don't you go in and sleep it off, kid?"

"You're the god damned reason she went to her mother's last week. You told her to!"

And then he lunged at Murch and I was up out of my chair. He was too drunk to swing with any grace or precision but he caught me on the side of the head with the punch he'd intended for Murch, and for a dizzy moment I felt my knees go. He could hit. No doubt about that.

And then he was on me, having given up on Murch, and I had to take four or five more punches while I tried to gather myself and bring some focus to my fear and rage.

I finally got him in the ribs with a good hooking right, and I felt real exhilaration when I heard the air *whoof* out of him, and then I banged another one just to the right of his jaw and backed him up several inches and then—

Then Kelly was on the porch crying and screaming and putting herself between us, a child trying to separate two mindless mastodons from killing each other and—

"You promised you wouldn't drink no more!" she kept screaming over and over at Briney.

All he could do was stand head hung and shamed like some whipped giant there in the dirty porch light she'd turned on. "But honey . . ." he'd mumble. Or "But sweetheart . . ." Or "But Kelly, jeeze I . . ."

"Now you get inside there, and right now!" she said, no longer his wife but his mother. And she sternly pointed to the door. And he shambled toward it, not looking back at any of us, just shuffling and shambling, drunk and dazed and sweaty, depleted of rage and pride, and no longer fierce at all.

When he was inside, the apartment door closed, she said, "I'm real sorry, Todd. I heard everything from inside."

"It's all right."

"You hurt?"

"I'm fine."

"I'm real sorry."

"I know."

She went over to Murch and touched him tenderly on the shoulder. He was standing up, this tired and suddenly very old looking man, and he had good gray Caesar in his arms. Kelly leaned over and petted Caesar and said, "I wish I had a husband like you Caesar."

She went back inside. The rest of our time on the porch, the Brineys spoke again in whispers.

Just before he went up to bed, Murch said, "He's going to kill her someday. You know that, don't you, Todd?"

This time I was ready for it. Six hours had gone by. I'd watched the late movie and then lay on the bed smoking a cigarette in the darkness and just staring at the play of street-light and tree shadow on the ceiling.

The first sound from below was very, very low and I wasn't even sure what it was. But I threw my legs off the bed and sat up, grabbing for my cigarettes as I did so.

When the sound came again, I recognized it immediately for what it was. A soft sobbing. Kelly.

Voices. Muffled. Bedsprings squeaking. A curse—Briney.

And then, sharp and unmistakable, a slap.

And then two, three slaps.

Kelly screaming. Furniture being shoved around.

I was up from the sweaty bed and into my jeans, not bothering with a shirt, and down the stairs two-at-a-time.

By now, Kelly's screams filled the entire house. Behind me, at the top of the stairs, I could hear Murch shouting down, "You gotta stop him, son! You gotta stop him!"

More slaps; the muffled thud of closed fists pounding into human flesh and bone.

I stood back from the door and raised my foot and kicked with the flat of my heel four times before shattering the wood into jagged splinters.

Briney had Kelly pinned on the floor as he had last week, and he was putting punches into her at will. Even at a glance, I could see that her nose was broken. Ominously, blood leaked from her ear.

I got him by the hair and yanked him to his feet. He still wasn't completely sober so he couldn't put up the resistance he might have at another time.

I meant to make him unconscious and that was exactly what I did. I dragged him over to the door. He kept swinging at me and occasionally landing hard punches to my ribs and kidney but at the moment I didn't care. He smelled of sweat and pure animal rage and Kelly's fresh blood. I got him to the door frame and held him high by this hair and then slammed his temple against the edge of the frame.

It only took once. He went straight down to the floor in an unmoving heap.

Murch came running through the door. "I called the cops!"

He went immediately to Kelly, knelt by her. She was over on her side, crying crazily and throwing up in gasps that shook her entire body. Her face was a mask of blood. He had ripped her nightgown and dug fierce raking fingers over her breasts. She just kept crying.

Even this late at night, the neighbors were up for a good show, maybe two dozen of them standing in the middle of the street as the whipping red lights of police cars and ambulance gave the crumbling neighborhood a nervous new life.

Kelly had slipped into unconsciousness and was brought out strapped to a stretcher.

Two uniformed cops questioned Briney on the porch. He kept pointing to me and Murch, who stood holding Caesar and stroking him gently.

There was an abrupt scuffle as Briney bolted and took a punch at one of the cops. He was a big man, this cop, and he brought Briney down with two punches. Then he cuffed him and took him to the car.

From inside the police vehicle, Briney glared at me and kept glaring until the car disappeared into the shadows at the end of the block.

✸ ✸ ✸

Kelly was a week in the hospital. Murch and I visited her twice. In addition to a broken nose, she'd also suffered a broken rib and two broken teeth. She had a hard time talking. She just kept crying softly and shaking her head and patting the hands we both held out to her.

Her brother, a burly man in his twenties, came over to the house two days later with a big U-Haul and three friends and cleaned out the Briney apartment. Murch and I gave him a hand loading.

The newspaper said that Peter James Briney had posted a $2500 bond and had been released on bail. He obviously wasn't going to live downstairs. Kelly's brother hadn't left so much as a fork behind, and the landlord had already nailed a Day-Glo FOR RENT sign on one of the front porch pillars.

As for me, the crew was getting ready to move on. In two more days, we'd pack up and head up the highway toward Des Moines.

I tried to make my last two nights with Murch especially good. There was a pizza and beer restaurant over on Ellis Boulevard and on the second to last night, I took him there for dinner. I even coerced him into telling me some of those good old WW II stories of his.

The next night, the last night in Cedar Rapids, we had to work overtime again.

I got home after nine, when it was full and starry dark.

I was walking up the street when one of the neighbors came down from his porch and said, "They took him away."

I stopped. My body temperature dropped several degrees. I knew what was coming. "Took who off?"

"Murch. You know, that guy where you live."

"The cops?"

The man shook his head. "Ambulance. Murch had a heart attack."

I ran home. Up the stairs. Murch's place was locked. I had a key for his apartment in my room. I got it and opened the place up.

I got the lights on and went through each of the four small rooms. Murch was an orderly man. Though all the furnishings were old, from the ancient horsehair couch to the scarred chest of drawers, there was an obstinate if shabby dignity about them, much like Murch himself.

I found what I was looking for in the bathtub. Apparently the ambulance attendants hadn't had time to do anything more than rush Murch to the hospital.

Caesar, or what was left of him anyway, they'd left behind.

He lay in the center of the old claw-footed bathtub. He had been stabbed dozens of times. His gray fur was matted and stiff with his own blood. He'd died in the midst of human frenzy.

I didn't have to wonder who'd done this or what had given Murch his heart attack.

I went over to the phone and called both hospitals. Murch was at Mercy. The nurse I spoke with said that he had suffered a massive stroke and was unconscious. The prognosis was not good.

After I hung up, I went through the phone book looking for Brineys. It took me six calls to get the right one but finally I found Peter Briney's father. I convinced him that I was a good friend of Pete's and that I was just in town for the night and that I really wanted to see the old sonofagun. "Well," he said, "he hangs out at the Log Cabin a lot."

The Log Cabin was a tavern not far away. I was there within fifteen minutes.

The moment I stepped through the bar, into a working class atmosphere of clacking pool balls and whiney country western music, I saw him.

He was in a booth near the back, laughing about something with a girl with a beehive hair-do and a quick beery smile.

When he saw me, he got scared. He left the booth and ran toward the back door. By now, several people were watching. I didn't care.

I went out the back door after him. I stood beneath a window unit air-conditioner that sounded like a B-52 starting up and bled water like a wound. The air was hot and pasty and I slapped at two mosquitoes biting my neck.

Ahead of me was a gravel parking lot. The only light was spill from the back windows of the tavern. The lot was about half full. Briney hadn't had time to get into that nice golden Mercury convertible at the end of the lot. He was hiding somewhere behind one of the cars.

I walked down the lot, my heels adjusting to the loose and wobbly feel of the gravel beneath.

He came lunging out from behind a pick-up truck. Because I'd been expecting him, I was able to duck without much problem.

I turned and faced him. He was crouched down, ready to jump at me.

"I'd still have a wife if it wasn't for you two bastards," he said.

"You're a pretty brave guy, Briney. You wait till Murch goes somewhere and then you sneak in and kill his cat. And then Murch comes home and finds Caesar dead and—"

But I was through talking.

I kicked him clean and sharp. I broke his nose. He gagged and screamed and started puking—he must have had way too much to drink that night—and sank to his knees and then I went over and kicked him several times in the ribs.

I kicked him until I heard the sharp brittle sound of bones breaking, and until he pitched forward, still screaming and crying, to the gravel. Then I went up and kicked him in the back of the head.

A couple of his friends from the tavern came out and started toward me but I was big enough and angry enough that they were wary.

"Personal dispute," I said. "Nothing to do with you boys at all."

Then they went over and tried to help their friend to his feet. It wasn't easy. He was a mess.

Murch died an hour and ten minutes after I got to the hospital. I went into his room and looked at all the alien tentacles stretching from beeping cold metal boxes to his warm but failing body. I stood next to his bed until a doctor came in and asked very softly and politely if I'd mind waiting in the hall while they did some work.

It was while the doctor was in there that Murch died. He had never regained consciousness and so we'd never even said proper goodbyes.

At the house, I went into Murch's apartment and found the shoebox and took it into the bathroom and gathered up the remains of poor Caesar.

I took the box down the stairs and out to the garage where I got the garden spade. Then I went over and in the starry prairie night, buried Caesar properly. I even blessed myself, though I wasn't a Catholic, and then knelt down and took the rich damp earth and covered Caesar's grave.

I didn't sleep that night. I just sat up in my little room with my last quart of Canadian Ace and my last pack of Pall Malls and thought about Kelly and thought about Caesar and especially I thought about Murch.

Just at dawn, it started to rain, a hot dirty city rain that would neither cool nor cleanse, and I packed my bags and left.

Stalker

1

Eleven years, two months, and five days later, we caught him. In an apartment house on the west edge of Des Moines. The man who had raped and murdered my daughter.

Inside the rental Pontiac, Slocum said, "I can fix it so we have to kill him." The dramatic effect of his words was lost somewhat when he waggled a bag of Dunkin' Donuts at me.

I shook my head, "No."

"No to the donuts. Or no to killing him?"

"Both."

"You're the boss."

I suppose I should tell you about Slocum. At least two hundred pounds overweight, given to western clothes too large for even his bulk (trying to hide that slope of belly, I suppose), Slocum is thirty-nine, wears a beard the angriest of Old Testament prophets would have envied, and carries at all times in his shoulder holster a Colt King Cobra, one of the most repellent-looking weapons I've ever seen. I don't suppose someone like me—former economics professor at the state university and antigun activist of the first form—ever quite gets used to the look and feel and smell of such weapons. Never quite.

I had been riding shotgun in an endless caravan of rented cars, charter airplanes, Greyhound buses, Amtrak passenger cars, and even a few motorboats for the past seven months, ever since that day in Chicago when I turned my life over to Slocum the way others turned their lives over to Jesus or Republicanism.

I entered his office, put twenty-five thousand dollars in cash on his desk, and said, "Everybody tells me you're the best. I hope that's true, Mr. Slocum."

He grinned at me with teeth that Red Man had turned the color of peach wine. "Fortunately for you, it is true. Now what is it you'd like me to do?" He turned down the Hank Williams, Jr. tape he'd been listening to and waved to me, with a massive beefy hand bearing two faded blue tattoos, to start talking.

I had worked with innumerable police departments, innumerable private investigators, two soldiers of fortune, and a psychic over the past eleven years in an effort to find the man who killed my daughter.

That cold, bright January day seven months ago, and as something of a last resort, I had turned to a man whose occupation sounded far too romantic to be any good to me: Slocum was a bounty hunter.

"Maybe you should wait here."

"Why?" I said.

"You know why."

"Because I don't like guns? Because I don't want to arrange it so we have to kill him?"

"It could be dangerous."

"You really think I care about that?"

He studied my face. "No, I guess you don't."

"I just want to see him when he gets caught. I just want to see his expression when he realizes he's going to go to prison for the rest of his life."

He grinned at me with his stained teeth. "I'd rather see him when he's been gut-shot. Still afraid to die but at the same time wanting to. You know? I gut-shot a gook in Nam once and watched him the whole time. It took him an hour. It was one long hour, believe me."

Staring at the three-story apartment house, I sighed. "Eleven years."

"I'm sorry for all you've gone through."

"I know you are, Slocum. That's one of the things a good liberal like me can't figure out about a man like you."

"What's that?"

"How you can enjoy killing people and still feel so much compassion for the human race in general."

He shrugged. "I'm not killing humanity in general, Robert. I'm killing animals." He took out the Cobra, grim gray metal almost glowing in the late June sunlight, checked it, and put it back. His eyes scanned the upper part of the red brick apartment house. Many of the screens were torn and a few shattered windows had been taped up. The lawn needed mowing and a tiny black baby walked around wearing a filthy too-small T-shirt and nothing else. Twenty years ago this had probably been a very nice middle-class place. Now it had the feel of an inner-city housing project.

"One thing," he said, as I started to open the door. He put a meaty hand on my shoulder for emphasis.

"Yes?"

"When this is all over—however it turns out—you're going to feel let down."

"You maybe; not me. All I've wanted for the past eleven years was finding Dexter. Now we have found him. Now I can start my life again."

"That's the thing," he said. "That's what you don't understand."

"What don't I understand?"

"This has changed you, Robert. You start hunting people—even when you've got a personal stake in it—and it changes you."

I laughed. "Right. I think this afternoon I'll go down to my friendly neighborhood recruiting office and sign up for Green Beret school."

Occasionally, he got irritated with me. Now seemed to be one of those times. "I'm just some big dumb redneck, right, Robert? What would I know about the subtleties of human psychology, right?"

"Look, Slocum, I'm sorry if—"

He patted his Cobra. "Let's go."

2

They found her in a grave that was really more of a wide hole up in High Ridge forest where the scrub pines run heavy down to the river. My daughter Debbie. The coroner estimated she had been there at least thirty days. At the time of her death she'd been seventeen.

This is the way the official version ran: Debbie, leaving her job at the Baskin-Robbins, was dragged into a car, taken into the forest, raped, and killed. Only when I pressed him on the subject did the coroner tell me the extent to which she had been mutilated, the mutilation coming, so far as could be determined, after she had died. At the funeral the coffin was closed.

At the time I had a wife—small, tanned, intelligent in a hard sensible way I often envied, quick to laugh, equally quick to cry—and a son. Jeff was twelve the year his sister died. He was seventeen when he died five years later.

When you're sitting home watching the sullen parade of faceless murders flicker and die on your screen—the weeping mother of the victim, the carefully spoken detective in charge, the sexless doll-like face of the reporter signing off on the story—you don't take into account the impact that the violent death of a loved one has on a family. I do; after Debbie's death, I made a study of the subject. Like so many things I've studied in my life, I ended up with facts that neither enlightened nor comforted. They were just facts.

My family's loss was measured in two ways—my wife's depression (she came from a family that suffered mental illness the way some families suffered freckles) and my son's wildness.

Not that I was aware of either of these problems as they began to play out. When it became apparent to me that the local police were never going to solve the murder—their entire investigation centered on an elusive 1986 red Chevrolet—I virtually left home. Using a generous inheritance left to me by an uncle, I began—in tandem with the private eyes and soldiers of fortune and psychics I've already mentioned—to pursue my daughter's killer. I have no doubt that my pursuit was obsessive, and clinically so. Nights I would lie on the strange, cold, lonely bed of a strange, cold, lonely motel room thinking of tomorrow, always tomorrow, and how we were only hours away from a man we now knew to be one William K. Dexter, age thirty-seven, twice incarcerated for violent crimes, unduly attached to a very aged mother, perhaps guilty of two similar killings in two other Midwestern states. I thought of nothing else—so much so that sometimes, lying there in the motel room, I wanted to take a butcher knife and cut into my brain until I found the place where memory dwelt—and cut it away. William K. Dexter was my only thought.

During this time, me gone, my wife began a series of affairs (I learned all this later) that only served to increase the senseless rage she felt (she seemed to resent the men because they could not give her peace)—she still woke up screaming Debbie's name. Her drinking increased also and she began shopping around for new shrinks the way you might shop around for a new car. A few times during her last two months we made love when I came home on the weekend from pursuing Dexter in one fashion or another—but afterward it was always the same. "You weren't a good father to her, Robert." "I know." "And I wasn't a good mother. We're such goddamned selfish people." And then the sobbing, sobbing to the point of passing out (always drunk of course) in a little-girl pile in the bathroom or the center of the hardwood bedroom floor.

Jeff found her. Just home from school, calling her name, not really expecting her to be there, he went upstairs to the TV room for the afternoon ritual of a dance show and there he found her. The last images of a soap opera flickering on the screen. A drink of bourbon in the Smurf glass she always found so inexplicably amusing. A cigarette guttering out in the ashtray.

Dressed in one of Jeff's T-shirts with the rock-and-roll slogan on its front and a pair of designer jeans that pointed up the teenage sleekness of her body. Dead. Heart attack.

On the day of her funeral, up in the TV room where she'd died, I was having drinks of my own, wishing I had some facts to tell me what I should be feeling now . . . when Jeff came in and sat down next to me and put his arm around my neck the way he used to when he was three or four. "You can't cry, can you, Dad?" All I could do was sigh. He'd been watching me. "You should cry, Dad. You really should. You didn't even cry when Debbie was killed. Mom told me." He said all this in the young man's voice I still couldn't quite get used to—the voice he used so successfully with ninth-grade girls on the phone. He wasn't quite a man yet but he wasn't a kid, either. In a moment of panic I felt he was an imposter, that this was a joke; where was my little boy? "That's all I do, Dad. Is cry, I mean. I think it helps me. I really do."

So I'd tried, first there with Jeff in the TV room, later alone in my bedroom. But there were just dry choking sounds and no tears at all. At all. I would think of Debbie, her sweet soft radiance; and of my wife, the years when it had been good for us, her so tender and kind in the shadows of our hours together; and I wanted to cry for the loss I felt. But all I could see was the face of William K. Dexter. In some way, he had become more important to me even than the two people he'd taken from me.

Jeff died three years later, wrapped around a light pole on the edge of a country park, drugs and vodka found in the front seat of the car I'd bought him six months earlier.

Left alone at the wake, kneeling before his waxen corpse, an Our Father faint on my lips, I'd felt certain I could cry. It would be a tribute to Jeff; one he'd understand; some part of the process by which he'd forgive me for being gone so much, for pursuing William K. Dexter while Jeff was discovering drugs and alcohol and girls too young to know about nurturing. I put out my hand and touched his cheek, his cold waxen cheek, and I felt something die in me. It was the opposite of crying, of bursting forth with poisons that needed to be purged. Something was dead in me and would never be reborn.

It was not too long after this that I met Frank Slocum and it was not long after Slocum took the case that we began to close inexorably in on William K. Dexter.

And soon enough we were here, at the apartment house just outside Des Moines.

Eleven years, two months, and five days later.

3

The name on the hallway mailbox said Severn, George Severn. We knew better, of course.

Up carpeted stairs threadbare and stained, down a hallway thick with dusty sunlight, to a door marked 4-A.

"Behind me," Slocum whispered, waving me to the wall.

For a moment, the only noises belonged to the apartment building; the thrum of electricity snaking through the walls; the creak of roof in summer wind; a toilet exploding somewhere on the floor below us.

Slocum put a hefty finger to his thick mouth, stabbing through a thistle of beard to do so. Sssh.

Slocum stood back from the door himself. His Cobra was in his hand, ready. He reached around the long way and set big knuckles against the cheap faded pine of the door.

On the other side of the door, I heard chair legs scrape against tile.

Somebody in there.

William K. Dexter.

Chair legs scraped again; footsteps. They did not come all the way to the door, however, rather stopped at what I imagined was probably the center of the living room.

"Yeah?"

Slocum put his finger to his lips again. Reached around once more and knocked.

"I said 'Yeah'. Who the hell is it?"

He was curious about who was in the hall, this George Severn was, but not curious enough to open the door and find out.

One more knock. Quick rap really; nothing more.

Inside, you could sense Severn's aggravation.

"Goddammit," he said and took a few loud steps toward the door but then stopped.

Creak of floor; flutter of robin wings as bird settled on hallway window; creak of floor again from inside the apartment.

Slocum held up a halting hand. Then he pantomimed Don't Move with his lips. He waited for my reaction. I nodded.

He looked funny, a man as big as he was, doing a very broad, cartoon version of a man walking away. Huge noisy steps so that it sounded as if he were very quickly retreating. But he did all this in place. He did it for thirty seconds and then he eased himself flat back against the wall. He took his Cobra and put it man-high on the edge of the door frame.

Severn didn't come out in thirty seconds but he did come out in about a minute.

For eleven years I'd wondered what he'd look like. Photos deceive. I always pictured him as formidable. He would have to be, I'd reasoned; the savage way he'd mutilated her . . . He was a skinny fortyish man in a stained white T-shirt and Levis that looked a little too big. He wore the wide sideburns of a hillbilly trucker and the scowl of a mean drunk. He stank of sleep and whiskey. He carried a butcher knife that appeared to be new. It still had the lime-green price sticker on the black handle.

When he came out of his apartment, he made the mistake of looking straight ahead.

Slocum did two things at the same time: slammed the Cobra's nose hard against Severn's temple and yanked a handful of hair so hard, Severn's knees buckled. "You're dead, man, in case you haven't figured it out already," Slocum said. He seemed enraged; he was a little frightening to watch.

He grabbed some more hair and then he pushed Severn all the way back into his apartment.

4

Slocum got him on a straight-backed chair, hit him so hard in the mouth that you could hear teeth go, and then handcuffed him, still in the chair, to the aged Formica dining-room table.

Slocum then cocked his foot back and kicked Severn clean and hard in the ribs. Almost immediately, Severn's mouth started boiling with red mucus that didn't seem quite thick enough to be blood.

Slocum next went over to Severn and ripped his T-shirt away from his shoulder. Without a word, Slocum motioned me over.

With his Cobra, Slocum pointed to a faded tattoo on Severn's right shoulder. It read: *Mindy* with a rose next to it. Not many men had such a tattoo on their right shoulder. It was identical to the one listed in all of Dexter's police records.

Slocum slapped him with stunning ferocity directly across the mouth, so hard that both Severn and his chair were lifted from the floor.

For the first time, I moved. Not to hit Severn myself but to put a halting hand on Slocum's arm. "That's enough."

"We've got the right guy!" It was easy to see he was crazed in some profound animal way I'd never seen in anybody before.

"I know we do."

"The guy who killed your daughter!"

"I know," I said, "but—"

"But what?"

I sighed. "But I don't want to be like him and if we sat here and beat him, that's exactly what we'd be. Animals—just like him."

Slocum's expression was a mixture of contempt and disbelief. I could see whatever respect he'd had for me—or perhaps it had been nothing more than mere pity—was gone now. He looked at me the same way I looked at him—as some alien species.

"Please, Slocum," I said.

He got one more in, a good solid right hand to the left side of Severn's head. Severn's eyes rolled and he went out. From the smell, you could tell he'd wet his pants.

I kept calling him Severn. But of course he wasn't Severn. He was William K. Dexter.

Slocum went over to the ancient Kelvinator, took out a can of Hamms and opened it with a great deal of violence, and then slammed the refrigerator door.

"You think he's all right?" I said.

"What the hell's that supposed to mean?"

"It means did you kill him?"

"Kill him?" He laughed. The contempt was back in his voice. "Kill him? No, but I should have. I keep thinking of your daughter, man. All the things you've told me about her. Not a perfect kid—no kid is—but a real gentle little girl. A girl you supposedly loved. Your frigging daughter, man." He sloshed his beer in the general direction of Dexter. "I should get out my hunting knife and cut his balls off. That's what I should do. And that's just for openers. Just for openers."

He started pacing around, then, Slocum did, and I could gauge his rage. I suppose at that moment he wanted to kill us both—Dexter for being an animal, me for being a weakling—neither of us the type of person Slocum wanted in his universe.

The apartment was small and crammed with threadbare and wobbly furniture. Everything had been burned with cigarettes and disfigured with beer-can rings. The sour smell of bad cooking lay on the air; sunlight poured through filthy windows; and even from here you could smell the rancid odors of the bathroom. On the bureau lay two photographs, one of a plump woman in a shabby housedress standing with her arm around Dexter, obviously his mother; and a much younger Dexter squinting into the sun outside a gray metal barracks where he had served briefly as an army private before being pushed out on a mental.

Peeking into the bedroom, I found the centerfolds he'd pinned up. They weren't the centerfolds of the quality men's magazines where the women were beautiful to begin with and made even more so with careful lighting and gauzy effects; no, these were the women of the street, hard-eyed, flabby-bodied, some even tattooed like Dexter himself. They covered the walls on either side of his sad little cot where he slept in a room littered with empty beer cans and hard-crusted pizza boxes. Many of the centerfolds he'd defaced, drawing penises in black ballpoint aimed at their vaginas or their mouths, or putting huge blood-dripping knives into their breasts or eyes or even their vaginas. All I could think of was Debbie and what he'd done to her that long ago night . . .

A terrible, oppressive nausea filled me as I backed out of the bedroom and groped for the couch so I could sit down.

"What's the matter?" Slocum said.

"Shut up."

"What?"

"Shut the fuck up!"

I sank to the couch—the sunlight through the greasy window making me ever warmer—and cupped my hands in my face and swallowed again and again until I felt the vomit in my throat and esophagus and stomach recede.

I was shaking, chilled now with sweat.

"Can you wake him up?"

"What?"

"Can you wake him up?"

"Sure," Slocum said, "Why?"

"Because I want to talk to him."

Slocum gulped the last of his beer, tossed the can into a garbage sack overflowing with coffee grounds and tomato rinds, and then went over to the sink. He took down a big glass with the Flintstones on it and filled it with water, then took the glass over to where he had Dexter handcuffed. With a certain degree of obvious pleasure, he threw the water across Dexter's head. He threw the glass—as if it were now contaminated—into the corner where it shattered into three large jagged pieces.

He grabbed Dexter by the hair and jerked his head back.

Groaning, Dexter came awake.

"Now what?" Slocum said, turning to me.

"Now I want to talk to him."

"Talk to him," Slocum said. "Right."

He pointed a large hand at Dexter as if he were a master of ceremonies introducing the next act.

It wasn't easy, getting up off that couch and going over to him. In a curious way, I was terrified of him. If I pushed him hard enough, he would tell me the exact truth about the night. The truth in detail. What she had looked like and sounded like—her screams as he raped her; her screams as she died—and then I would have my facts . . . but facts so horrible I would not be able to live with them. How many times—despite myself—I had tried to recreate that night. But there would be no solace in this particular truth; no solace at all.

I stood over him. "Have you figured out who I am yet?"

He stared up at me. He started crying. "Hey, man, I never did nothing to you."

"You raped and killed a girl named Debbie eleven years ago."

"I don't know what you're talking about, man. Honest. You got the wrong guy."

I knew by the way I studied his face—every piece of beard stubble, the green matter collected in the corners of his eyes, the dandruff flaked off at the front of his receding hairline—that I was trying to learn something about him, something that would grant me peace after all these years.

A madman, this Dexter, and so not quite responsible for what he'd done and perhaps even deserving of pity in my good liberal soul.

But he didn't seem insane, at least not insane enough to move me in any way. He was just a cheap trapped frightened animal.

"Really, man; really I don't know what the hell you're talking about."

"I've been tracking you for eleven years now—"

"Jesus, man; listen—"

"You're going to hate prison, Dexter. Or maybe they'll even execute you. Did you ever read anything about the injections they give? They make it sound so humane but it's the waiting, Dexter. It's the waiting—"

"Please," he said, "please," and he writhed against his handcuffs, scraping the table across the floor in the process.

"Eleven years, Dexter," I said.

I could hear my voice, what was happening to it—all my feelings about Dexter were merging into my memories of those defaced centerfolds in his bedroom—and Slocum must have known it too, with his animal wisdom, known at just what moment I would be right for it

because just then and just so

the Cobra came into my hands and I

shot Dexter once in the face and once in the

chest and I

5

Slocum explained to me—though I really wasn't listening—that they were called by various names (toss guns or throw away guns) but they were carried by police officers in case they wanted to show that the person they'd just killed had been armed.

From a holster strapped to his ankle, Slocum took a .38, wiped it clean of prints, and set it next to Dexter's hand.

Below and to the side of us the apartment house was a frenzy of shouts and cries—fear and panic—and already in the distance sirens exploded red on the soft blue air of the summer day.

6

That evening I cried.

I sat in a good room in a good hotel with the air-conditioning going strong, a fine dinner and many fine drinks in my belly, and I cried.

Wept, really.

Whatever had kept me from crying for my daughter and then my wife and then my son was gone now and so I could love and mourn them in a way I'd never been able to. I thought of each of them—their particular ways of laughing, their particular sets of pleasures and dreams, their particular fears and apprehensions—and it was as if they joined me there in that chill antiseptic hotel room, Debbie in her blue sweater and jeans, my wife in her white linen sheath, Jeff in his Kiss T-shirt and chinos—came around in the way the medieval church taught that angels gathered around the bed of a dying person . . . only I wasn't dying.

My family was there to tell me that I was to live again. To seek some sort of peace and normalcy after the forced march of these past eleven years.

"I love you so much," I said aloud to each of them, and wept all the more; "I love you so much."

And then I slept.

7

"I talked to the district attorney," Slocum said in the coffee shop the following morning. "He says it's very unlikely there will be any charges."

"He really thought Dexter was armed?"

"Wouldn't you? A piece of trash like Dexter?"

I stared at him. "You know something terrible?"

"What?"

"I don't feel guilty."

He let go with one of those cigarette-raspy laughs of his. "Good."

Then it was his turn to stare at me, there in the hubbub of clattering dishes and good sweet coffee smells and bacon sizzling on the grill. "So what now?"

"See if I can get my job back."

"At the university?"

"Umm-hmm."

He kept staring. "You don't feel any guilt do you?"

"No. I mean, I know I should. Whatever else, he was a human being. But—"

He smiled his hard Old Testament smile. "Now don't you go giving me any of those mousy little liberal 'buts,' all right?"

"All right."

"You just go back and live your life and make it a good one."

"I owe you one hell of a lot, Slocum."

He put forth a slab of hand and a genuine look of affection in his eyes. "Just make it a good one," he said. "Promise?"

"Promise."

"And no guilt?"

"No guilt."

He grinned. "I knew I could make a man out of you."

8

Her name was Anne Stevens and she was to dominate my first year back at the university. Having met at the faculty picnic—hot August giving way to the fierce melancholy of Indian summer—we began what we both hoped (her divorced; me not quite human yet) would be a pleasant but slow-moving relationship. We were careful to not introduce real passion, for instance, until we both felt certain we could handle it, about the time the first of the Christmas decorations blew in the gray wind of Harcourt Square.

School itself took some adjusting. First, there was the fact that the students seemed less bright and inquisitive, more conservative than the students I remembered. Second, the faculty had some doubts about me; given my experiences over the past eleven years, they wondered how I would fit into a setting whose goals were at best abstract. I wondered, too . . .

After the first time we made love—Anne's place, unplanned, satisfying if slightly embarrassing—I went home and stared at the photograph of my wife I keep on my bureau. In whispers, I apologized for what I'd done. If I'd been a better husband I would have no guilt now. But I had not, alas, been a better husband at all . . .

In the spring, a magazine took a piece on inflation I wrote and the academic dean made a considerable fuss over this fact. Also in the spring Anne and I told each other that we loved each other in a variety of ways, emotionally, sexually, spiritually. We set June 23 as our wedding day.

It was on May 5 that I saw the item in the state newspaper. For the following three weeks I did my best to forget it, troubling as it was. Anne began to notice a difference in my behavior, and to talk about it. I just kept thinking of the newspaper item and of something Slocum had said that day when I killed Dexter.

In the middle of a May night—the breeze sweet with the newly blooming world—I typed out a six-page letter to Anne, packed two bags, stopped by a 7-

11 and filled the Volvo and dropped Anne's letter in a mailbox, and then set out on the Interstate.

Two mornings later, I walked up a dusty flight of stairs inside an apartment house. A Hank Williams, Jr. record filled the air.

To be heard above the music, I had to pound.

I half-expected what would happen, that when the door finally opened a gun would be shoved in my face. It was.

A Cobra.

I didn't say anything. I just handed him the news clipping. He waved me in—he lived in a place not dissimilar from the one Dexter had lived in—read the clipping as he opened an 8:48 A.M. beer.

Finished reading it, he let it glide to the coffee table that was covered with gun magazines.

"So?"

"So I want to help him. I don't want him to go through what I did."

"You know him or something?"

"No."

"Just some guy whose daughter was raped and killed and the suspect hasn't been apprehended."

"Right."

"And you want what?"

"I've got money and I've got time. I quit my job."

"But what do you want?"

"I want us to go after him. Remember how you said that I'd changed and that I didn't even know it?"

"Yeah, I remember."

"Well, you were right. I have changed."

He stood up and stated laughing, his considerable belly shaking beneath his Valvoline T-shirt. "Well, I'll be goddamned, Robert. I'll be goddamned. I did make a man out of you, after all. So how about having a beer with me?"

At first—it not being nine A.M. yet—I hesitated. But then I nodded my head and said, "Yeah, Slocum. That sounds good. That really sounds good."

Duty

Earlier this morning, just as the sun had begun to burn the dew off the farm fields, Keller got out his old Schwinn and set off. In less than a minute, he'd left behind the tar-paper shack where he lived with a goat, three chickens he'd never had the heart to eat, four cats, and a hamster. The hamster had been Timmy's.

Today he traveled the old two-lane highway. The sun hot on his back, he thought of how it used to Be on this stretch of asphalt, the bright red convertibles with the bright pink blondes in them and the sound of rock and roll waving like a banner in the wind. Or the green John Deere tractors moving snail-slow, trailing infuriated city drivers behind.

The old days. Before the change. He used to sit in a chair in front of his shack and talk to his wife, Martha, and his son, Timmy, till Timmy went to sleep in Martha's lap. Then Keller would take the boy inside and lay him gently in bed and kiss the boy-moist brow good night. The Kellers had always been referred to locally, and not unkindly, as "that hippie family." Keller had worn the tag as a badge of honor. In a world obsessed with money and power, he'd wanted to spend his days discovering again and again the simple pleasures of starry nights, of clear quick country streams, of mountain music strummed on an old six-string and accompanied by owls and kitties and crocuses. Somehow back in time he'd managed to get himself an advanced degree in business and finance. But after meeting Martha, the happiest and most contented person he'd ever known, he'd followed her out here and he never once yearned for the treacherous world he'd deserted.

He thought of these things as he angled the Schwinn down the center of the highway, his golden collie, Andy, running alongside, appreciative of the exercise. Across Keller's shoulder was strapped his ancient backpack, the one he'd carried twenty years ago in college. You could see faintly where the word *Adidas* had been.

He rode on. The Schwinn's chain was loose and banged noisily sometimes, and so on a particularly hard bump the front fender sometimes rubbed the tire. He fixed the bike methodically, patiently, at least once a week, but the Schwinn was like a wild boy and would never quite be tamed. Timmy had been that way.

The trip took two hours. By that time, Andy was tired of running, his pink tongue lolling out of his mouth, exhausted, and Keller was tired of pedaling.

The farmhouse was up a high sloping hill, east of the highway.

From his backpack Keller took his binoculars. He spent ten minutes scanning the place. He had no idea what he was looking for. He just wanted to reassure himself that the couple who'd sent the message with Conroy—a pig farmer ten miles to the west of Keller's—were who and what they claimed to be.

He saw a stout woman in a faded housedress hanging laundry on a backyard clothesline. He saw a sun-reddened man in blue overalls moving among a waving carpet of white hungry chickens, throwing them golden kernels of corn. He saw a windmill turning with rusty dignity in the southern wind.

After returning his binoculars to his backpack, he mounted the Schwinn again, patted Andy on the head, and set off up the steep gravel hill.

The woman saw Keller first. He had come around the edge of the big two-story frame house when she was just finishing with her laundry.

She looked almost angry when she saw who he was.

She didn't speak to him; instead, she called out in a weary voice for her husband. Somehow, the man managed to hear her above the squawking chickens. He set down the tin pan that held the kernels of corn then walked over and stood by his wife.

"You're a little early," the farmer said. His name was Dodds, Alcie Dodds; and his wife was Myrna. Keller used to see them at the potluck dinners the community held back before the change.

"I wasn't sure how long it would take. Guess I left a little before I needed to."

"You enjoy what you do, Mr. Keller? Does it give you pleasure?" Myrna Dodds said.

"Now, Myrna, don't be—"

"I just want him to answer the question. I just want him to answer honestly."

By now, Keller was used to being treated this way. It was, he knew, a natural reaction.

Alcie Dodds said, "She hasn't had much sleep the last couple of nights, Keller. You know what I'm saying."

Keller nodded.

"You want a cup of coffee?" Alcie Dodds said.

"I'd appreciate it."

Suddenly the woman started crying. She put her hands to her face and simply began wailing, her fleshy body shaking beneath the loose fitting housedress.

Keller saw such grief everywhere he went. He wished there was something he could do about it.

Dodds went over and slid his arm around his wife. "Why don't you go in and see Beth, honey?"

Mention of the name only caused the woman to begin sobbing even more uncontrollably.

She took her hands from her face and glared at Keller. "I hope you rot in hell, Mr. Keller. I hope you rot in hell."

Shadows cooled the kitchen. The air smelled of the stew bubbling on the stove, of beef and tomatoes and onions and paprika.

The two men sat at a small kitchen table beneath a funeral home calendar that had a picture of Jesus as a young and very handsome bearded man. By now, they were on their second cup of coffee.

"Sorry about the missus."

"I understand. I'd feel the same way."

"We always assume it won't happen to us."

"Ordinarily, they don't get out this far. It isn't worth it for them. They stick to cities, or at least areas where the population is heavy."

"But they do get out here," Dodds said. "More often than people like to admit."

Keller sighed. He stared down into his coffee cup. "I guess that's true."

"I hear it happened to you."

"Yes."

"Your boy."

"Right."

"The fucking bastards. The fucking bastards." Dodds made a large fist and brought it down thunderously on the table that smelled of the red-and-white checkered oilcloth. In the window above the sink the sky was very blue and the blooming trees very green.

After a time, Dodds said, "You ever seen one? In person, I mean?"

"No."

"We did once. We were in Chicago. We were supposed to get back to our hotel room before dusk, before they came out into the streets but we got lost. Anybody ever tell you about their smell?"

"Yes"

"It's like rotting meat. You can't believe it. Especially when a lot of them are in one place at the same time. And they've got these sores all over them. Like leprosy. We made it back to the hotel all right, but before we did we saw these two young children—they'd turned already—they found this old lady and they started chasing her, having a good time with her, really prolonging it, and then she tripped in the street and one of them knelt beside her and went to work. You heard about how they puke afterward?"

"Yes. The shock to their digestive systems. All the blood."

"Never saw anybody puke like this. And the noise they made when they were puking. Sickening. Then the old lady got up and let out this cry. I've never heard anything even close to it. Just this loud animal noise. She was already starting to turn."

Keller finished his coffee.

"You want more?"

"No, thanks, Mr. Dodds."

"You want a Pepsi? Got a six-pack we save for special occasions." He shrugged. "I'm not much of a liquor drinker."

"No, thanks, Mr. Dodds."

Dodds drained his own coffee. "Can I ask you something?"

"Sure."

It was time to get it over with. Dodds was stalling. Keller didn't blame him.

"You ever find that you're wrong?"

"How so, Mr. Dodds?"

"You know, that you think they've turned he they really haven't?"

Keller knew what Dodds was trying to say, of course. He was trying to say—to whatever God existed—please let it be a mistake. Please let it not be what it seems to be.

"Not so far, I haven't, Mr. Dodds. I'm sorry."

"You know how it's going to be on her, don't you, on my wife?"

"Yes, I'm afraid I do, Mr. Dodds."

"She won't ever be the same."

"No, I don't suppose she will."

Dodds stared down at his hands and turned them into fists again. Under his breath, he said, "Fucking bastards."

"Maybe we'd better go have a look, Mr. Dodds."

"You sure you don't want another cup of coffee?"

"No, thanks, Mr. Dodds. I appreciate the offer, though."

Dodds led them through the cool, shadowy house. The place was old. You could tell that by all the mahogany trim and the height of the ceilings and the curve of the time-swollen floor. But even given its age it was a pleasant and comfortable place, a nook of sweet shade on a hot day.

Down the hall Keller could hear Mrs. Dodd singing, humming really, soft noises rather than words.

"Forgive her if she acts up again, Mr. Keller."

Keller nodded.

And it was then the rock came sailing through the window in the front room. The smashing glass had an almost musical quality to it on the hot silent afternoon.

"What the hell was that?" Dodds wondered. He turned around and ran back down the pink wallpapered hall and right out the front door, almost slamming the screen door in Keller's face.

There were ten of them on the lawn, in the shade of the elm, six men, four women. Two of the men held carbines.

"There he is," one of the men said.

"That sonofabitch Keller," another man said.

"You people get out of here, and now," Dodds said, coming down off the porch steps. "This is my land."

"You really gonna let him do it, Alcie?" a man said.

"That's my business," Dodds said, pawing at the front of his coveralls.

A pretty woman leaned forward. "I'm sorry we came, Alcie. The men just wouldn't have it any other way. Us women just came along to make sure there wasn't no violence."

"Speak for yourself, honey," a plump woman in a man's checkered shirt and jeans said. "Personally, I'd like to cut Keller's balls off and feed 'em to my pigs."

Two of the men laughed at her. She'd said it to impress them and she'd achieved her end.

"Go on, now, before somethin' is said or done that can't be unsaid or undone," Dodds said.

"Your wife want this done?" the man with the second carbine said. He answered his own question: "Bet she don't. Bet she fought you on it all the way."

A soft breeze came. It was an afternoon for drinking lemonade and watching monarch butterflies and seeing the foals in the pasture running up and down the summer green hills. It was not an afternoon for angry men with carbines.

"You heard me now," Dodds said.

"How 'bout you, chickenshit? You got anything to say for yourself, Keller?"

"Goddamnit, Davey—" Dodds started to say.

"Won't use my gun, Alcie. Don't need it." And with that the man named Davey tossed his carbine to one of the other men and then stepped up near the steps where Dodds and Keller stood. Keller recognized Davey. He ran the feed and grain in town and was a legendary tavern bully. God forbid you should ever beat him at snooker. He had freckles like a pox and fists like anvils.

"You hear what I asked you, chickenshit?"

"Davey—" Dodds started to say again.

Keller stepped down off the steps. He was close enough to smell the afternoon beer on Davey's breath.

"This wasn't easy for Mr. Dodds, Davey," Keller said. He spoke so softly Davey's friends had to lean forward to hear. "But it's his decision to make. His and his wife's."

"You enjoy it, don't you, chickenshit?" Davey said. "You're some kind of pervert who gets his kicks that way, aren't you?"

Behind him, his friends started cursing Keller, and that only emboldened Davey all the more.

He threw a big roundhouse right and got Keller right in the mouth.

Keller started to drop to the ground, black spots alternating with yellow spots before his eyes, and then Davey raised his right foot and kicked Keller square in the chest.

"Kill that fucker, Davey! Kill that fucker!" one of the men with the carbines shouted.

And then, on the sinking afternoon, the shotgun was fired.

The bird shot got so close to Davey that it tore tiny holes in his right sleeve, like something that had been gnawed on by a puppy.

"You heard my husband," Mrs. Dodds said, standing on the porch with a sawed-off double barrel that looked to be one mean and serious weapon. "You get off our land."

Davey said, "We was only tryin' to help you, missus. We knew you didn't want—"

But she silenced him. "I was wrong about Keller here. If he didn't care about them, he couldn't do it. He had to do it to his own wife and son, or are you forgetting that?"

Davey said, "But—"

And Mrs. Dodds leveled the shotgun right at his chest. "You think I won't kill you, Davey, you're wrong."

Davey's wife took him by the sleeve. "C'mon, honey; you can't see she's serious."

But Davey had one last tnmg to say. "It ain't right what he does. Don't you know that, Mrs. Dodds? It ain't right!"

But Mrs. Dodds could only sadly shake her head. "You know what'd become of 'em if he didn't do it, don't you? Go into the city sometime and watch 'em. Then tell me you'd want one of your own to be that way."

Davey's wife tugged on his sleeve again. Then she looked up at Mrs. Dodds and said, "I'm sorry for this, Mrs. Dodds. I really am. The boys here just had too much to drink and—" She shook her head. "I'm sorry."

And in ones and twos they started drifting back to the pickup trucks they'd parked on the down-slope side of the gravel drive.

"It's a nice room," Keller said twenty minutes later. And it was. The wallpaper was blue. Teddy bears and unicorns cavorted across it. There was a tiny table and chairs and a globe and a set of junior encyclopedias, things she would grow up to use someday. Or would have, anyway.

In the corner was the baby's bed. Mrs. Dodds stood in front of it, protecting it. "I'm sorry how I treated you when you first came."

"1 know."

"And I'm sorry Davey hit you."

"Not your fault."

By now he realized that she was not only stalling. She was also doing something else—pleading. "You look at little Beth and you be sure."

"I will."

"I've heard tales of how sometimes you think they've turned but it's just some other illness with the same symptoms."

"I'll be very careful."

Mr. Dodds said, "You want us to leave the room?"

"It'd be better for your wife."

And then she spun around and looked down into the baby's bed where her seven-month-old daughter lay discolored and breathing as if she could not catch her breath, both primary symptoms of the turning.

She picked the infant up and clutched it to her chest. And began sobbing so loudly, all Keller could do was put his head down.

It fell to Mr. Dodds to pry the baby from his wife's grip and to lead Mrs. Dodds from the baby's room.

On his way out, starting to cry a man's hard embarrassed tears, Mr. Dodds looked straight at Keller and said, "Just be sure, Mr. Keller. Just be sure."

Keller nodded that he'd he sure.

The room smelled of sunlight and shade and baby powder.

The bed had the sort of slatted sides you could pull up or down. He put it down and leaned over to the baby. She was very pretty, chunky, blond, with a cute little mouth. She wore diapers. They looked very white compared to the blue, asphyxiated color of her skin.

His examination was simple. The Dodds could easily have done it themselves, but of course they didn't want to. It would only have confirmed their worst fears.

He opened her mouth. She started to cry. He first examined her gums and then her teeth. The tissue on the former had started to harden and scab; the latter had started to elongate.

The seven-month-old child was in the process of turning.

Sometimes they roamed out here from the cities and took what they could find. One of them had broken into the Dodds' two weeks ago and had stumbled on the baby's room.

He worked quickly, as he always did, as he'd done with his wife and son when they'd been ambushed in the woods one day and had then started to turn.

All that was left of civilization was in the outlands such as these. Even though you loved them, you could not let them turn because the life ahead for them was so unimaginably terrible. The endless hunt for new bodies, the feeding frenzies, the constant illness that was a part of the condition and the condition was forever—

No, if you loved them, you had only one choice.

In this farming community no one but Keller could bring himself to do what was necessary.

They always deluded themselves that their loved hadn't really been infected, hadn't really begun turning—

And so it fell to Keller.

He rummaged quickly through his Adidas backpack now, finding hammer and wooden stake.

He returned to the bed and leaned over and kissed the little girl on the forehead. "You'll be with God, honey," he said. "You'll be with God."

He stood up straight, took the stake in his left hand and set it against her heart, and then with that sad weariness raised the hammer.

He killed her as he killed them all, clean and quick, hot infected blood splattering his face and shirt, her final cry one more wound in his soul.

On the porch, Mrs. Dodds inside in her bedroom, Mr. Dodds put his hand on Keller's shoulder and said, "I'll pray for you, Mr. Keller."

"I'll he needing your prayers, Mr. Dodds," Keller said, and then nodded goodbye and left.

In half an hour, he was well down the highway again, Andy getting another good run for the day, pink tongue lolling. In his backpack he could feel the sticky hammer and stake, the same tools he used over and over again as the sickness of the cities spread constantly outward.

In a while it began to rain. He was still thinking of the little Dodds girl, of her innocent eyes there at the very last.

He did not seem to notice the rain, or the soft quick darkness.

He rode on, the bicycle chain clattering, the front wheel wobbling from the twisted fender, and Andy stopping every quarter mile or so to shake the rain off.

The fucking sonsofbitches, he thought.

The fucking sonsofbitches.

Out There in the Darkness

1

The night it all started, the whole strange spiral, we were having our usual midweek poker game—four fortyish men who work in the financial business getting together for beer and bawdy jokes and straight poker. No wild card games. We hate them.

This was summer, and vacation time, and so it happened that the game was held two weeks in a row at my house. Jan had taken the kids to see her Aunt Wendy and Uncle Verne at their fishing cabin, and so I offered to have the game at my house this week, too. With nobody there to supervise, the beer could be laced with a little bourbon, and the jokes could get even bawdier. With the wife and kids in the house, you're always at least a little bit intimidated.

Mike and Bob came together, bearing gifts, which in this case meant the kind of sexy magazines our wives did not want in the house in case the kids might stumble across them. At least that's what they say. I think they sense, and rightly, that the magazines might give their spouses bad ideas about taking the secretary out for a few after-work drinks, or stopping by a singles bar some night.

We got the chips and cards set up at the table, we got the first beers open (Mike chasing a shot of bourbon with his beer), and we started passing the dirty magazines around with tenth-grade glee. The magazines compensated, I suppose, for the balding head, the bloating belly, the stooping shoulders. Deep in the heart of every hundred-year-old man is a horny fourteen-year-old boy.

All this, by the way, took place up in the attic. The four of us got to know each other when we all moved into what city planners called a "transitional neighborhood." There were some grand old houses that could be renovated with enough money and real care. The city designated a ten-square-block area as one it wanted to restore to shiny new luster. Jan and I chose a crumbling

Victorian. You wouldn't recognize it today. And that includes the attic, which I've turned into a very nice den.

"Pisses me off," Mike O'Brien said. "He's always late."

And that was true. Neil Solomon was always late. Never by that much but always late nonetheless.

"At least tonight he has a good excuse," Bob Genter said.

"He does?" Mike said. "He's probably swimming in his pool."

Neil recently got a bonus that made him the first owner of a full-size outdoor pool in our neighborhood.

"No, he's got Patrol. But he's stopping at nine. He's got somebody trading with him for next week."

"Oh, hell," Mike said, obviously sorry that he'd complained. "I didn't know that."

Bob Genter's handsome black head nodded solemnly.

Patrol is something we all take very seriously in this newly restored "transitional neighborhood." Eight months ago, the burglaries started, and they'd gotten pretty bad. My house had been burglarized once and vandalized once. Bob and Mike had had curb-sitting cars stolen. Neil's wife, Sheila, was surprised in her own kitchen by a burglar. And then there was the killing four months ago, man and wife who'd just moved into the neighborhood, savagely stabbed to death in their own bed. The police caught the guy a few days later trying to cash some of the traveler's checks he'd stolen after killing his prey. He was typical of the kind of man who infested this neighborhood after sundown: a twentyish junkie stoned to the point of psychosis on various street drugs, and not at all averse to murdering people he envied and despised. He also knew a whole hell of a lot about fooling burglar alarms.

After the murders there was a neighborhood meeting and that's when we came up with the Patrol, something somebody'd read about being popular back East. People think that a nice middle-sized Midwestern city like ours doesn't have major crime problems. I invite them to walk many of these streets after dark. They'll quickly be disabused of that notion. Anyway, the Patrol worked this way: each night, two neighborhood people got in the family van and patrolled the ten-block area that had been restored. If they saw anything suspicious, they used their cellular phones and called the police. We jokingly called it the Baby Boomer Brigade. The Patrol had one strict rule: you were never to take direct action unless somebody's life was at stake. Always, always use the cellular phone and call the police.

Neil had Patrol tonight. He'd be rolling in here in another half hour. The Patrol had two shifts: early, 8:00-10:00; late, 10:00-12:00.

Bob said, "You hear what Evans suggested?"

"About guns?" I said.

"Yeah."

"Makes me a little nervous," I said.

"Me, too," Bob said. For somebody who'd grown up in the worst area of the city, Bob Genter was a very polished guy. Whenever he joked that he was the token black, Neil always countered with the fact that he was the token Jew, just as Mike was the token Catholic, and I was the token Methodist. We were friends of convenience, I suppose, but we all really did like each other, something that was demonstrated when Neil had a cancer scare a few years back. Bob, Mike and I were in his hospital room twice a day, all eight days running.

"I think it's time," Mike said. "The bad guys have guns, so the good guys should have guns."

"The good guys are the cops," I said. "Not us."

"People start bringing guns on Patrol," Bob said, "somebody innocent is going to get shot."

"So some night one of us here is on Patrol and we see a bad guy and he sees us and before the cops get there, the bad guy shoots us? You don't think that's going to happen?"

"It could happen, Mike," I said. "But I just don't think that justifies carrying guns."

The argument gave us something to do while we waited for Neil.

"Sony I'm late," Neil Solomon said after he followed me up to the attic and came inside.

"We already drank all the beer," Mike O'Brien said loudly.

Neil smiled. "That gut you're carrying lately, I can believe that you drank all the beer."

Mike always enjoyed being put down by Neil, possibly because most people were a bit intimidated by him—he had that angry Irish edge—and he seemed to enjoy Neil's skilled and fearless handling of him. He laughed with real pleasure.

Neil sat down, I got him a beer from the tiny fridge I keep up here, cards were dealt, seven card stud was played.

Bob said, "How'd Patrol go tonight?"

Neil shrugged. "No problems."

"I still say we should carry guns," Mike said.

"You're not going to believe this but I agree with you," Neil said.

"Seriously?" Mike said.

"Oh, great," I said to Bob Genter, "another beer-commercial cowboy."

Bob smiled. "Where I come from we didn't have cowboys, we had 'mothas'." He laughed. "Mean mothas, let me tell you. And practically all of them carried guns."

"That mean you're siding with them?" I said.

Bob looked at his cards again then shrugged. "Haven't decided yet, I guess."

I didn't think the antigun people were going to lose this round. But I worried about the round after it, a few months down the line when the subject of carrying guns came up again. All the TV coverage violence gets in this city, people are more and more developing a siege mentality.

"Play cards," Mike said, "and leave the debate society crap till later."

Good idea.

We played cards.

In forty-five minutes, I lost $63.82. Mike and Neil always played as if their lives were at stake. All you had to do was watch their faces. Gunfighters couldn't have looked more serious or determined.

The first pit stop came just after ten o'clock and Neil took it. There was a john on the second floor between the bedrooms, and another john on the first floor.

Neil said, "The good Doctor Gottesfeld had to give me a finger-wave this afternoon, gents, so this may take a while."

"You should trade that prostate of yours in for a new one," Mike said.

"Believe me, I'd like to."

While Neil was gone, the three of us started talking about the Patrol again, and whether we should go armed.

We made the same old arguments. The passion was gone. We were just marking time waiting for Neil and we knew it.

Finally, Mike said, "Let me see some of those magazines again."

"You got some identification?" I said.

"I'll show you some identification," Mike said.

"Spare me," I said, "I'll just give you the magazines."

"You mind if I use the john on the first floor?" Bob said.

"Yeah, it would really piss me off," I said.

"Really?"

That was one thing about Bob. He always fell for deadpan humor.

"No, not 'really'," I said. "Why would I care if you used the john on the first floor?"

He grinned. "Thought maybe they were segregated facilities or something."

He left.

Mike said, "We're lucky, you know that?"

"You mean me and you?"

"Yeah."

"Lucky how?"

"Those two guys. They're great guys. I wish I had them at work." He shook his head. "Treacherous bastards. That's all I'm around all day long."

"No offense, but I'll bet you can be pretty treacherous yourself."

He smiled. "Look who's talking."

The first time I heard it, I thought it was some kind of animal noise from outside, a dog or a cat in some kind of discomfort maybe. Mike, who was dealing himself a hand of solitaire, didn't even look up from his cards.

But the second time I heard the sound, Mike and I both looked up. And then we heard the exploding sound of breaking glass. "What the hell is that?" Mike said.

"Let's go find out."

Just about the time we reached the bottom of the attic steps, we saw Neil coming out of the second-floor john. "You hear that?"

"Sure as hell did," I said.

We reached the staircase leading to the first floor. Everything was dark. Mike reached for the light switch but I brushed his hand away.

I put a *ssshing* finger to my lips and then showed him that Louisville Slugger I'd grabbed from Tim's room. He's my nine-year-old and his most devout wish is to be a good baseball player. His mother has convinced him that just because I went to college on a baseball scholarship, I was a good player. I wasn't. I was a lucky player.

I led the way downstairs, keeping the bat ready at all times.

"You sonofabitch!"

The voice belonged to Bob.

More smashing glass.

I listened to the passage of the sound. Kitchen. Had to be the kitchen.

In the shadowy light from the street, I saw their faces, Mike and Neil's. They looked scared.

I hefted the bat some more and then started moving fast to the kitchen.

Just as we passed through the dining room, I heard something heavy hit the kitchen floor. Something human and heavy.

I got the kitchen light on.

He was at the back door. White. Tall. Blond shoulder-length hair. Filthy tan T-shirt. Greasy jeans. He had grabbed one of Jan's carving knives from the huge iron rack that sits atop the butcher-block island. The one curious thing about him was the eyes: there was a malevolent iridescence to the blue pupils, an angry but somehow alien intelligence, a silver glow.

Bob was sprawled facedown on the tile floor. His arms were spread wide on either side of him. He didn't seem to be moving. Chunks and fragments of glass were strewn everywhere across the floor. My uninvited guest had smashed two or three of the colorful pitchers we'd bought the winter before in Mexico.

"Run!" the burglar cried to somebody on the back porch.

He turned, waving the butcher knife back and forth to keep us at bay.

Footsteps out the back door.

The burglar held us off a few more moments but then I gave him a little bit of tempered Louisville Slugger wood right across the wrist. The knife went clattering.

By this time, Mike and Neil were pretty crazed. They jumped him, hurled him back against the door, and then started putting in punches wherever they'd fit.

"Hey!" I said, and tossed Neil the bat. "Just hold this. If he makes a move, open up his head. Otherwise leave him alone."

They really were crazed, like pit bulls who'd been pulled back just as a fight was starting to get good.

"Mike, call the cops and tell them to send a car."

I got Bob up and walking. I took him into the bathroom and sat him down on the toilet lid. I found a lump the size of an egg on the back of his head. I soaked a clean washcloth with cold water and pressed it against the lump. Bob took it from there.

"You want an ambulance?" I said.

"An ambulance? Are you kidding? You must think I'm a ballet dancer or something."

I shook my head. "No, I know better than that. I've got a male cousin who's a ballet dancer and he's one tough sonofabitch, believe me. You—" I smiled. "You aren't that tough, Bob."

"I don't need an ambulance. I'm fine."

He winced and tamped the rag tighter against his head. "Just a little headache is all." He looked young suddenly, the aftershock of fear in his brown eyes. "Scared the hell out of me. Heard something when I was leaving the john. Went out to the kitchen to check it out. He jumped me."

"What'd he hit you with?"

"No idea."

"I'll go get you some whiskey. Just sit tight."

"I love sitting in bathrooms, man."

I laughed. "I don't blame you."

When I got back to the kitchen, they were gone. All three of them. Then I saw the basement door. It stood open a few inches. I could see dusty light in the space between door and frame. The basement was our wilderness. We hadn't had the time or money to really fix it up yet. We were counting on this year's Christmas bonus from the Windsor Financial Group to help us set it right.

I went down the stairs. The basement is one big, mostly unused room except for the washer and drier in the corner. All the boxes and odds and ends that should have gone to the attic instead went down here. It smells damp most of the time. The idea is to turn it into a family room for when the boys are older. These days it's mostly inhabited by stray waterbugs.

When I reached the bottom step, I saw them. There are four metal support poles in the basement, near each corner. They had him lashed to a pole in the east quadrant, lashed his wrists behind him with rope found in the tool room. They also had him gagged with what looked like a pillowcase. His eyes were big and wide. He looked scared and I didn't blame him. I was scared, too.

"What the hell are you guys doing?"

"Just calm down, Papa Bear," Mike said. That's his name for me whenever he wants to convey to people that I'm kind of this old fuddy-duddy. It so happens that Mike is two years older than I am and it also happens that I'm not a fuddy-duddy. Jan has assured me of that, and she's completely impartial.

"Knock off the Papa Bear bullshit. Did you call the cops?"

"Not yet," Neil said. "Just calm down a little, all right?"

"You haven't called the cops. You've got some guy tied up and gagged in my basement. You haven't even asked how Bob is. And you want me to calm down."

Mike came up to me, then. He still had that air of pit-bull craziness about him, frantic, uncontrollable, alien.

"We're going to do what the cops can't do, man," he said. "We're going to sweat this son of a bitch. We're going to make him tell us who he was with tonight, and then we're going to make him give us every single name of every single bad guy who works this neighborhood. And then we'll turn all the names over to the cops."

"It's just an extension of the Patrol," Neil said. "Just keeping our neighborhood safe is all."

"You guys are nuts," I said, and turned back toward the steps. "I'm going up and calling the cops."

That's when I realized just how crazed Mike was. "You aren't going anywhere, man. You're going to stay here and help us break this bastard down. You're going to do your goddamned neighborhood duty."

He'd grabbed my sleeve so hard that he'd torn it at the shoulder. We both discovered this at the same time.

I expected him to look sorry. He didn't. In fact, he was smirking at me. "Don't be such a wimp, Aaron," he said.

2

Mike led the charge getting the kitchen cleaned up. I think he was feeling guilty about calling me a wimp with such angry exuberance. Now I understood how lynch mobs got formed. One guy like Mike stirring people up by alternately insulting them and urging them on.

After the kitchen was put back in order, and after I'd taken inventory to find that nothing had been stolen, I went to the refrigerator and got beers for everybody. Bob had drifted back to the kitchen, too.

"All right," I said, "now that we've all calmed down, I want to walk over to that yellow kitchen wall phone there and call the police. Any objections?"

"I think blue would look better in here than yellow," Neil said.

"Funny," I said.

They looked themselves now, no feral madness on the faces of Mike or Neil, no winces on Bob's.

I started across the floor to the phone.

Neil grabbed my arm. Not with the same insulting force Mike had used on me. But enough to get the job done.

"I think Mike's right," Neil said. "I think we should grill that bastard a little bit."

I shook my head, politely removed his hand from my forearm, and proceeded to the phone.

"This isn't just your decision alone," Mike said.

He'd finally had his way. He'd succeeded in making me angry. I turned around and looked at him. "This is my house, Mike. If you don't like my decisions, then I'd suggest you leave."

We both took steps toward each other. Mike would no doubt win any battle we had but I'd at least be able to inflict a little damage and right now that's all I was thinking about.

Neil got between us.

"Hey," he said. "For God's sake you two, c'mon. We're friends, remember?"

"This is my house," I said, my words childish in my ears.

"Yeah, but we live in the same neighborhood, Aaron," Mike said, "which makes this 'our' problem."

"He's right, Aaron," Bob said from the breakfast nook. There's a window there where I sometimes sit to watch all the animals on sunny days. I saw a mother raccoon and four baby raccoons one day, marching single file across the grass. My grandparents were the last generation to live on the farm. My father came to town here and ended up working at a ball bearing company. Raccoons are a lot more pleasant to gaze upon than people.

"He's not right," I said to Bob. "He's wrong. We're not cops, we're not bounty hunters, we're not trackers. We're a bunch of goddamned guys who peddle stocks and bonds. Mike and Neil shouldn't have tied him up downstairs—that happens to be illegal, at least the way they went about it—and now I'm going to call the cops."

"Yes, that poor thing," Mike said, "aren't we just picking on him, though? Tell you what, why don't we make him something to eat?"

"Just make sure we have the right wine to go with it," Neil said. "Properly chilled, of course."

"Maybe we could get him a chick," Bob said.

"With bombers out to here," Mike said, indicating with his hands where "here" was.

I couldn't help it. I smiled. They were all being ridiculous. A kind of fever had caught them.

"You really want to go down there and question him?" I said to Neil.

"Yes. We can ask him things the cops can't."

"Scare the bastard a little," Mike said. "So he'll tell us who was with him tonight, and who else works this neighborhood." He came over and put his hand out. "God, man, you're one of my best friends. I don't want you mad at me."

Then he hugged me, which is something I've never been comfortable with men doing, but to the extent I could, I hugged him back.

"Friends?" he said.

"Friends," I said. "But I still want to call the cops."

"And spoil our fun?" Neil said.

"And spoil your fun."

"I say we take it to a vote," Bob said.

"This isn't a democracy," I said. "It's my house and I'm the king, I don't want to have a vote."

"Can we ask him one question?" Bob said.

I sighed. They weren't going to let go. "One question?"

"The name of the guy he was with tonight."

"And that's it?"

"That's it. That way we get him and one other guy off the street."

"And then I call the cops?"

"Then," Mike said, "you call the cops."

"One question," Neil said.

While we finished our beers, we argued a little more, but they had a lot more spirit left than I did. I was tired now and missing Jan and the kids and feeling lonely. These three guys had become strangers to me tonight. Very old boys eager to play at boy games once again.

"One question," I said. "Then I call the cops."

I led the way down, sneezing as I did so.

There's always enough dust floating around in the basement to play hell with my sinuses.

The guy was his same sullen self, glaring at us as we descended the stairs and then walked over to him. He smelled of heat and sweat and city grime. The long bare arms sticking out of his filthy T-shirt told tattoo tales of writhing snakes and leaping panthers. The arms were joined in the back with rope. His jaw still flexed, trying to accommodate the intrusion of the gag.

"Maybe we should castrate him," Mike said, walking up close to the guy. "You like that, scumbag? If we castrated you?"

If the guy felt any fear, it wasn't evident in his eyes. All you could see there was the usual contempt.

"I'll bet this is the jerk who broke into the Donaldsons' house a couple weeks ago," Neil said.

Now he walked up to the guy. But he was more ambitious than Mike had been. Neil spat in the guy's face.

"Hey," I said, "cool it."

Neil glared at me. "Yeah, I wouldn't want to hurt his feelings, would I?"

Then he suddenly turned back on the guy, raised his fist and started to swing. All I could do was shove him. That sent his punch angling off to the right, missing our burglar by about half a foot.

"You asshole," Neil said, turning back on me now.

But Mike was there, between us.

"You know what we're doing? We're making this jerk happy. He's gonna have some nice stories to tell all his criminal friends."

He was right. The burglar was the one who got to look all cool and composed. We looked like squabbling brats. As if to confirm this, a hint of amusement played in the burglar's blue eyes.

"Oh, hell, Aaron, I'm sorry," Neil said, putting his hand out. This was like a political convention, all the handshaking going on.

"So am I, Neil," I said. "That's why I want to call the cops and get this over with."

And that's when he chose to make his move, the burglar. As soon as I mentioned the cops, he probably realized that this was going to be his last opportunity.

He waited until we were just finishing up with the handshake, when we were all focused on each other. Then he took off running. We could see that he'd slipped the rope. He went straight for the stairs, angling out around us like a running back seeing daylight. He even stuck his long, tattooed arm out as if he was trying to repel a tackle.

"Hey," Bob shouted. "He's getting away."

He was at the stairs by the time we could gather ourselves enough to go after him. But when we moved, we moved fast, and in virtual unison.

By the time I got my hand on the cuff of his left jean, he was close enough to the basement door to open it.

I yanked hard and ducked out of the way of his kicking foot. By now I was as crazy as Mike and Neil had been earlier. There was adrenaline and great anger. He wasn't just a burglar, he was all burglars, intent not merely on stealing things from me, but hurting my family, too. He hadn't had time to take the gag from his mouth.

This time, I grabbed booted foot and leg and started hauling him back down the stairs. At first he was able to hold on to the door but when I wrenched his foot rightward, he tried to scream behind the gag. He let go of the doorknob.

The next half minute is still unclear in my mind. I started running down the stairs, dragging him with me. All I wanted to do was get him on the basement floor again, turn him over to the others to watch, and then go call the cops.

But somewhere in those few seconds when I was hauling him back down the steps, I heard edge of stair meeting back of skull. The others heard it, too, because their shouts and curses died in their throats.

When I turned around, I saw the blood running fast and red from his nose. The blue eyes no longer held contempt. They were starting to roll up white in the back of his head.

"God," I said. "He's hurt."

"I think he's a lot more than hurt," Mike said.

"Help me carry him upstairs."

We got him on the kitchen floor. Mike and Neil rushed around soaking paper towels. We tried to revive him. Bob, who kept wincing from his headache, tried the guy's wrist, ankle and throat for a pulse. None. His nose and mouth were bloody. Very bloody.

"No way you could *die* from hitting your head like that," Neil said.

"Sure you could," Mike said. "You hit it just the right way."

"He can't be dead," Neil said. "I'm going to try his pulse again."

Bob, who obviously took Neil's second opinion personally, frowned and rolled his eyes. "He's dead, man. He really is."

"Bullshit."

"You a doctor or something?" Bob said.

Neil smiled nervously. "No, but I play one on TV."

So Neil tried the pulse points. His reading was exactly what Bob's reading had been.

"See," Bob said.

I guess none of us were destined to ever quite be adults.

"Man," Neil said, looking down at the long, cold unmoving form of the burglar. "He's really dead."

"What the hell're we gonna do?" Mike said.

"We're going to call the police," I said, and started for the phone.

"The hell we are," Mike said. "The hell we are."

3

Maybe half an hour after we laid him on the kitchen floor, he started to smell. We'd looked for identification and found none. He was just the Burglar.

We sat at the kitchen table, sharing a fifth of Old Grandad and innumerable beers.

We'd taken two votes and they'd come up ties. Two for calling the police, Bob and I; two for not calling the police, Mike and Neil.

"All we have to tell them," I said, "is that we tied him up so he wouldn't get away."

"And then they say," Mike said, "so why didn't you call us before now?"

"We just lie about the time a little," I said. "Tell them we called them within twenty minutes."

"Won't work," Neil said.

"Why not?" Bob said.

"Medical examiner can fix the time of death," Neil said.

"Not that close."

"Close enough so that the cops might question our story," Neil said. "By the time they get here, he'll have been dead at least an hour, hour and a half."

"And then we get our names in the paper for not reporting the burglary or the death right away," Mike said. "Brokerages just love publicity like that."

"I'm calling the cops right now," I said, and started up from the table.

"Think about Tomlinson a minute," Neil said.

Tomlinson was my boss at the brokerage. "What about him?"

"Remember how he canned Dennis Bryce when Bryce's ex-wife took out a restraining order on him?"

"This is different," I said.

"The hell it is," Mike said. "Neil's right, none of our bosses will like publicity like this. We'll all sound a little—crazy—you know, keeping him tied up in the basement. And then killing him when he tried to get away."

They all looked at me.

"You bastards," I said. "I was the one who wanted to call the police in the first place. And I sure as hell didn't try to kill him on purpose."

"Looking back on it," Neil said, "I guess you were right, Aaron. We should've called the cops right away."

"Now's a great time to realize that," I said.

"Maybe they've got a point," Bob said softly, glancing at me, then glancing nervously away.

"Oh, great. You, too?" I said.

"They just might kick my black ass out of there if I had any publicity that involved somebody getting killed," Bob said.

"He was a frigging burglar," I said.

"But he's dead," Neil said.

"And we killed him," Mike said.

"I appreciate you saying 'we'," I said.

"I know a good place," Bob said.

I looked at him carefully, afraid of what he was going to say next. "Forget it," I said.

"A good place for what?" Neil said.

"Dumping the body," Bob said.

"No way," I said.

This time when I got up, nobody tried to stop me. I walked over to the yellow wall telephone.

I wondered if the cozy kitchen would ever feel the same to me now that a dead body had been laid upon its floor.

I had to step over him to reach the phone. The smell was even more sour now.

"You know how many bodies get dumped in the river that never wash up?" Bob said.

"No," I said, "and you don't, either."

"Lots," he said.

"There's a scientific appraisal for you. 'Lots.'"

"Lots and lots, probably," Neil said, taking up Bob's argument. Mike grinned. "Lots and lots and lots."

"Thank you, Professor," I said.

I lifted the receiver and dialed 0.

"Operator."

"The police department, please."

"Is this an emergency?" asked the young woman. Usually I would have spent more time wondering if the sweetness of her voice was matched by the sweetness of her face and body. I'm still a face man. I suppose it's my romantic side. "Is this an emergency?" she repeated.

"No; no, it isn't."

"I'll connect you," she said.

"You think your kids'll be able to handle it?" Neil said.

"No mind games," I said.

"No mind games at all," he said. "I'm asking you a very realistic question. The police have some doubts about our story and then the press gets ahold of it and bam. We're the lead story on all three channels. 'Did four middle-class men murder the burglar they captured?' The press even goes after the kids these days. 'Do you think your daddy murdered that burglar, son?'"

"Good evening. Police Department."

I started to speak but I couldn't somehow. My voice wouldn't work. That's the only way I can explain it.

"The six o'clock news five nights running," Neil said softly behind me. "And the DA can't endorse any kind of vigilante activity so he nails us on involuntary manslaughter."

"Hello? This is the Police Department," said the black female voice on the phone.

Neil was there then, reaching me as if by magic.

He took the receiver gently from my hand and hung it back up on the phone again.

"Let's go have another drink and see what Bob's got in mind, all right?"

He led me, as if I were a hospital patient, slowly and carefully back to the table where Bob, over more whiskey, slowly and gently laid out his plan.

The next morning, three of us phoned in sick. Bob went to work because he had an important meeting.

Around noon—a sunny day when a softball game and a cold six-pack of beer sounded good—Neil and Mike came over. They looked as bad as I felt, and no doubt looked myself.

We sat out on the patio eating the Hardee's lunch they'd bought. I'd need to play softball to work off some of the calories I was eating.

Birdsong and soft breezes and the smell of fresh cut grass should have made our patio time enjoyable. But I had to wonder if we'd ever enjoy anything again. I just kept seeing the body momentarily arced above the roaring waters of the dam; and dropping into white churning turbulence.

"You think we did the right thing?" Neil said.

"Now's a hell of a time to ask that," I said.

"Of course we did the right thing," Mike said. "What choice did we have? It was either that or get our asses arrested."

"So you don't have any regrets?" Neil said.

Mike sighed. "I didn't say that. I mean, I wish it hadn't happened in the first place."

"Maybe Aaron was right all along," Neil said.

"About what?"

"About going to the cops."

"Goddamn," Mike said, sitting up from his slouch. We all wore button-down shirts without ties and with the sleeves rolled up. Somehow there was something profane about wearing shorts and T-shirts on a workday. We even wore pretty good slacks. We were that kind of people. "Goddamn."

"Here he goes," Neil said.

"I can't believe you two," Mike said. "We should be happy that everything went so well last night—and what are we doing? Sitting around here pissing and moaning."

"That doesn't mean it's over," I said.

"Why the hell not?" Mike said.

"Because there's still one left."

"One what?"

"One burglar."

"So?"

"So you don't think he's going to get curious about what the hell happened to his partner?"

"What's he gonna do?" Mike said. "Go to the cops?"

"Maybe."

"Maybe? You're crazy. He goes to the cops, he'd be setting himself up for a robbery conviction."

"Not if he tells them we murdered his pal."

Neil said, "Aaron's got a point. What if this guy goes to the cops?"

"He's not going to the cops," Mike said. "No way he's going to the cops at all."

4

I was dozing on the couch, a Cubs game on the TV set, when the phone rang around nine that evening. I hadn't heard from Jan yet so I expected it would be her. Whenever we're apart, we call each other at least once a day.

The phone machine picks up on the fourth ring so I had to scramble to beat it.

"Hello?"

Nothing. But somebody was on the line. Listening.

"Hello?"

I never play games with silent callers. I just hang up. I did so now.

Two innings later, having talked to Jan, having made myself a tuna fish sandwich on rye, found a package of potato chips I thought we'd finished off at the poker game, and gotten myself a new can of beer, I sat down to watch the last inning. The Cubs had a chance of winning. I said a silent prayer to the God of Baseball.

The phone rang.

I mouthed several curses around my mouthful of tuna sandwich and went to the phone.

"Hello?" I said, trying to swallow the last of the bite.

My silent friend again.

I slammed the phone.

The Cubs got two more singles, I started on the chips and I had polished off the beer and was thinking of getting another one when the phone rang again.

I had a suspicion of who was calling and then saying nothing—but I didn't really want to think about it.

Then I decided there was an easy way to handle this situation. I'd just let the phone machine take it. If my anonymous friend wanted to talk to a phone machine, good for him.

Four rings. The phone machine took over, Jan's pleasant voice saying that we weren't home but would be happy to call you back if you'd just leave your number.

I waited to hear dead air then a click.

Instead a familiar female voice said: "Aaron, it's Louise. Bob—" Louise was Bob's wife. She was crying. I ran from the couch to the phone machine in the hall.

"Hello, Louise. It's Aaron."

"Oh, Aaron. It's terrible."

"What happened, Louise?"

"Bob—" More tears. "He electrocuted himself tonight out in the garage." She said that a plug had accidentally fallen into a bowl of water, according to the fire captain on the scene, and Bob hadn't noticed this and put the plug into the outlet and

Bob had a woodcraft workshop in his garage, a large and sophisticated one. He knew what he was doing.

"He's dead, Aaron. He's dead."

"Oh, God, Louise. I'm sorry."

"He was so careful with electricity, too. It's just so hard to believe—"

Yes, I thought. Yes, it was hard to believe. I thought of last night. Of the burglars—one who'd died. One who'd gotten away. "Why don't I come over?"

"Oh, thank you, Aaron, but I need to be alone with the children. But if you could call Neil and Mike—"

"Of course."

"Thanks for being such good friends, you and Jan."

"Don't be silly, Louise. The pleasure's ours."

"I'll talk to you tomorrow. When I'm—you know."

"Good night, Louise."

Mike and Neil were at my place within twenty minutes. We sat in the kitchen again, where we were last night.

I said, "Either of you get any weird phone calls tonight?"

"You mean just silence?" Neil said.

"Right."

"I did," Mike said. "Carrie was afraid it was that pervert who called all last winter."

"I did, too," Neil said. "Three of them."

"Then a little while ago, Bob dies out in his garage," I said. "Some coincidence."

"Hey, Aaron," Mike said. "Is that why you got us over here? Because you don't think it was an accident?"

"I'm sure it wasn't an accident," I said. "Bob knew what he was doing with his tools. He didn't notice a plug that had fallen into a bowl of water?"

"He's coming after us," Neil said.

"Oh, God," Mike said. "Not you, too."

"He calls us, gets us on edge," I said. "And then he kills Bob. Making it look like an accident."

"These are pretty bright people," Mike said sarcastically.

"You notice the burglar's eyes?" Neil said.

"I did," I said. "He looked very bright."

"And spooky," Neil said. "Never saw eyes like that before."

"I can shoot your theory right in the butt," Mike said.

"How?" I said.

He leaned forward, sipped his beer. I'd thought about putting out some munchies but somehow that seemed wrong given poor Bob's death and the phone calls. The beers we had to have. The munchies were too festive.

"Here's how. There are two burglars, right? One gets caught, the other runs. And given the nature of burglars, keeps on running. He wouldn't even know who was in the house last night, except for Aaron, and that's only because he's the owner and his name would be in the phone book. But he wouldn't know anything about Bob or Neil or me. No way he'd have been able to track down Bob."

I shook my head. "You're overlooking the obvious."

"Like what?"

"Like he runs off last night, gets his car and then parks in the alley to see what's going to happen."

"Right," Neil said. "Then he sees us bringing his friend out wrapped in a blanket. He follows us to the dam and watches us throw his friend in."

"And," I said, "everybody had his car here last night. Very easy for him to write down all the license numbers."

"So he kills Bob," Neil said. "And starts making the phone calls to shake us up."

"Why Bob?"

"Maybe he hates black people," I said.

Mike looked first at me and then at Neil. "You know what this is?"

"Here he goes," Neil said.

"No; no, I'm serious here. This is Catholic guilt."

"How can it be Catholic guilt when I'm Jewish?" Neil said.

"In a culture like ours, everybody is a little bit Jewish and a little bit Catholic, anyway," Mike said. "So you guys are in the throes of Catholic guilt. You feel bad about what we had to do last night—and we did have to do it, we really didn't have any choice—and the guilt starts to play on your mind. So poor Bob electrocutes himself accidentally and you immediately think it's the second burglar."

"He followed him," Neil said.

"What?" Mike said.

"That's what he did, I bet. The burglar. Followed Bob around all day trying to figure out what was the best way to kill him. You know, the best way that would look like an accident. So then he finds out about the workshop and decides it's perfect."

"That presumes," Mike said, "that one of us is going to be next."

"Hell, yes," Neil said. "That's why he's calling us. Shake us up. Sweat us out. Let us know that he's out there somewhere, just waiting. And that we're next."

"I'm going to follow you to work tomorrow, Neil," I said. "And Mike's going to be with me."

"You guys are having breakdowns. You really are," Mike said.

"We'll follow Neil tomorrow," I said. "And then on Saturday you and Neil can follow me. If he's following us around, then we'll see it. And then we can start following him. We'll at least find out who he is."

"And then what?" Mike said. "Suppose we do find out where he lives? Then what the hell do we do?"

Neil said, "I guess we worry about that when we get there, don't we?"

In the morning, I picked Mike up early. We stopped off for doughnuts and coffee. He's like my brother, not a morning person. Crabby. Our conversation was at a minimum, though he did say, "I could've used the extra hour's sleep this morning. Instead of this crap, I mean."

As agreed, we parked half a block from Neil's house. Also as agreed, Neil emerged exactly at 7:35. Kids were already in the wide suburban streets on skateboards and rollerblades. No other car could be seen, except for a lone silver BMW in a driveway far down the block.

We followed him all the way to work. Nobody followed him. Nobody.

When I dropped Mike off at his office, he said, "You owe me an hour's sleep."

"Two hours," I said.

"Huh?"

"Tomorrow, you and Neil follow me around."

"No way," he said.

There are times when only blunt anger will work with Mike. "It was your idea not to call the police, remember? I'm not up for any of your sulking, Mike. I'm really not."

He sighed: "I guess you're right."

I drove for two and a half hours Saturday morning. I hit a hardware store, a lumberyard, and a Kmart. At noon, I pulled into a McDonald's. The three of us had some lunch.

"You didn't see anybody even suspicious?"

"Not even suspicious, Aaron," Neil said. "I'm sorry."

"This is all bullshit. He's not going to follow us around."

"I want to give it one more chance," I said.

Mike made a face. "I'm not going to get up early, if that's what you've got in mind."

I got angry again. "Bob's dead, or have you forgotten?"

"Yeah, Aaron," Mike said. "Bob is dead. He got electrocuted. Accidentally."

I said, "You really think it was an accident?"

"Of course I do," Mike said. "When do you want to try it again?"

"Tonight. I'll do a little bowling."

"There's a fight on I want to watch," Mike said.

"Tape it," I said.

"'Tape it,'" he mocked. "Since when did you start giving us orders?"

"Oh, for God's sake, Mike, grow up," Neil said. "There's no way that Bob's electrocution was an accident or a coincidence. He's probably not going to stop with Bob, either."

The bowling alley was mostly teenagers on Saturday night. There was a time when bowling was mostly a working-class sport. Now it's come to the suburbs and the white-collar people. Now the bowling lane is a good place for teenage boys to meet teenage girls.

I bowled two games, drank three beers, and walked back outside an hour later.

Summer night. Smell of dying heat, car exhaust, cigarette smoke, perfume. Sound of jukebox, distant loud mufflers, even more distant rushing train, lonely baying dogs.

Mike and Neil were gone.

I went home and opened myself a beer.

The phone rang. Once again, I was expecting Jan.

"Found the bastard," Neil said. "He followed you from your house to the bowling alley. Then he got tired of waiting and took off again. This time we followed him."

"Where?"

He gave me an address. It wasn't a good one.

"We're waiting for you to get here. Then we're going up to pay him a little visit."

"I need twenty minutes."

"Hurry."

Not even the silver touch of moonlight lent these blocks of crumbling stucco apartment houses any majesty or beauty. The rats didn't even bother to hide. They squatted red-eyed on the unmown lawns, amidst beer cans, and broken bottles, and wrappers from Taco John's, and used condoms that looked like deflated mushrooms.

Mike stood behind a tree.

"I followed him around back," Mike said. "He went up the fire escape on the back. Then he jumped on this veranda. He's in the back apartment on the right side. Neil's in the backyard, watching for him."

Mike looked down at my ball bat. "That's a nice complement," he said. Then he showed me his handgun. "To this."

"Why the hell did you bring that?"

"Are you kidding? You're the one who said he killed Bob."

That, I couldn't argue with.

"All right," I said, "but what happens when we catch him?"

"We tell him to lay off us," Mike said.

"We need to go to the cops."

"Oh, sure. Sure we do." He shook his head. He looked as if he were dealing with a child. A very slow one. "Aaron, going to the cops now won't bring Bob back. And it's only going to get us in trouble."

That's when we heard the shout. It sounded like Neil.

Maybe five feet of rust-colored grass separated the yard from the alley that ran along the west side of the apartment house.

We ran down the alley, having to hop over an ancient drooping picket fence to reach the backyard where Neil lay sprawled, face down, next to a twenty-year-old Chevrolet that was tireless and up on blocks. Through the windshield, you could see the huge gouges in the seats where the rats had eaten their fill.

The backyard smelled of dog shit and car oil.

Neil was moaning. At least we knew he was alive.

"The sonofabitch," he said, when we got him to his feet. "I moved over to the other side, back of the car there, so he wouldn't see me if he tried to come down that fire escape. I didn't figure there was another fire escape on the side of the building. He must've come around there and snuck up on me. He tried to kill me but I had this—"

In the moonlight, his wrist and the switchblade knife he held in his fingers were wet and dark with blood. "I got him a couple of times in the arm. Otherwise, I'd be dead."

"We're going up there," Mike said.

"How about checking Neil first?" I said.

"I'm fine," Neil said. "A little headache from where he caught me on the back of the neck." He waved his bloody blade. "Good thing I had this."

The landlord was on the first floor. He wore Bermuda shorts and no shirt. He looked eleven or twelve months pregnant with little male titties and enough coarse black hair to knit a sweater with. He had a plastic-tipped cigarillo in the left corner of his mouth.

"Yeah?"

"Two-F," I said.

"What about it?"

"Who lives there?"

"Nobody."

"Nobody?"

"If you were the law, you'd show me a badge."

"I'll show you a badge," Mike said, making a fist.

"Hey," I said, playing good cop to his bad cop. "You just let me speak to this gentleman."

The guy seemed to like my reference to him as a gentleman. It was probably the only flattering name he'd never been called.

"Sir, we saw somebody go up there."

"Oh," he said, "the vampires."

"Vampires?"

He sucked down some cigarillo smoke. "That's what we call 'em, the missus and me. They're street people, winos and homeless and all like that. They know that sometimes some of these apartments ain't rented for a while, so they sneak up there and spend the night."

"You don't stop them?"

"You think I'd get my head split open for something like that?"

"I guess that makes sense." Then: "So nobody's renting it now?"

"Nope, it ain't been rented for three months. This fat broad lived there then. Man, did she smell. You know how fat people can smell sometimes? *She* sure smelled." He wasn't svelte.

Back on the front lawn, trying to wend my way between the mounds of dog shit, I said, "'Vampires.' Good name for them."

"Yeah it is," Neil said. "I just keep thinking of the one who died. His weird eyes."

"Here we go again," Mike said. "You two guys love to scare the shit out of each other, don't you? They're a couple of nickel-dime crooks, and that's all they are."

"All right if Mike and I stop and get some beer and then swing by your place?"

"Sure," I said. "Just as long as Mike buys Bud and none of that generic crap."

"Oh, I forgot," Neil laughed. "He does do that when it's his turn to buy, doesn't he?"

"Yeah," I said, "he certainly does."

I was never sure what time the call came. Darkness. The ringing phone seemed part of a dream from which I couldn't escape. Somehow I managed to lift the receiver before the phone machine kicked in.

Silence. That special kind of silence.

Him. I had no doubt about it. The vampire, as the landlord had called him. The one who'd killed Bob. I didn't say so much as hello. Just listened, angry, afraid, confused.

After a few minutes, he hung up.

Darkness again; deep darkness, the quarter moon in the sky a cold golden scimitar that could cleave a head from a neck.

5

About noon on Sunday, Jan called to tell me that she was staying a few days extra. The kids had discovered archery and there was a course at the Y they were taking and wouldn't she please please *please* ask good old Dad if they could stay. I said sure.

I called Neil and Mike to remind them that at nine tonight we were going to pay a visit to that crumbling stucco apartment house again.

I spent an hour on the lawn. My neighbors shame me into it. Lawns aren't anything I get excited about. But they sort of shame you into it. About halfway through, Byrnes, the chunky advertising man who lives next door, came over and clapped me on the back. He was apparently pleased that I was a real human being and taking a real human being's interest in my lawn. As usual he wore an expensive T-shirt with one of his client products on it and a pair of Bermuda shorts. As usual he tried hard to be the kind of winsome neighbor you always had in sitcoms of the fifties. But I knew somebody who knew him. Byrnes had fired his number two man so he wouldn't have to keep paying the man's insurance. The man was unfortunately dying of cancer. Byrnes was typical of all the ad people I'd met. Pretty treacherous people who spent most of their time cheating clients out of their money and putting on awards banquets so they could convince themselves that advertising was actually an endeavor that was of consequence.

Around four *Hombre* was on one of the cable channels so I had a few beers and watched Paul Newman doing the best acting of his career. At least that was my opinion.

I was just getting ready for the shower when the phone rang.

He didn't say hello. He didn't identify himself. "Tracy call you?"

It was Neil. Tracy was Mike's wife. "Why should she call me?"

"He's dead. Mike."

"What?"

"You remember how he was always bitching about that elevator at work?"

Mike worked in a very old building. He made jokes about the antiquated elevators. But you could always tell the joke simply hid his fears. He'd gotten stuck innumerable times, and it was always stopping several feet short of the upcoming floor.

"He opened the door and the car wasn't there. He fell eight floors."

"Oh, God."

"I don't have to tell you who did it, do I?"

"Maybe it's time—"

"I'm way ahead of you, Aaron. I'll pick you up in half an hour. Then we go to the police. You agree?"

"I agree."

Late Sunday afternoon, the second precinct parking lot is pretty empty. We'd missed the shift change. Nobody came or went.

"We ask for a detective," Neil said. He was dark sportcoat-white shirt-necktie earnest. I'd settled for an expensive blue sport-shirt Jan had bought me for my last birthday.

"You know one thing we haven't considered?"

"You're not going to change my mind."

"I'm not trying to change your mind, Neil, I'm just saying that there's one thing we haven't considered."

He sat behind his steering wheel, his head resting on the back of his seat.

"A lawyer."

"What for?"

"Because we may go in there and say something that gets us in very deep shit."

"No lawyers," he said. "We'd just look like we were trying to hide something from the cops."

"You sure about that?"

"I'm sure."

"You ready?" I said.

"Ready."

The interior of the police station was quiet. A muscular bald man in a dark uniform sat behind a desk that read Information.

He said, "Help you?"

"We'd like to see a detective," I said.

"Are you reporting a crime?"

"Uh, yes," I said.

"What sort of crime?" he said.

I started to speak but once again lost my voice. I thought about all the reporters, about how Jan and the kids would be affected by it all. How my job would be affected. Taking a guy down to the basement and tying him up and then accidentally killing him

Neil said: "Vandalism."

"Vandalism?" the cop said. "You don't need a detective, then. I can just give you a form." Then he gave us a leery look, as if he sensed we'd just changed our minds about something.

"In that case, could I just take it home with me and fill it out there?" Neil said.

"Yeah, I guess." The cop still watched us carefully now.

"Great."

"You sure that's what you wanted to report? Vandalism?"

"Yeah; yeah, that's exactly what we wanted to report," Neil said. "Exactly."

"Vandalism?" I said, when we were back in the car.

"I don't want to talk right now."

"Well, maybe I want to talk."

"I just couldn't do it."

"No kidding."

He looked over at me. "You could've told him the truth. Nobody was stopping you."

I looked out the window. "Yeah, I guess I could've."

"We're going over there tonight. To the vampire's place."

"And do what?"

"Ask him how much he wants."

"How much he wants for what?" I said.

"How much he wants to forget everything. He goes on with his life, we go on with ours."

I had to admit, I'd had a similar thought myself. Neil and I didn't know how to do any of this. But the vampire did. He was good at talking, good at harassing, good at violence.

"We don't have a lot of money to throw around."

"Maybe he won't want a lot of money. I mean, this guy isn't exactly sophisticated."

"He's sophisticated enough to make two murders look like accidents."

"I guess that's the point."

"I'm just not sure we should pay him anything, Neil."

"You got any better ideas?"

I didn't, actually; I didn't have any better ideas at all.

6

I spent an hour on the phone with Jan that afternoon. The last few days I'd been pretty anxious and she'd sensed it and now she was making sure that everything was all right with me. In addition to being wife and lover, Jan's also my best friend. I can't kid her. She always knows when something's wrong. I'd put off telling her about Bob and Mike dying. I'd been afraid that I might accidentally say more than I should and make her suspicious. But now I had to tell her about their deaths. It was the only way I could explain my tense mood.

"That's awful," she said. "Their poor families."

"They're handling it better than you might think."

"Maybe I should bring the kids home early."

"No reason to, hon. I mean, realistically there isn't anything any of us can do."

"Two accidents in that short a time. It's pretty strange."

"Yeah, I guess it is. But that's how it happens sometimes."

"Are you going to be all right?"

"Just need to adjust is all." I sighed. "I guess we won't be having our poker games anymore."

Then I did something I hadn't intended. I started crying and the tears caught in my throat.

"Oh, honey," Jan said. "I wish I was there so I could give you a big hug."

"I'll be OK."

"Two of your best friends."

"Yeah." The tears were starting to dry up now.

"Oh, did I tell you about Tommy?" Tommy was our six-year-old. "No, what?"

"Remember how he used to be so afraid of horses?"

"Uh-huh."

"Well, we took him out to this horse ranch where you can rent horses?"

"Uh-huh."

"And they found him a little Shetland pony and let him ride it and he loved it. He wasn't afraid at all." She laughed. "In fact, we could barely drag him home." She paused. "You're probably not in the mood for this, are you? I'm sorry, hon. Maybe you should go do something to take your mind off things. Is there a good movie on?"

"I guess I could check."

"Something light, that's what you need."

"Sounds good," I said. "I'll go get the newspaper and see what's on."

"Love you."

"Love you, too, sweetheart," I said.

I spent the rest of the afternoon going through my various savings accounts and investments. I had no idea what the creep would want to leave us alone. We could always threaten him with going to the police, though he might rightly point out that if we really wanted to do that, we would already have done it.

I settled in the five-thousand-dollar range. That was the maximum cash I had to play with. And even then I'd have to borrow a little from one of the mutual funds we had earmarked for the kids and college.

Five thousand dollars. To me, it sounded like an enormous amount of money, probably because I knew how hard I'd had to work to get it.

But would it be enough for our friend the vampire?

Neil was there just at dark. He parked in the drive and came in. Meaning he wanted to talk.

We went in the kitchen. I made us a couple of highballs and we sat there and discussed finances.

"I came up with six thousand," he said.

"I got five."

"That's eleven grand," he said. "It's got to be more cash than this creep has ever seen."

"What if he takes it and comes back for more?"

"We make it absolutely clear," Neil said, "that there is no more. That this is it. Period."

"And if not?"

Neil nodded. "I've thought this through. You know the kind of lowlife we're dealing with? A) He's a burglar which means, these days, that he's a junkie. B) If he's a junkie then that means he's very susceptible to AIDS. So between being a burglar and shooting up, this guy is probably going to have a very short lifespan."

"I guess I'd agree."

"Even if he wants to make our lives miserable, he probably won't live long enough to do it. So I think we'll be making just the one payment. We'll buy enough time to let nature take its course—his nature."

"What if he wants more than the eleven grand?"

"He won't. His eyes'll pop out when he sees this."

I looked at the kitchen clock. It was going on nine now. "I guess we could drive over there."

"It may be a long night," Neil said.

"I know."

"But I guess we don't have a hell of a lot of choice, do we?"

As we'd done the last time we'd been here, we split up the duties. I took the backyard, Neil the apartment door. We waited until midnight. The rap music had died by now. Babies cried and mothers screamed; couples fought. TV screens flickered in dark windows.

I went up the fire escape slowly and carefully. We'd talked about bringing guns then decided against it. We weren't exactly marksmen and if a cop stopped us for some reason, we could be arrested for carrying unlicensed firearms. All I carried was a flashlight in my back pocket.

As I grabbed the rungs of the ladder, powdery rust dusted my hands. I was chilly with sweat. My bowels felt sick. I was scared. I just wanted it to be over with. I wanted him to say yes he'd take the money and then that would be the end of it.

The stucco veranda was filled with discarded toys—a tricycle, innumerable games, a space helmet, a Wiffle bat and ball. The floor was crunchy with dried animal feces. At least I hoped the feces belonged to animals and not human children.

The door between veranda and apartment was open. Fingers of moonlight revealed an overstuffed couch and chair and a floor covered with the debris of fast food. McDonald's sacks. Pizza Hut wrappers and cardboards. Arby's wrappers, and what seemed to be five or six dozen empty beer cans. Far toward the hall that led to the front door I saw four red eyes watching me; a pair of curious rats.

I stood still and listened. Nothing. No sign of life. I went inside. Tiptoeing.

I went to the front door and let Neil in. There in the murky light of the hallway, he made a face. The smell was pretty bad.

Over the next ten minutes, we searched the apartment. And found nobody.

"We could wait here for him," I said.

"No way."

"The smell?"

"The smell, the rats, God; don't you just feel unclean?"

"Yeah, guess I do."

"There's an empty garage about halfway down the alley. We'd have a good view of the back of this building."

"Sounds pretty good."

"Sounds better than this place, anyway."

This time, we both went out the front door and down the stairway. Now the smells were getting to me as they'd earlier gotten to Neil. Unclean. He was right.

We got in Neil's Buick, drove down the alley that ran along the west side of the apartment house, backed up to the dark garage, and whipped inside.

"There's a sack in back," Neil said. "It's on your side."

"A sack?"

"Brewskis. Quart for you, quart for me."

"That's how my old man used to drink them," I said. I was the only blue-collar member of the poker game club. "Get off work at the plant and stop by and pick up two quart bottles of Hamms. Never missed."

"Sometimes I wish I would've been born into the working class," Neil said.

I was the blue-collar guy and Neil was the dreamer, always inventing alternate realities for himself.

"No, you don't," I said, leaning over the seat and picking up the sack damp from the quart bottles. "You had a damned nice life in Boston."

"Yeah, but I didn't learn anything. You know I was eighteen before I learned about cunnilingus?"

"Talk about cultural deprivation," I said.

"Well, every girl I went out with probably looks back on me as a pretty lame lover. They went down on me but I never went down on them. How old were you when you learned about cunnilingus?"

"Maybe thirteen."

"See?"

"I learned about it but I didn't do anything about it."

"I was twenty years old before I lost my cherry," Neil said.

"I was seventeen."

"Bullshit."

"Bullshit what? I was seventeen."

"In sociology, they always taught us that blue-collar kids always lost their virginity a lot earlier than white-collar kids."

"That's the trouble with sociology. It tries to particularize from generalities."

"Huh?" He grinned. "Yeah, I always thought sociology was full of shit, too, actually. But you were really seventeen?"

"I was really seventeen."

I wish I could tell you that I knew what it was right away, the missile that hit the windshield and shattered and starred it, and then kept right on tearing through the car until the back window was also shattered and starred.

But all I knew was that Neil was screaming and I was screaming and my quart bottle of Miller's was spilling all over my crotch as I tried to hunch down behind the dashboard. It was a tight fit because Neil was trying to hunch down behind the steering wheel.

The second time, I knew what was going on: somebody was shooting at us. Given the trajectory of the bullet, he had to be right in front of us, probably behind the two dumpsters that sat on the other side of the alley.

"Can you keep down and drive this sonofabitch at the same time?"

"I can try," Neil said.

"If we sit here much longer, he's going to figure out we don't have guns. Then he's gonna come for us for sure."

Neil leaned over and turned on the ignition. "I'm going to turn left when we get out of here."

"Fine. Just get moving."

"Hold on."

What he did was kind of slump over the bottom half of the wheel, just enough so he could sneak a peek at where the car was headed. There were no more shots.

All I could hear was the smooth-running Buick motor.

He eased out of the garage, ducking down all the time.

When he got a chance, he bore left.

He kept the lights off.

Through the bullet hole in the windshield I could see an inch or so of starry sky.

It was a long alley and we must have gone a quarter block before he said, "I'm going to sit up. I think we lost him."

"So do I."

"Look at that frigging windshield."

Not only was the windshield a mess, the car reeked of spilled beer.

"You think I should turn on the headlights?"

"Sure," I said. "We're safe now."

We were still crawling at maybe ten miles per hour when he pulled the headlights on.

That's when we saw him, silver of eye, dark of hair, crouching in the middle of the alley waiting for us. He was a good fifty yards ahead of us but we were still within range.

There was no place we could turn around.

He fired.

This bullet shattered whatever had been left untouched of the windshield. Neil slammed on the brakes.

Then he fired a second time.

By now, both Neil and I were screaming and cursing again.

A third bullet.

"Run him over!" I yelled, ducking behind the dashboard.

"What?" Neil yelled back.

"Floor it!"

He floored it. He wasn't even sitting up straight. We might have gone careening into one of the garages or dumpsters. But somehow the Buick stayed in the alley. And very soon it was traveling eighty-five miles per hour. I watched the speedometer peg it.

More shots, a lot of them now, side windows shattering, bullets ripping into fender and hood and top.

I didn't see us hit him but I felt us hit him, the car traveling that fast, the creep so intent on killing us he hadn't bothered to get out of the way in time.

The front of the car picked him up and hurled him into a garage near the head of the alley.

We both sat up, watched as his entire body was broken against the edge of the garage, and he then fell smashed and unmoving to the grass.

"Kill the lights," I said.

"What?"

"Kill the lights and let's go look at him."

Neil punched off the headlights.

We left the car and ran over to him.

A white rib stuck bloody and brazen from his side. Blood poured from his ears, nose, mouth. One leg had been crushed and also showed white bone. His arms had been broken, too.

I played my flashlight beam over him.

He was dead, all right.

"Looks like we can save our money," I said. "It's all over now."

"I want to get the hell out of here."

"Yeah," I said. "So do I."

We got the hell out of there.

7

A month later, just as you could smell autumn on the summer winds, Jan and I celebrated our twelfth wedding anniversary. We drove up to Lake Geneva, in Wisconsin, and stayed at a very nice hotel and rented a Chris-Craft for a couple of days. This was the first time I'd been able to relax since the thing with the burglar had started.

One night when Jan was asleep, I went up on the deck of the boat and just watched the stars. I used to read a lot of Edgar Rice Burroughs when I was a boy. I always remembered how John Carter felt—that the stars had a very special destiny for him—and that night there on the deck, that was to be a good family man, a good stockbroker, and a good neighbor. The bad things were all behind me now. I imagined Neil was feeling pretty much the same way. Hot bitter July seemed a long ways behind us now. Fall was coming, bringing with it football and Thanksgiving and Christmas. July would recede even more with snow on the ground.

The funny thing was, I didn't see Neil much anymore. It was as if the sight of each other brought back a lot of bad memories. It was a mutual feeling, too. I didn't want to see him any more than he wanted to see me. Our wives thought this was pretty strange. They'd meet at the supermarket or shopping center and wonder why "the boys" didn't get together anymore. Neil's wife, Sarah, kept inviting us over to "sit around the pool and watch Neil pretend he knows how to swim." September was summer hot. The pool was still the centerpiece of their life.

Not that I made any new friends. The notion of a midweek poker game had lost all its appeal. There was work and my family and little else.

Then one sunny Indian summer afternoon, Neil called and said, "Maybe we should get together again."

"Maybe."

"It's over, Aaron. It really is."

"I know."

"Will you at least think about it?"

I felt embarrassed. "Oh, hell, Neil. Is that swimming pool of yours open Saturday afternoon?"

"As a matter of fact, it is. And as a matter of fact, Sarah and the girls are going to be gone to a fashion show at the club."

"Perfect. We'll have a couple of beers."

`You know how to swim?"

"No," I said, laughing. "And from what Sarah says, you don't, either."

I got there about three, pulled into the drive, walked to the back where the gate in the wooden fence led to the swimming pool. It was eighty degrees and even from here I could smell the chlorine.

I opened the gate and went inside and saw him right away. The funny thing was, I didn't have much of a reaction at all. I just watched him. He was floating. Facedown. He looked pale in his red trunks. This, like the others, would be judged an accidental death. Of that I had no doubt at all.

I used the cellular phone in my car to call 911.

I didn't want Sarah and the girls coming back to see an ambulance and police cars in the drive and them not knowing what was going on.

I called the club and had her paged.

I told her what I'd found. I let her cry. I didn't know what to say. I never do.

In the distance, I could hear the ambulance working its way toward the Neil Solomon residence.

I was just about to get out of the car when my cellular phone rang. I picked up. "Hello?"

"There were three of us that night at your house, Mr. Bellini. You killed two of us. I recovered from when your friend stabbed me, remember? Now I'm ready for action. I really am, Mr. Bellini."

Then the emergency people were there, and neighbors, too, and then wan, trembling Sarah. I just let her cry some more. Gave her whiskey and let her cry.

8

He knows how to do it, whoever he is.

He lets a long time go between late-night calls. He lets me start to think that maybe he changed his mind and left town. And then he calls.

Oh, yes, he knows just how to play this little game.

He never says anything, of course. He doesn't need to. He just listens. And then hangs up.

I've considered going to the police, of course, but it's way too late for that. Way too late.

Or I could ask Jan and the kids to move away to a different city with me. But he knows who I am and he'd find me again.

So all I can do is wait and hope that I get lucky, the way Neil and I got lucky the night we killed the second of them.

Tonight I can't sleep.

It's after midnight.

Jan and I wrapped presents until well after eleven. She asked me again if anything was wrong. We don't make love as much as we used to, she said; and then there are the nightmares. Please tell me if something's wrong. Aaron. Please.

I stand at the window watching the snow come down. Soft and beautiful snow. In the morning, a Saturday, the kids will make a snowman and then go sledding and then have themselves a good old-fashioned snowball fight, which invariably means that one of them will come rushing in at some point and accuse the other of some terrible misdeed.

I see all this from the attic window.

Then I turn back and look around the poker table. Four empty chairs. Three of them belong to dead men.

I look at the empty chairs and think back to summer.

I look at the empty chairs and wait for the phone to ring.

I wait for the phone to ring.

The Brasher Girl

For Stephen King

I guess by now you pretty much know what happened the last year or so in the Valley here—with Cindy and I, I mean.

All I can hope for is that you'll give me time to tell my side of things. Nobody ever did. Not the cops, not the press, not even my own parents. They all just assumed

Well, they all assumed wrong, each and every one of them.

It took me 19 dates to have my way with Cindy Marie Brasher, who was not only the prettiest girl in Central Consolidated High, but the prettiest girl in the entire Valley, though I will admit to some prejudice on that particular judgment.

Night we met, I was 23 and just out of the Army, and she was 17 and about to be voted Homecoming queen. She was not only good looking, she was popular, too.

Consolidated being my own alma mater, I went along with my 16-year-old brother to the season's first football game, and afterward to a party.

Things hadn't changed much as far as high schools rituals went. There was a big bonfire down by the river and a couple kegs of Bud and a few dozen joints of some of the worst marijuana I'd ever smoked. Couple hours in, several of the couples snuck off into the woods to make out more seriously than they could around the bonfire, at least ten different boys and maybe two girls rushed down to the riverbank to throw up, and two farm boys about the same size got into a fist fight that I let run three, four minutes before I stepped in and broke it up. One thing you learn in the Army, drinking and fist fights can lead to some serious damage.

Now it'd be real nice here to tell you that Cindy took one look at me in my Army clothes (face it, might as well get some mileage out of my Paratrooper uniform) and fell right in love with me. But she didn't. For one thing, she was the date of Michael Henning, whose old man was president of the oldest bank in the Valley. And Michael himself was no slouch, either—took the basketball team twice to state, and had a swimming scholarship waiting for him at any of three Big 10 schools.

No, she didn't rush into my arms; but she did look me over. Subtly. Very subtly. Because that was her style. But a few times our gazes met over the flickering flames and—there was some mutual interest. No doubt about it.

She left early, and on Michael Henning's arm, but just before she vanished into the prairie darkness surrounding the bonfire, she looked at me a last time and I knew I hadn't been imagining things earlier.

Three weeks went by before I saw her again, during which time I carried her in my mind like a talisman. Always there, burning brightly.

Autumn had come to our small town. On sunny mornings, I walked down to the State employment office to take aptitude tests and to see if they'd found anything for me yet. Then I'd drift over to the library and check out a book by Hemingway or John Steinbeck or Robert Stone. They were my favorite writers. Most of the time, I'd read in the town square, the fierce fall leaves of red and gold and bronze scraping along the walk, pushed by a chill wind. The bandstand was closed for the season and even the two men on the Civil War statues appeared to be hunkering down for winter.

That was where I had my first real talk with her, sitting on a park bench reading Steinbeck's *In Dubious Battle*.

She was cutting through the park on her way back to school. I heard her and looked up.

She looked quickly away but I could tell she'd been staring at me. "Hey," I said, "you're Cindy Brasher, right?"

She grinned. "You were at the bonfire party? You're Ted's brother, right?"

I walked her back to school. And after school, I just happened to be sitting in Lymon's, which is the Rexall drug store downtown where the kids all go, and where Cindy had told me she just might be if I stopped in. Unfortunately, I'd no more than picked up my cherry Coke and started walking back to the booths than Michael Henning showed up and sat down next to her.

Things went on like this for another month. I got a job selling men's clothes, just a temporary sort of thing, at Wallingham's Fine Fashions, and I also got a loan from my Dad so I could pay down on a three-year-old Pontiac convertible, a red job that shined up real well.

Of course, my main interest remained Cindy. We saw each other three, four times a week, but always in a sneaky kind of way—one time we sat in the grassy railroad tracks behind G&H Supermarket—and there was never anything romantic. She told me that she was in the process of breaking up with Michael Henning and that he was having a hard time with it. She said he cried a lot and one time even threatened to kill himself. She said she felt terribly guilty and responsible and that Michael was a fine person whom people disliked just because he came from money and that she wished she still loved him but she didn't and that nothing between us could happen until her break with Michael was final and official and she wouldn't blame me if I'd go find somebody else, having to wait around like this and all, but of course she knew better. By now there was nobody else for me and never would be.

To be honest, I felt a little guilty about Michael Henning, too. From what Cindy said, she'd been drifting away from Michael before I got back from the Army but my presence certainly accelerated things. Back in eleventh grade I'd been going with Laurie McKee, a very appealing blonde, and she dumped me for a senior named Sam Hampton. I didn't take it well. I drank a lot and got into a lot of fights and one night I even ran away from home, loading up my car and taking off down the highway like a character in a Kerouac novel. Came back four days later, broke and aggrieved and scared as hell of just about everything. That was why I finished up my high school at St. Pius, the Catholic school. My folks weren't all that crazy about papists but they knew I'd never make it through Consolidated, having to see Laurie every day. Far as that went, that was no magic formula, either, I was still depressed a lot, and still occasionally hinted that I'd like to take my Dad's hunting rifle down and do a Hemingway on myself, and still had notions of taking Sam Hampton out into the woods and kicking his ass real good.

So I pretty much knew what Michael Henning was going through and, believe me, that's not something I'd wish on anybody.

The break-up didn't come until after Christmas. The kids all joked that she'd wanted to drag it out so she could get a nice Christmas present but in fact when Michael gave her that brand-new coat rumored to have cost $500, she told him that it wasn't right that he'd give her something like this, and would he please take it back.

Same night he took it back, he showed up on my parents' doorstep and asked me if I wanted to go for a ride. I had a lot of quick spooky premonitions. He might have a gun in his car and blow my brains out. Or he might drive us both off a cliff up at Manning State Park. Or he might drag me over to Cindy's house for a real humiliating scene.

But I went. Poor bastard was shaking so bad I couldn't say no, big lanky handsome kid who looked real scared.

Christmas night, the highways were empty. You saw the occasional cannonball sixteen wheeler whooshing through the Midwestern night but that was about all. We drove west, paralleling the State Park. And we drove fast. He had a Trans-Am that did 110 and you barely had to turn the ignition on.

And then he started crying. Weeping, really. And so hard that he pulled off the road and I just sat there and watched him and listened to him, not knowing what to do or say.

"I got to tell you something, Spence," he said, Spencer being my last name, and Spence being forever my nickname, "I just want you to take care of her. I want you to be good to her, you understand?"

I nodded.

"She doesn't think much of herself, Spence, which you've probably noticed." I nodded again. I had noticed that.

"That old man of hers—boy would I like to get him in a fight sometime—he always told her she wasn't worth shit, and now she believes that. She ever tell you how he'd beat her?"

I shook my head. She hadn't told me that.

"She used to come out to the car with black eyes sometimes, and once she had a compound fracture from where he'd thrown her into a wall, and another time he cracked her ankle and she was hobbling around almost a week before I got her to go to the doctor's."

It was real strange, the two of us there, talking about the girl we both loved, and him saying that all he cared about was that I loved her true and took gentle care of her.

And then his tears seemed to dry up and he turned more toward me in the seat—the heater pushing out warm air and the radio real low with a Van Morrison song—and he said, "But you don't know the truth yet, do you?"

"The truth?"

"About Cindy?"

I felt a chill. And I shuddered. And I wasn't sure why. Maybe it was just the way he said it there in the dashlight darkness. The Truth.

"I guess I don't."

"She has a friend."

"A friend?"

"Yeah."

"What kind of friend? You mean another boyfriend?"

He shook his head. "Not exactly." He smiled. "You, I could've dealt with. But her friend—"

Then he turned around and put the Trans-Am into gear and we squealed out. We didn't say a word until we were halfway back to my house.

"Michael?"

"Yeah?"

"You going to tell me any more?"

"About what?"

"About this friend of hers?"

He looked over at me and smiled but it was a cold and sinister smile and I saw in it his hatred of me. He knew something that I didn't and he was going to enjoy the hell out of me finding out what it was.

When he reached my curb, he reached over and slapped forth a handshake. "Good luck, Spence. You're a lot tougher guy than I am." The quick chill smile again. "And believe me, with Cindy that'll come in handy."

I went in and said some more Merry Christmas kind of things to my parents and my brother and sister and then I went down to the family room and put in a Robert Mitchum tape, Mitch being my favorite actor, and settled in with a Pepsi and some popcorn.

At the same time I was watching Mitch and Jane Russell try to outfox William Bendix in *Macao*, Michael Henning was up in his bedroom pulling a Hemingway.

Coroner said that the entire back of his head had been blown out and town rumor had it that try as his parents might over the next few weeks to scrape blood and bone and brains off the wall, they were having no luck at all. Finally, a carpenter came in, cut out that entire section of the wall, and then replastered and repainted it.

Three hundred people came to Michael Henning's funeral. Not wanting to be hypocritical, I stayed home.

I mentioned in the beginning that it took me 19 dates to seduce Cindy. I am counting only those dates we had after her month long mourning of Michael Henning, during which time the town had a change of heart about her. Where before she'd been their pride, the poor girl with the drunken father who constantly humiliated her, they now saw her as the whore who'd betrayed her lover and driven him to suicide. Townsfolk knew about me, too, and liked me no better.

We did a lot of driving, mostly to Iowa City and Cedar Rapids, on our dates. Couple town people were so angry about seeing us together, they came right up to us and started arguing that we had no business enjoying ourselves with poor Michael barely cold in his grave. One guy even tried to pick a fight with me but my paratrooper tricks were a little too wily for him. Fat slob ending up on his back, huffing and puffing and panting out dirty words.

The worst, of course, was seeing Michael's parents. We were leaving the Orpheum one night after seeing a Barbara Streisand movie—I guess you can guess which one of us chose that particular picture—and there they were in the lobby, waiting with a small crowd for the next feature to stop. The Mrs. got tears in her eyes and looked away; the Mr. just glared right at me, staring me down. He won. I couldn't look at him very long.

Odd thing was, the night we saw them in the lobby was the night that Cindy let me go all the way, which is how she always referred to it.

Friend of mine had an apartment over a tavern and we went up there because he was out of town on a four-day Army Reserve weekend.

I figured it was going to be the same thing as usual, bringing each other to satisfaction with eager hands and fingers, but this night, she said, "Why don't we do it tonight, Spence? I need to know you love me and you need to know I love you and this is the best way to prove it. Just please let's keep the lights off. You know, my breasts." She really had a hang-up about her breasts. So they were small, I didn't care. But she sure did. A lot of times I'd be petting her or kissing her nipples and she'd push me gently away and say, "That's enough for now, all right, hon?" Michael had been absolutely right. She really was ashamed of herself in a lot of ways.

After that night, we were closer than ever, and a few weeks later I uttered, for the very first time, the word "marriage."

She just looked at me all funny and said, "Spence, you know what your parents think of me."

"It isn't that they don't like you, Cindy, it's just that they worry about me."

"Worry? Why?"

"I told you about Laurie. You know, how screwed up I got and all."

"I'm not like Laurie."

"I know, sweetheart, but they think—well, a young girl doesn't know her mind. We'll announce our engagement and everybody'll start making a fuss and everything—and then you'll feel a lot better."

"That really makes me mad, Spence. I'm not like Laurie at all. I love you. Deeply and maturely. The way a woman loves a man."

How could a guy go wrong with a girl like that?

By spring, I had a better job, this one at a lumber company out on 151. I worked the front desk and handled all the wholesale orders. Salary plus commission. Kept me hopping but I enjoyed it. Nights were all free and only half a day Saturdays.

Couple nights a week we drove up to an old high school haunt of mine, place where kids back in the days of the Bee Gees and Donna Summer liked to make out. It was great because now the high school kids used the state park. Hardly anybody came up here.

One night as I sat there, looking down at the lights of the little prairie town where I'd grown up, Cindy all snug in my arms, she said, "Spence? If I asked you an honest question would you give me an honest answer?"

"Sure I would."

"Well . . ."

And right away, I thought of my folks and how smug they'd look when I told them what I feared she was about to say—that she'd been thinking real hard and had decided that maybe I really was just a tad old for her; or that she'd met this senior boy, see, and without wanting to, without planning for it or even wanting it to happen in any way, well she'd gone and fallen in love with somebody else.

"You're trembling," she said.

"I just know this is going to be real bad news."

"Oh, honey, no it's not. Honest. You're so silly."

And then she tickled me the way she always did, and then gave me one of those big warm creamy kisses of hers, and then she said, "It's just that I've got this friend I'd like you to meet some time."

Right away, of course, I remembered what Michael had told me that night in her car. About her friend.

"This is a male friend?"

"Yes, hon, but nothing to be jealous of." She smiled. "When you meet him, you'll see how silly you are. Honest." Then she gave me another one of those creamy kisses.

"How'd you meet him?"

"Let's not talk about him any more tonight, all right? Let's just sit here and look at the stars. I love looking at the stars—and thinking about life in outer space." Pause. "You believe in that?"

"In what?"

"You know, that there is life on other planets."

I made a scary sound and a monster face but she didn't laugh. Didn't even smile.

"I'm serious, Spence. Do you?"

"Guess I haven't thought about it much."

"Well, I do."

"Believe that there's life on other planets?"

"Uh-huh."

I gave her a very long kiss. My crotch started getting real tight. "Well, if you do, I do."

"Believe in life on other planets?"

"Uh-huh."

We had another kiss on it.

Three nights later, Cindy suggested that we drive up by Dubuque which, for a rainy night, was something of a hike, being over 100 miles away. When I asked her why, she just shrugged and said, "I just like looking at the Mississippi. Makes me feel peaceful. But if you don't want to—"

Makes her feel peaceful. What was I going to say, No, I don't want you to feel peaceful?

We drove up by Dubuque and it was nice, even with the rain. When we reached the Mississippi, I pulled up and parked. In the distance you could see the tugs and barges, and then a fervent bright gambling boat, and then just the dark river rushing down to New Orleans and the Gulf. We sat there for an hour and then she suggested we head back.

When we were 40 miles from Cedar Rapids when she spotted a convenience store shining like a mirage on a dark hill. "Could I get you to pull in there?"

"Sure."

"Thanks."

When we got to the drive, she said to just park and she'd run in. "Just need to tinkle," she grinned.

Ten minutes later, we were back on the highway. She kind of scooched up to me the rest of the way home.

Following day, I must've heard the story on the news six, seven times before I finally figured it out. At first, I rejected the whole idea, of course. What a stupid idea it was. That Cindy, good Cindy, could possibly have—

That night, no place better to go, we parked up in the state park and got in the back seat and made love and afterward I said, "I've had this really crazy idea all day."

"Yeah? What kind of crazy idea?"

"You hear the news?"

"News about what?"

But soon as I said it, I felt her slender body tense beneath mine. She hadn't put her bra back on yet and her sweet little breasts were very cold. Usually she would have covered up right away but soon as I mentioned having this idea, she just kind of froze in place. I could smell her perfume and the cold night air and the jism in the condom I'd set in the rear ashtray.

"You remember when we stopped at that convenience store last night? Commg back from Dubuque?"

"Sure."

"Place got robbed. And the kid working got killed."

"Oh? Really? I hadn't heard that."

Now she started getting dressed real fast. "You mind if I have a cigarette?"

"Thought you quit."

Smoking was her only bad habit. Winston Lights.

"I just carry one around, hon. just one. You know that."

"How come you need it all of a sudden?"

She shrugged, twisting her bra cups around so they'd cover her breasts.

"Just get jittery sometimes. You know how I get."

"You did it, didn't you?"

"What, hon?"

"Robbing that place, killing that kid. You."

"Well, thank you very fucking much. Isn't that a nice thing to say to the girl you love?"

We didn't talk for a long time. We took our respective places up in the front seat and I got the car all fired up and we drove back into town but we still didn't talk.

When I pulled up in front of her house, I said, "I don't know what came over me, Cindy. God, I really don't. Of course you didn't rob that place or kill that guy. Of course, you didn't."

She sat way over against the window in the shadows. I couldn't see her very well but I could sense her warm full mouth and the gentling warmth between her legs. I wanted to hide in that warmth and never see sunshine again.

"You were right, Spence. I took the money and I killed the kid."

"Bullshit."

"Huh-uh. True. And I've done it before, too."

"Robbed places?"

"Uh-huh."

"And killed guys?"

"Uh-huh."

"Bullshit."

"God, Spence, you think I'd make up something like this?"

I absolutely didn't know what to say.

"He makes me do it."

"Who?"

"My friend."

I thought of poor dead Michael Henning and the warning he'd given me.

"How does he make you do it?"

"He controls my mind."

I grinned. "Boy, you had me going there, Cindy. I mean, for a minute there I thought you were serious. You were robbin' guys and killin' guys and—"

"You want to meet him?"

"Your friend?"

"Yeah."

"When?"

"Tomorrow night."

"You serious?"

"Yes. But I better warn you, when Michael met him?"

"Yeah."

"Really freaked him out."

"How come?"

"You'll see. Tomorrow night."

"Is this all bullshit, Cindy?"

"None of it's bullshit, Spence, and you know it. You're just afraid to admit it's true."

"If it's true, I should go to the law."

"Then maybe that's what you should do. Lord knows, I couldn't stop you. Big strapping paratrooper like you."

"But why do you kill them?"

"He makes me." She leaned over to me and now I could see her face in the faint streetlight, see that tears were streaming down her cheeks. "I don't want to do any of it, Spence. But he makes me."

"Nobody has that kind of control over somebody else."

"Nobody human."

"He's not human?"

She kissed me with that luxurious mouth of hers and I have to say that I went a little insane with my senses so full of her—the taste of her mouth, the scent of her skin, the soft warmth of her lips behind the denim covering her crotch . . . I went a little insane.

"Tomorrow night, Spence," she said.

I wanted to say a lot more, of course, but she was gone, her door opening and the dome light coming on, night rushing in like a cold black tide.

Not human. Those were the two words I thought about all next day. Not human. And around three o'clock, just when the wholesale business was slowing down, I started thinking about two words of my own. Temporarily insane. Sure, why not? A girl who'd grown up without a mother, constantly being beaten by her father? A girl who secretly blamed herself for the death of her boyfriend, as I secretly suspected she did? That could cause her to lose her mind. It happened all the time.

"You not hungry tonight?" my Dad said over dinner.

I saw them glance at each other, Mom and Dad. Whenever I did anything they found out of the ordinary, they'd exchange that same kind of glance. The Cindy glance, I called it.

"One of the women at work got a box of birthday candy and she passed it around. Guess I ate too much of it."

Another Cindy glance. They knew that I wasn't much for sweets and that I'd certainly never stuff myself with them. I decided that then would be a good time to tell them.

"I'll be moving out next week."

"Moving out?" Mom said, startled.

I laughed. "Well, I'll be twenty-four this year. Don't you think it's about time?"

"Is—Cindy—moving in with you?" Dad asked. Sometimes they both had a hard time saying her name. Got downright tongue-tied. The way Christians do when they have to say the name Satan.

I nodded to Jeff and Suzie. "These are very young, impressionable children. I don't think we should discuss such matters in front of them." I smiled at Suzie.

"Who would have thought," said fourteen-year-old Suzie, "my very own brother, shacking up."

Jeff laughed. Mom said, "That'll be enough of that, young lady."

"Is she?" Dad said.

I reached across the table and took their hands, the way we hold hands during Grace on Thanksgiving and Christmas. "She's not moving in with me. And I'm not going to start dealing crack out of my apartment. I'm just going to live there alone the way any normal red-blooded twenty-four-year-old guy would."

I could tell they weren't happy—I mean, even if Cindy wasn't going to live there, she was obviously going to spend a lot of time there—but at least they let me change the subject. The rest of the meal we talked about some of the new cars I'd been looking at. Last month's bonus at the lumber yard had been pretty dam good.

Funny thing was, that night Cindy went two hours before even bringing up the subject of her friend. We drove to Cedar Rapids to Westdale Mall where she bought some new clothes. Always before, I'd wondered where Cindy got the money for her seemingly endless supply of fashionable duds. After the robbery the other night, I no longer wondered.

On the way back, radio real low with a Bob Seger tape, windows open to let the warm May breeze bring the scents of new mown grass and hay into the car, she said, "You know where the old Parkinson cabin is?"

"Sure. Up in the hills."

"That's where he lives."

"Your friend?"

"Uh-huh."

"You want to go up there?"

"Do you?"

"I got to admit," I said, "I'm kinda curious."

"Michael was afraid. He put it off for a real long time." She leaned over and kissed me, making it hard to concentrate on my driving. Like I cared. What better way to die than Cindy kissing me?

"No," I said, "I'm not afraid." But I was.

Little kids in our town believe that there are two long-haunted places. One is the old red brick school abandoned back in the fifties. The tale five different generations of boys and girls have told is that there was this really wicked principal, a warted crone who looked a lot like Miss Grundy in "Archie" comics, who on two occasions took two different first-graders to the basement and beat them so badly that they died. Legend had it that she cracked the concrete floor, buried them beneath it, and then poured fresh concrete. Legend also had it that even today the spirits of those two little kids still haunt the old schoolhouse and that on certain nights, the ghost of the principal can be seen carrying a blood-dripping ax.

The other legend concerns Parkinson's cabin, a place built in the mid-1800s by a white man who planned to do a lot of business with the Mesquakie Indians. Except something went wrong. The local newspaper—and for the hell of it, I once spent a day in the library confirming the fact that an 1861 paper did run this story—noted that a huge meteor was spotted by many townspeople one night, and that it crashed to earth not far from Trapper Parkinson's crude cabin. Odd thing was, nobody ever saw or talked to Parkinson after the meteor crash. Perfect soil for a legend to grow.

Took us thirty-five minutes to reach the cabin from the road. Bramble and first-growth pine trees made the passage slow. But then we stood on a small hill, the moon big and round and blanch white, and looked down on this disintegrating lean-to of boards and tar paper, which a bunch of hobos had added in the forties when they were trying to fix the place up with not much luck. An ancient plow-all blade—rusted and wood-rotted—stood stuck in a stand of buffalo grass. A silver snake of moon-touched creek ran behind the cabin.

And then Cindy said, "You see it over there? The well?"

Sometime in the early part of this century, when the last of the Mormons were trekking their way across the country to Utah, a straggling band stopped here long enough to help a young couple finish the well they'd started digging. The Mormons, being decent folks indeed, even built the people a pit made of native stone and a roof made of birch. And the well itself hadn't been easy to dig. You started with a sharp-pointed auger looking for water and then you dug with a shovel when you found it. Sometimes you dug 200 feet, sending up buckets of rock and dirt and shale for days before you were done. It was all tumbledown now, of course, but you could see in the remnants of the pit how impressive it must have been when it was new

We went over to the well. Cindy ducked beneath the shabby roof and peered straight down into the darkness. I dropped a rock down there. Echoes rose of its plopping through the surface. I shone my light down. This was what they call a dug well, about the only kind a fella could make back then. Most of the dug wells in this area went down into clay and shale about 50 feet.

I shone my light down. Dirty black water was still spiderwebbed from the rock.

"He probably doesn't like the light."

I stood up, clipping off the light. "You going to get mad if I start laughing?"

"You better not, Spence. This is real serious."

"Your friend lives down in the well?"

"Uh-huh. In the water."

"Nobody could live below the water, Cindy."

"I told you last night. He's not human."

"What is he, then?"

"Some kind of space alien."

"I see."

"You better not laugh."

"Where'd he come from, this space alien?"

"Where do you think, dopey? He was inside the meteor that crashed here that time. Parkinson's meteor."

"And he stays down in the well?"

"Right."

"Because why?"

"Because if humans ever laid their eyes on him, they'd go insane. Right on the spot."

"And how do you know that?"

"He told me. Or rather, It. It's more of an It than a He, though it's also sort of a He. It told me. But It's also a He."

"So he just stays down there."

"Uh-huh."

"Doing what?"

"Now how the hell would I know that, Spence?"

"And he tells you to do things?"

"Uh-huh. Once he establishes telepathic contact with you."

"Telepathic. I see."

"Don't be a prick and start laughing, Spence."

"How'd he make contact with you?"

She shrugged. "One night I was real lonely—Michael went to some basketball game with his father—and I didn't know where else to go so I walked up to the park and then I wandered over here and before I knew it I saw the old cabin and I just kind of drifted down the hill and—He started talking to me. Inside my mind, I mean."

"Telepathically."

"Exactly, you smart-ass. Telepathically."

"Then you brought Michael up here?"

"Uh-huh."

"And he started talking to Michael?"

"Not right away. Michael and He, well, they didn't like each other much. I always felt kinda sorry for Michael. I had such a good relationship with Him but Michael—but at least Michael did what He told him."

"Which was?"

"You remember when O'Banyon's trailer burned that night?"

My stomach tightened. Brice O'Banyon was a star baseball pitcher for Consolidated. He lived in a trailer with his folks. One night it burned down and the three of them died.

"Michael did that?"

"He didn't want to. He put up a fight. He even told me he thought about going to the police. But you can imagine what the police would say when Michael told them that some kind of alien being was controlling his mind."

"He do anything else?"

"Oh, yes. Lots of things."

"Like what?"

"We drove up to Minnesota and robbed eleven convenience stores in two nights."

"God."

"Then in Chicago, we set two homeless people on fire. It was kind of weird, watching them all on fire and running down the street screaming for help. Michael shot both of them. In the back."

"While they were on fire?"

"Uh-huh."

I laughed. "Now I know it's bullshit."

"It isn't, Spence. You just want to think it is."

"But setting people on fire—"

"I didn't want to do it, Spence. I really didn't. And neither did Michael. But we kept coming back up here to the well all the time and—"

We didn't talk for a while. We just listened to the dark soughing night and all the strange little creatures that hop and slither and sidle in the undergrowth. And the wind was trapped in the pines and not far away a windmill sang and then—

She startled me, moving up against me, her hands in my hair, her tongue forcing my mouth open with a ferocity that was one part comic and one part scary—

She pushed me up against the well and deftly got my fly open and fell to her knees and did me. I felt a whole lot of things just then, lust and fear and disbelief and then a kind of shock when I realized that this had been the one thing she'd said she'd never wanted to do, take anybody in her mouth that way, but she kept right on doing it till I spent my seed on the earth surrounding the well.

Then she was in my arms again, her face buried in my neck, and her hands gripping me so tight I felt pain—

And then: "He's talking to me, Spence. Couple minutes, He'll be talking to you, too. You'll be scared at first, hearing Him in your mind this way, but just hold me tight and everything will be all right. I promise."

But I was scared already because I knew now that what I was seeing was the undoing of Cindy Brasher. She probably felt a whole lot guiltier about Michael than she'd realized. And now her guilt was taking its toll. Friend of mine worked at the U of I hospital. He'd be able to help me get her in to see a shrink. I'd call him tonight, soon as I dropped Cindy off.

And then I heard it.

I didn't want to hear it, I pretended not to hear it, but I heard it. This voice, this oddly sexless voice inside my head, saying: *You're just what I've been looking for, Spence. You're a lot tougher than Michael could ever have been.*

And then I saw Cindy's face break into a little girl smile, all radiance and joy, and she said, "He's speaking to you, isn't He?"

I nodded.

And started to tear up and I didn't even know why.

Just standing there in the chill prairie night with this gal I was crazy in love with and this telepathic alien voice in my head—and my eyes just filled up with tears.

Filled way up and started streaming down my cheeks.

And then the alien voice started talking to me again, telling of its plans, and then Cindy was saying, "We're one now, Spence. You, me and the thing in the well. One being. Do you know what I mean?"

I killed my first man two weeks later.

One rainy night we drove over to Davenport and walked along the river and then started back to Cedar Rapids. Cindy was all snuggled up to me when, through the rain and steam on the windshield, I saw the hitchhiker. He was old and skinny and gray and might have been part Indian. He wore a soaked-through red windbreaker and jeans and this sweat-stained Stetson.

The voice came to me so fast and so strong that I didn't have any time to think about it at all.

"Is He saying the same thing to you?" Cindy said, as the hitchhiker got bigger in the windshield.

"Yeah."

"You going to do it?"

I gulped. "Yeah."

We pulled over to him. He had a real ancient weary smile. And real bad brown teeth. He was going to get his ride.

Cindy rolled down the window.

"Evening, sir," I said.

He looked a mite surprised that we were going to talk to him rather than just let him hop in.

He put his face in through the window and that's when I shot him. Twice in the forehead. Knocked him back maybe ten, twelve feet. And then he stumbled backwards and disappeared into a ravine.

"Wow," Cindy said.

"Man, I really did it, didn't I?"

"You sure did, Spence. You sure did."

That night we made love with a hunger that was almost painful, the way we hurled ourselves at each other in the darkness of my apartment.

Thing was, I wanted to feel guilty. I wanted to feel that I'd just gone crazy and done something so reprehensible that I'd turn myself in and take my punishment. But I didn't feel anything at all except this oneness with Cindy. She was right. Ever since the voice had been in my mind, I did feel this spiritual closeness to her. So there was no thought of turning myself in.

Oh, no, next night we went back to the well and He spoke to us again. Inside our minds. I had a strange thought that maybe what we heard was our own voices inside our respective heads— telling to do things we'd ordinarily be afraid or unwilling to do. But the voice seemed so real—

In the next week, there were six robberies, two arsons and a beating. I had never been tough. Never. But one night Cindy and I strolled all fearless into this biker bar and had a couple of beers and of course a couple of the bikers started making remarks about how good looking Cindy was and what was she doing with a fag like me, things like that, so I picked the toughest one I could see, this really dramatic bastard who had a skull and bones tattoo on the left side of his forehead, and rings with tiny spikes sticking up. I gave him a bad concussion, two broken ribs and a nose he'd never quite be able to breathe out of again. I guess I got carried away. He was all the bullies who'd hurt and humiliated me growing up and in the Army. He was every single one of them in one body—even in the Paratroopers, I was afraid of being beaten up. But now those fears were gone. Long gone.

The lovemaking got more and more violent and more and more bedeviling. It was all I could think of. Here I was working a lumber yard front office, not a place that's conducive to daydreaming what with the front door constantly banging open and closed, open and closed, and the three phone lines always screaming—but all I could do was stare out the window with my secret hard-on in my pants and think about how good it would be that night with Cindy. My boss, Mr. Axminster, he even remarked on it, said I was acting moony as a high school kid. He didn't say it in a very friendly way, either. There was no bonus in my check at the end of that month.

Stopped by a few times to see my folks. They looked sad when they saw me, probably not a whole lot different than they'd look if I'd died in a car accident or something. A real sense of loss, their first and eldest torn away from them and made a stranger. I felt bad for them. I gave them long hugs and told them how much I loved them several times but all they could do was say that I looked different somehow and was I feeling all right and did I ever think of going to old Doc Hemple for a physical.

And of course I went back to the Parkinson cabin and the well. I say "I." While most of the time I went, with Cindy, sometimes I went alone. Figured that was all right now that I was with the program. I mean I was one with Cindy and He but I was also still myself.

That's why I was alone when I got the Mex down by the railroad tracks.

He was maybe twenty, a hobo just off a freight, looking for shelter for the night.

I'd been covering the tracks for the past hour, watching the lonesome stars roll down the lonesome sky, waiting for somebody just like him.

The voice this time had suggested a knife. Said there was a great deal of difference in killing a man with a knife and killing a man with a gun. So I drove over to Wal-Mart and got me the best hunting knife I could find. And here I was.

I crouched beneath one of three boxcars sitting dead on the tracks. The Mex walked by, I let him get ten feet ahead of me, then I jumped him.

Got him just under the chin with my forearm and then slashed the knife right across the throat. Man, did he bleed. I just let him sink to the gravel. Blood was everywhere. He was grasping his throat and gasping, dumb brown eyes frantic and looking everywhere. I saw why this was different. And it was real different. With guns, you were at one remove, impersonal. But this was real real personal. I watched till I was sure he was dead then I drove back to my apartment and took a shower.

Twenty-five minutes later, I pulled up to Cindy's place and she came out. In the dome light, I could see she was irritated.

"I hope you plan to start by apologizing."

"I'm really sorry, Cindy."

"Almost two hours late."

"I said I'm sorry."

"Where were you?"

So I told her.

"You've been going up to the well alone?"

Somehow I'd sensed that she wouldn't like that. That's why I hadn't told her about it.

"I don't want you to do that anymore."

"Go to the well?"

"Not by yourself, Spence."

"But why?"

"Because--" She looked out the window for a while. Said nothing. Every few minutes, her drunken old man would peek out the living room window to see if we were still sitting at the curb.

"Because why, Cindy?"

She turned and looked at me. "Because He's my friend."

"He's my friend, too."

"Well, He wouldn't be your friend—you wouldn't even know anything about Him—if I hadn't taken you up there."

Kind of a funny night, that one. We never really got over our initial mood. Even the lovemaking was off a little. Sometimes you can feel when a woman is losing interest in you. Isn't anything they say or do; there's just something in the air. Laurie had been like that when she'd dropped me back in high school. I'd gone weeks with this sense that she found me vaguely distasteful before she actually dumped me. I was getting the same sense with Cindy. I just prayed to God I was sensing things wrong.

But next night, things were pretty much back to normal. Drove to an Italian restaurant in Iowa City, little place with candle light and a chunky guy wandering around with a violin, a kind of make-up dinner. After that, we went straight back to my place and made up for all the great sex we'd missed out on the night previous. Or at least I did. But Cindy—there was a certain vagueness to her sentiments now. No passion in the I-love-you's. No clinging to me after we made love.

Just before I took her home, she said, "Promise me you'll never go to the well again by yourself."

"God, I just don't understand what you're so upset about."

"Just promise me, Spence."

"All right. I promise."

She kissed me with a tenderness that rattled me, that made me think that we really were going to be as tight and true as we'd once been.

Next two visits to the well, we went together. By now, I knew why she always wanted to go there. It was addictive, that voice in your head, the sense that you were an actor in some cosmic drama you couldn't even begin to comprehend. I suppose religious people feel this way when they're contemplating Jesus or Jehovah or Buddha. I needed my fix every few days, and so did Cindy.

Following these two particular visits, we drove to Des Moines and found a darkened building we could climb to the top of. Kind of cold on the fourteenth floor. And it was late May. My knuckles were numb as I assembled the scope rifle. There was a motel and a bar a quarter block away. Must be where the really well-fixed swingers hung out because the cars ran to BMWs and Porsches. There was even a Maserati.

Cindy crouched right next to me, rubbing my crotch as I sighted the gun. Gray-haired guy came out and started to climb into his Caddy. The dark city sprawled all around him, tattered clouds covering the moon.

"Him?"

"Huh-uh," she said.

Few minutes later a real drunk lady with a fur wrap came wobbling out. "Her?"

"Huh-uh."

Then a couple real slick types. Probably in advertising.

"Them?"

"Yeah."

"Both?"

"Uh-huh."

"That'll be tricky."

"You can do it, Spence."

I had to hurry.

Bam.

Guy's head exploded in big bloody chunks. Man, it was hard to believe that a bullet could—

"Get him!" Cindy cried as the other guy, stunned, looked up at the roof we were firing from.

Knocked him a good clean five yards backwards. Picked him up. Hurled him onto the trunk of a Lincoln Towncar. Even had time to put another bullet in him before he rolled off the trunk and hit the pavement.

And then she was all over me, lashing me and licking me with her tongue, and she kept grinding her crotch against the barrel of the gun and I kept saying "Cindy, God, listen we have to get out of here!"

I just about had to drag her.

She wanted to do it right there on the roof.

She seemed crazy. I'd never seen her like this.

She couldn't calm down.

We rolled out of Des Moines about ten minutes later. She had my hand between her legs and her head back and her eyes were all white and dazed-looking. She just kept rubbing against my hand. We must have gone twenty miles that way.

Later, in bed, she said, "We're good again, aren't we, you and me?"

"We sure are."

"I was scared for a few days there."

"So was I."

"I just wouldn't want to live without you, Spence."

"I wouldn't want to live without you, either."

Her craziness had gone. We made gentle love and then I took her home.

And then next day, despite all my promising, I took the afternoon off and went to the well. I wanted to see it in daylight, see if I could see anything I missed at night.

But I couldn't.

I sat on the edge of the pit and watched squirrels and field mice dart in and out of the buffalo grass. And then for a while I watched a hawk ride the air currents and I thought again, as I had all my boyhood, of how fine and free it would be to be a hawk. There was Indian lore that said that hawks were actually spies from another dimension and that had always intrigued me.

And then the voice filled my head.

I turned around real fast so I could look down the well and see if the water boiled or bubbled when the voice spoke but it didn't. Just dirty brackish water. Still. Very still.

But I wasn't still. I was agitated. I said, *No, that's not right. I won't do that.* But the voice wouldn't let go. I tried to walk away but something stopped me. I tried to shut the voice out but I couldn't.

I had to listen to His plan. His terrible terrible plan.

At dinner that night, a burger and fries with coupons at Hardee's, Cindy said, "I called you after school this afternoon."

"Oh. I should've told you."

"You took off, huh?"

"Yeah."

"Where'd you go?" She wasn't real good at hiding her suspicions.

"Iowa City."

"How come?"

I shrugged. "Check out one of the bookstores."

"Which one?"

"Prairie Lights."

"I guessed that was what you'd say."

"What's that supposed to mean?"

"I figured you'd lie and I figured it would have something to do with Iowa City so I called some of the places you go. And one of the places I called was Prairie Lights. And guess what?"

"What?"

"They're dosed down this week. Doing some kind of remodeling."

"Bullshit."

"Bullshit yourself, Spence. You want to call them? Find out for yourself?"

She leaned back on her side of the booth and crossed her arms over her chest. "You went to the well, didn't you?"

"No."

"You fucker."

She started crying, then, just like that, right there in the middle of Hardee's with all the moms and dads and kiddies watching us, some with great glee, some with embarrassment and a kind of pity

I put my head down. "I'm sorry, Cindy. I won't ever do it again."

"Oh, right, Spence. You won't ever do it again."

Must have been two hours later before she uttered another syllable.

We were lying in bed and she said, "I need to be honest with you, Spence."

"I was hoping we were done arguing. I said I wouldn't ever go to the well again alone. And I mean it."

"The way you meant it last week?"

"God, Cindy, I—"

"I met somebody, Spence."

"What?"

"A guy. College boy, actually."

"What's that mean, you 'met' him?"

"I met him. That's what it means. Some girls and I went to Cedar Rapids a few days ago, to one of the malls. That's where he works. One of the malls. Anyway, he called me and asked me if I'd go out with him." Pause. "I told him yes, Spence."

"What the fuck are you doing to me, Cindy?"

"I'm not doing anything to you, Spence. I'm just being a nice, normal eighteen-year-old girl who met a nice, normal young man who asked her out."

"We're going to get married."

Pause. "I'm not sure about that now, Spence." Pause. "I'm sorry."

I rolled off the bed, sat on the edge, face in my hands.

She slid her arms around me, kissed me gently on the back. "Maybe I just need a little break, Spence. Maybe that's all it is."

I took my face from my hands. "You're punishing me, aren't you, Cindy?"

"Punishing you?"

"For going to the well alone."

"God, Spence, that's crazy. I don't play games like that. I really don't."

"We have to get married, Cindy."

She laughed. "Why, are you pregnant?"

"The stuff we've done—"

"We didn't get caught, Spence. Nobody knows. We can just forget about it. Go on with our lives."

"Right. Just forget it. You know how many fucking people we've killed?"

I lost it, then, jumped up off the bed and stalked over to the bureau, and swept it clean with my arm. Brut and my graduation picture and my Army picture and Cindy's picture all smashed against the wall and fell to the floor in a rain of jagged glass.

The funny thing was, I wasn't thinking of Cindy at all, I was thinking of Laurie, and how she'd dumped me back in high school, and how even now I sometimes felt a sudden sharp pain from the memories . . . pain as dangerous as the pieces of glass now scattered all over my floor.

I turned to Cindy. "I'll tell you something, Cindy. If you go out with this guy, I'll kill you."

"God, that's real nice and mature, Spence. Maybe that's why I've lost interest in you. I thought that because you were older, you were an adult but—"

"Don't try and talk around it, Cindy. You heard what I said."

She got up and started putting her clothes on. We hadn't made love but we'd seemed on the verge of it. Until she'd told me about this guy at the mall.

"If you threaten me one more time, Spence, I'll go to the police. I swear I will."

"Right."

"I will. You wait and see."

I grabbed her. Couldn't control myself. Wanted to smash her face in but settled for throwing her up against the wall and grabbing a bunch of her button-down blouse and holding her several inches off the floor.

"I meant what I said, Cindy. I'll kill you. And that's a promise"

Three hours after she left, the rain started. I lay awake the rest of the night listening to the shutters bang and the wind cry like lost children weeping. How could you hate what you loved so dearly?

I tried not to think what the voice had told me the last time at the well, about killing Cindy. But that's exactly what it said. And that's why I'd threatened Cindy tonight, I realized now. I was only doing the bidding of the voice, acting on its suggestion.

I had been shocked, I had resisted it—but I saw now that He could also see the future. He saw that Cindy would meet a stranger at the mall, just as He saw that Cindy would soon be ready to dump me. That's why he'd suggested I kill her.

I didn't see or hear from Cindy for three days. Things were bad at work. I couldn't concentrate. I sent a wrong shipment to the new co-op they're building out on the edge of the old Galton Farm and my boss did something he'd never done before—started yelling at me right in front of customers. It was pretty embarrassing.

Lonesome, I even thought of going to see my folks but anything I said would just lead to I-told-you-so's.

Looked up a few buddies, too, but they were like strangers now. Oh, we went through some of the old routines, and made some plans for doing some autumn fishing up at Carter Lake, but I left the tavern that night feeling more isolated than ever.

I wondered what Cindy was doing. I kept seeing her naked and mounting the mall guy the way she sometimes mounted me. I drove and drove and drove, prairie highways leading to more prairie highways, cows and horses restless in the starry rolling Iowa darkness. Sometimes I merged Cindy and Laurie into one, sometimes I wanted to cry but being unable to. How could you hate what you loved so dearly?

Warm summer arrived like a gift a few days later. People out here always go a little crazy when summer comes. I think they get intoxicated by all the scents of the flowers and the trees and the sweet sad songs of the birds. I do. Ordinarily, anyway. But this summer was different. I couldn't appreciate any of it. It was as if I'd been entombed in my sorrow over Cindy leaving me. There was no room for anything but her.

I saw them, then. Town square. Around nine o'clock. Walking slowly past the Civil War memorial. Her arm through his. Same way we used to walk. He was handsome, of course. Cindy wouldn't have to settle for anything less.

I stumbled into an alley and was sick. Literally. Took the lid off a reeking garbage can and threw up.

Then I went into a grocery store and bought a pint of Jim Beam and went back to the alley and thought about what I was going to do. How I was going to handle all this.

I'm not much of a drinker. By the time I finished the pint, I was pretty foggy. I was also pretty sleepy. I leaned against the garbage can and slept.

A country western song woke me a few hours later. Some pore truck-drivin' sumbitch had lost his honey. You know how country songs go. I got up all stiff and chilly and reoriented myself. I took a leak while never taking my eye from the quarter-moon so brilliant in the midnight sky. I felt homesick; but I also felt as if I had no home to go to. And never would.

Twenty minutes later, I stood out in front of the police station. Town this size, the station is in the old courthouse. Neon sign above the westernmost entrance says: POLICE. There's a lock-up in the basement and a traffic court on second floor. On first floor is where the seven police officers work at various times of day and night.

I was going to do it. I was going to walk right up those stairs, right inside that building, and tell whichever cop was on duty just what Cindy and I had been up to.

"Hey, Spence."

Voice was familiar. I turned to see Donny Newton, whom I'd gone to high school with, walking up the street. He wore the dark uniform of the local gendarmes.

"Hey, Donny. Since when did you become a cop?"

"Took my test last year then went to the Police Academy in Des Moines for three months and *voila*, here I am. Doesn't pay jack shit for the first couple years but given all the layoffs we've been having, I'm lucky to have a steady paycheck." Then he ceased being plain Donny Newton and became Officer Donny Newton. Suspicious. "So what're you doing here?"

Maybe Donny could make it easy for me. I'd known him a long time. Maybe he'd let me tell it all my way and not get all self-righteous about it.

My mouth opened. My brain wrote three or four lines of dialogue for my tongue to speak, just to get things going. But somehow my tongue wouldn't speak them.

"Hey, you all right, man?"

Then I just wanted to get out of there. Fast.

"Little too much to drink."

"You all right to drive?"

I nodded. "Yeah."

"Sure?"

"Positive."

"I'd be happy to run you home."

"Thanks, Donny, but I'll be fine."

But he sure was giving me a funny look. I nodded a goodnight, and took off walking to my car, knowing he was watching me again.

Home I drank four beers and sat in the dark kitchen and listened to an owl who sounded every bit as lonely as I felt. Then I tumbled into bed and began seven hours of troubled and exhausting sleep.

At six I dragged myself from bed for a quick shave and shower. I'd just lathered up when I looked out the bathroom window and saw Donny Newton, still in uniform, doing something to my right rear tire. There's no garage or concrete drive. I just park on the grass on the east side of the house.

I couldn't figure out what the hell he was doing. He was down on one knee, spraying something in the tire tracks I'd made on the grass. Then he took this small wooden frame and put it over a portion of the tire marks he'd just sprayed.

Only then did I understand what he was doing—getting an impression of my tracks, the way the cops do at a crime scene.

But why the hell was he interested in my tire tracks? Had there been a hit-and-run last night and he suspected me of driving drunk and leaving the scene of the accident?

He left quickly. Probably had no idea I'd seen him. Probably figured I was still asleep.

At noon, I saw him again, Donny. When did he sleep?

He was out in the lumber yard with my boss Mr. Axminster. Couple times when they were talking, they'd both looked back at the front office where I was. Then he was gone.

The rest of the afternoon, Mr. Axminster acted pretty funny. He was already pissed that I'd been so preoccupied lately, and that I was making a lot of mistakes—but now it wasn't so much that he was mad—more that he wasn't quite sure what to make of me. As if I were some kind of alien being or something.

Just before quitting time, the phone rang. I was checking in some wallpaper kits so Mr. Axminster had to take it. He talked a few minutes, in a whispery kind of voice, so I figured it was his lady friend. Rumor had it that he was sweet on a waitress named Myrna over at the Chow Down cafe. I think it was true because she called here sometimes. He was always boasting about how good a Lutheran he was, so his being a family man and having a little strange on the side surprised me.

Then he said, "It's for you, Spence."

He tried to act like everything was just fine and dandy. But he was sweating a lot suddenly and it wasn't hot, and he couldn't look me directly in the eye. He handed me the phone. I said hello.

"Spence?"

"Uh-huh."

"Donny Newton."

I looked at Mr. Axminster, who looked quickly away.

"Wondered if we could get together?"

"When?"

"You're off in fifteen minutes, right?"

"Right."

"How about then?"

"Have a beer somewhere, you mean? Maybe a little bumper pool?" But I knew better, knew what he was really up to.

"Uh . . . well, actually, I was hoping you'd sort of stop over to the station."

"The station? How come?" I played it real dumb.

"Oh, just a couple things came up. Hoping you could help us dear them up a little."

"Well, sure, Donny. If it's important."

"I'd sure appreciate it."

"Sure thing, Donny. About fifteen minutes?"

"Fifteen minutes would be great. That'll give me time to empty the old bladder and grab us a pair of Pepsis."

"See you then, Donny."

Panic. Tried to control it. Closed my eyes. Forced myself to take deep breaths. Gripped the edge of the counter so I'd quit shaking.

Good old Cindy. The only person who could possibly have interested the police in my tire tracks. We'd used my car on all our murders and robberies. If Cindy had decided to blame me and to cooperate with authorities in reeling me in—

Cindy would likely avoid jail herself. And she'd have her brand-new beau.

"They asked me about you, Spence. In case you're wondering."

When I opened my eyes, Mr. Axminster was standing there. "You've gotten yourself in some serious trouble, Spence." He shook his head. "When Donny Newton told me, well—" He looked very said. "I've known your folks all my life, Spence. When they hear about this—"

But I wasn't waiting around for any more of his hand-wringing dramatic presentation.

I ran out to my car, hopped in, tore out of the driveway.

I drove. I have no idea where. Just—around. And fast. Very fast.

When I was aware of things again, it was an hour later and I was racing up a gravel road, leaving a plume of dust in my wake.

Instinctively, I headed for the only place I'd find any wisdom or solace.

I pulled into the surrounding woods so nobody could see my car from the highway. I waited till dark before finding the trail that led to the well.

Downhill, a crow sat on the rickety remains of the cabin. He was big and shiny in the cool dusk.

The well looked the same as I approached it, the native stone of the pit a dead white in the darkening shadows.

I knelt down next to the well and put my head down inside. I needed to hear Him. Needed His wisdom.

Right away, I started crying. I was going to lose it all. My job. My girl. My freedom.

All I'd done was what the voice in the well had told me to do. And I had no control over that.

You'll feel better soon.

I let those words echo in my mind for a time before asking Him what He meant.

And He told me that I'd soon know what he meant.

And right after that, I heard her laugh.

Cindy. Coming down the path. Then: a second voice. Male. The guy she'd met at the mall.

Everything was dark now. I staggered to my feet and scurried into the woods. They were holding hands. And laughing. And she was telling him about the well.

"You really love putting me on, don't you?" he said.

"It's not a put-on. Honest."

"There's this voice down the well."

"Not just a voice—an entity."

"Hey—big word. Entity"

"Right," Cindy said.

She slid her arm around him. Kissed him playfully on the chin. I was afraid I was going to be sick again. Real sick.

"It's an alien."

"From outer space?" he said.

"Exactly."

He laughed again. "What a con artist."

He sat on the edge of the well pit and took her to him and then kissed her long and deep and passionately.

And then the knife was in my hand. The knife I'd used on the Mex.

And suddenly I was screaming and running from the woods toward the well and I saw the mall guy looked startled and then terrified and I heard Cindy scream.

But I didn't stop.

I ran straight up to the guy and stabbed him in the chest. Stabbed him again and again and again.

He fell to the ground, all blood and dying gasps now, but I kept right on stabbing him until I heard Cindy's feet slapping up the path as she tried to escape. But she wasn't going to escape.

No way.

I went after her, grabbed her by the long hair, whipped her back to me until our faces were almost touching.

"I loved you and you didn't give a damn at all."

"I still love you, Spence. It's just that I'm so—confused—please don't—please understand that I love you Spence and we can be together again just the way we were and—"

I stabbed her in the chest.

She didn't scream or even cry.

In fact her hands fitted themselves around the hilt of the knife, as if she wanted to make sure that the blade stayed deep and true in her heart. And then she fell into my arms.

And that was the weird thing, you know.

She didn't scream. But I did.

She didn't cry. But I did.

She didn't call for help. But I did.

The way it was later told to me, a farmer looking for a couple stray head of cattle found me just like that—holding Cindy lifeless in my arms, and sobbing so hard he was afraid I was going to suffer some kind of seizure.

Later there were lights and harsh voices and then the tear-stained faces of my parents.

Oh my God Spence

How could you do this Spence

Spence we're going to get you the best lawyer we can afford but your father's not a rich man you know

Mr. Spencer this is your attorney Dan Myles

Seven different counts of murder, Mr. Spencer

Seven dfferent . . .

Same night they put me in jail they transferred me to a mental hospital on the outskirts of Iowa City. I was so cold I ended up with six wool blankets on me before they could stop me from shuddering. They gave me three different shots in my hip. Then I seemed to die. There was just—darkness.

Over the next few weeks, they gave me several tests a day. I saw medical doctors, psychologists, a priest though I'm not Roman Catholic, and then a young reporter named Donna Mannering who had just started working for our small-town newspaper.

They let her see me for twenty minutes in a room with an armed guard outside. I had told the MD that I wanted to talk to a reporter and he had seen to it that Donna was brought in.

"Dr. Wingate said you were saving something to tell me."

She was blonde and a little bit overweight but very pretty. She was also terrified. I'm sure I was the first killer she'd ever met in person.

"Yeah."

She flipped open her long skinny reporter's notebook. "I guess I'll just let you do the talking."

"I want to tell you about the well."

"You mean like a wishing well."

I thought a moment. "Yeah, I guess it is kind of like a wishing well. Only you don't make the wishes. The thing in the well does."

"The thing in the well?"

"This alien."

"I see."

Now she looked more frightened than ever. Her blue gaze fled to the door several times. She wanted to be sure she could get away from me if I suddenly went berserk.

"There's an alien in the well."

"Right," I said.

"And it told you to do things?"

"Everything I did. I mean the killing, the robberies, the arson fires."

"The alien?"

"Uh-huh. And you know what?"

"What?"

"I don't mind if you smile. Because I know how crazy it all must sound."

"Well, I guess it does sound a little—" But then she stopped herself. "Did the thing in the well tell you to kill Cindy and her new friend?"

"Yes."

"Would you have done it otherwise?"

"I don't think so." Pause. "I want you to go out there."

"Where?"

"The well." I told her where she'd find it.

"When?"

"Soon as you can. But I want you to go alone."

"Why?"

"Because the thing will be more apt to talk to you if you're alone."

"Were you alone when you first heard it?"

"No. I was with Cindy but she already knew about the alien so that was different."

"I see." She glanced at her watch. She was trembling and licking her lips frantically. Her mouth must have been very dry. "Boy, where has the time gone. I need to get out of here. Guard!" She practically shouted.

The guard came in and led her out.

She glanced over her shoulder when she reached the threshold.

I said, "Please go out there, all right?"

She looked anxiously away and followed the guard out the door.

My trial didn't start for seven months. Because we were pleading insanity, there wasn't much I had to do but wait for the trial date.

During this time, I started reading about the strange murders taking place in and around my small hometown. Old ladies viciously strangled to death with rosary beads.

On the first day of my trial, the day my lawyer spoke aloud my defense, that I had been taking orders from an alien being at the bottom of a well, I saw Donna Mannering sitting with several other reporters near the back of the courtroom. The other reporters were all smirking at the reference to the alien in the well.

But Donna wasn't.

At the end of the day, when I was being led back to county lockup, Donna pushed past the deputies surrounding me and pushed her face into mine. I saw in her eyes that same anger and same madness I'd known when I'd been under the sway of the voice in the well.

"You bastard," she spat at me.

And then she grabbed my right hand and shoved something into it and ran out of the court room.

I kept my hand closed all the way back to my cell for fear that one of the guards would see what she'd given me and confiscate it.

I sat on the edge of my bunk and opened my hand and stared down at the snake-like coil of black rosary beads.

Author's Note

Stephen King has been a big influence on me. Somebody once called him the Thomas Wolfe of popular fiction, but to me he's more the Thomas Hardy.

He has Hardy's social eye and his obsession with what time does to us all. And he has Hardy's generosity of spirit, too. The beautiful and forlorn poetry of *Pet Sematary* will tell you all you need to know about King's soul. I like just about everything he does, but I especially like some of the stories nobody seems to mention much: *Christine*, which is one of the great high school novels of our time; "Strawberry Spring," which is one of the best crime stories of the '70s; and "Nola," which I had in mind when I wrote "The Brasher Girl." Some people call this sort of thing homage; others, the more vigilant perhaps, call it theft.

Calculated Risk

By eleven o'clock that morning, three people had come up to Michael Brody and asked if he was feeling all right. He joked that he'd imbibed a little too much in the course of last night's TV football game. Most of the people who worked in the Parole Office had had the occasional hangover themselves, so they readily accepted his explanation.

He closed the door to his small office and prepared for his eleven-thirty appointment. As usual before seeing someone, he ran a pocket comb through his easily mussed dark hair. He was a rangy man with a melancholy face some women had been generous enough to call handsome.

The computer screen had all the information on one John Richard Cahill, thirty-four, recently paroled from state prison after serving five-and-a-half years for burglary and assault. Previous to that he'd been convicted of domestic abuse after beating up a young woman he'd been living with. He'd earned probation for that. As a juvenile he'd been in trouble for three other assaults. "A predilection to violence," as a judge had noted. According to the computer screen, Cahill was still married. Thirty-year-old Susan had visited him frequently in prison.

They'd tested his urine for drugs and alcohol this morning and found him clean. The test was standard before every parole office meeting.

When Nancy Daly, the administrative assistant who worked with all five parole officers, knocked on his door and said, "John Cahill is here," Brody felt acid burning up from his stomach into his throat.

"Send him in."

Even after almost six years of gray and treacherous prison life, Cahill had not lost the swagger in his step nor the amused contempt in his blue eyes. He had the sort of reckless good looks that had likely won him many, many women at least for brief periods of time. Of course, this being his initial visit to his parole officer, he aimed to impress as nothing more or less than an average, decent citizen. The clean, pressed white shirt, the blue dress trousers and the scent of Brut were meant to indicate that he was on his very best behavior. So was the quick, strong-but-not-too-strong handshake, the full smile and the boyishly rendered, "I'm kind of nervous about this, Mr. Brody."

"Nothing to be nervous about, John—if I may call you John."

"Sure, Mr. Brody."

"And please call me Michael. We'll be seeing each other pretty regularly so we might as well be on a first-name basis. Care for some coffee?"

"I'd love some."

As he filled two cups, Brody asked Cahill how things had been going his first week out.

"I've got a great little wife. She waited for me this whole time. Never asked for a divorce. Never ran around. We picked up right where we left off."

"You're a lucky man, John."

"Tell me about it," Cahill said as he accepted the coffee. "But I guess you know what I'm talking about." He nodded to the framed photo of Jane and their daughter.

"I'm a lucky man, too."

After a few more minutes of strained chatter, Brody began to explain the parole system and what Cahill could expect from it. He emphasized the need for monthly contact, for checking by phone if Brody had any questions about something that might violate the terms of his parole, and avoiding the obvious traps of alcohol and drugs.

"Some of your old friends will probably come around."

"A few already have. I told them to buzz off. I'm not going back. Ever." Anger in the voice now. Anger at being caught and sent up, probably. Resentment, really. "There's no way I'm going back to prison. No way." Cahill obviously sensed that he'd allowed his real feelings to show—he'd sounded threatening just now. He backed them off with a broad faked smile. "I learned my lesson."

Brody picked up a paper from his desk. "I see you like working with cars and trucks."

"Yeah. That was the only thing I enjoyed in the joint. My old man was a mechanic and I guess I picked it up from him. I worked in the prison garage five days a week, seven hours a day. Probably didn't miss more than four or five days the whole time. I get these sinus infections that really do me in."

Brody handed him the single sheet of paper. "There are three names with addresses and phone numbers on there. These are shops that are part of our Second Start program. They hire men who've been incarcerated. I'd make appointments with them right away."

This time the smile didn't seem contrived. "I get a job right away, my wife Susan'll be real happy."

"I think you've got a good chance with one of them. The economy's picking up some, so they all say they've been busy."

"And they don't mind ex-cons, huh?"

"All three of them have former convicts working for them."

"That's pretty nice." Once again Cahill managed to sound sincerely pleased.

"I'd appreciate it if you'd give me a call and let me know how the job hunting is going."

"Be happy to."

"Any questions?"

"You've laid it out pretty good. Especially about staying clean and reporting."

Brody studied him a moment. "You say you don't want to go back. We don't want you to go back, either." He wondered how many times he'd spoken those exact words. He should think about freshening up his routine. He stood up and offered his hand.

As they shook, Brody said, "The wife was worried about how I'd handle this meeting. But you've been such a nice guy it went pretty good, huh?"

Cahill was back to shining him on. The scorn in his eyes revealed how he felt about Brody. Just another nowhere hack in the justice system. A nerd, a square.

"Well, I'll keep you posted, man."

The "man" was another slip and they both realized it at the moment it was uttered. "Man" indicated Cahill was back swaggering down the street.

He gave Brody a nod then hurried out the door.

Before making the call, Brody walked over and poured himself more coffee. Sitting down again, he allowed himself a sigh. Then he dialed the number. He'd known better than to put it on his speed dial.

"Hi. He just left."

"How'd it go?"

"Pretty much the way you said it would. He knows how to put on a show. He's good at it. The only time I bought his act was when I told him that I thought he could get a job as a mechanic."

"In the old days, I always joked about how he loved cars more than he did me. That's one of the things I appreciate so much about you, Michael. I know you love me more than anybody else. Except your daughter, of course."

It used to come so easily, he thought. Eighteen months of lust and maybe even love. She was the romantic of the pair but he'd almost been able to match her soap opera-like patter. These days the patter was difficult, if not impossible, to come by. "That's very sweet of you to say."

"Well, it's true. That's why I can't wait for us to just go ahead and do what we have to and get married."

"Susan, I told you we need to take it slow. Carrie's having problems again. Doctor Wohlner says we have to be extra careful." Four months ago, realizing the trap he'd made for himself, he'd created mental problems for his nine-year-old daughter Carrie. He'd even invented a Dr. Wohlner. Much as he wanted to ask his wife for a divorce—he'd told her—he couldn't do it at a time when Dr. Wohlner said that if they weren't careful, Carrie could end up in an institution. He'd accompanied this with some very dramatic mumbo-jumbo about Carrie's alleged schizoid condition.

"I feel so sorry for her." But it was herself she felt sorry for of course, he realized.

"Thank you."

"I hate that you can't come over anymore. You can't even phone at night now."

"We knew it would be like this when he got out. We just have to accept it."

"We're still meeting at that motel tomorrow afternoon, aren't we?"

"Of course. Two o'clock."

"It'll be so nice when we're married."

"I can't wait, either." Sounding as smitten as he could. "But now I need to go. Your husband isn't my only client today."

"I love you so much."

"Me, too. I'll see you tomorrow."

He sat in the wake of all these words, realizing that he'd put on at least as much of a show as her husband had. And after that realization came the ironic one he'd had last night. After five or six years with his wife Jane, he'd become bored with her psychologically and sexually. Maybe it was the extra twenty pounds she'd put on despite her frustrating attempts to lose them. But now, after his time with Susan, he'd found Jane once again as powerful erotically as she'd been in the old days. And now her bossiness—which he'd always despised—struck him as amusing, even charming. And he had to admit most of the unwanted "advice" she gave him was often much sounder and more productive than the advice he gave himself.

The affair had been a calculated risk. Most of the time he'd felt that he'd gotten away with it. He hadn't ever considered the possibility that the roles of the two women in his life would reverse themselves.

Now it was dull, bossy Susan he needed to escape from . . .

❦ ❦ ❦

Three months before Susan came to his office Brody had had his first taste of adultery. At the good old office Christmas party that Jane hadn't been able to attend because of the flu Carrie had dragged home from school, he'd drunkenly found himself entangled, in a stockroom no less, with a married secretary from a judge's office three floors down. He'd seen her before but they had never even spoken. She was buxom, and generally he didn't care for buxom, but that night as he'd sped through first, second and third base—the elusive home run eluding him—he felt what the evangelicals say when they claim to be born again. Except here he was born again in carnality. And in the hangover morning he felt not guilt but exhilaration. Wanting more.

But what with family life and work, more was not to be. He'd never cared for bars and he certainly didn't want to start up with anyone in the office, and the few times he'd seen the woman from the Christmas party she'd looked humiliated. He felt sorry for her.

But Susan came to him. For all the wrong reasons, as it turned out.

She sat in his office in a cheap tan trench coat with her dishwater blond hair in a chignon the wind had played hell with and watched him with pleading brown eyes that he found beautiful. Once again she played against the type he ordinarily fantasized about, the middle-class women of ripe bodies, poise and playful humor. Many of Jane's friends were this way.

When she told him that she was a waitress at a decent restaurant and that after being struck by a car in a crosswalk she'd had to go on welfare while she recovered, he began to understand the wounded gaze. But for all of it she was quite pretty and when she finally took off her coat—Brody found himself eager to keep the conversation going—she was one of those women who managed to be thin but sumptuous.

The reason she'd come here was to seek advice on her husband's parole. Any points he could give her on how he should handle himself during the hearing. She said that she'd been told by a friend whose husband had also faced parole that Brody had given her good advice. He dimly remembered that woman; the advice he'd given had been cursory at best, designed to get rid of her because he knew she'd come to the wrong place.

At one point Susan had started to cry. Out came the tissues and the soothing words. He found himself ridiculously jealous that she could love a man like her husband—he'd punched him up on the computer as they'd spoken—so passionately. Hell, she'd once reported him for domestic abuse but had withdrawn the charge so that he wouldn't be arrested.

She stayed nearly an hour, long enough for him to find himself completely taken with her. Still shaken, she had thanked him and left. The rest of the day his skin tingled where she'd touched his hand in gratitude. A day later, pretending to be concerned about her and apologetic that he hadn't been more help, he called her and said that he'd contacted a parole board member he knew and asked him a number of questions about the kind of convict who tended to win parole. It was all bullshit but it won Brody a lunch with her the following day, lunch with Susan always being at two o'clock. That was when she got her midday break until five o'clock when she returned for her dinner shift.

She was so fixated on the fate of her husband that it took a month and a half of lunches and phone calls before she realized that she and Brody had become, in her words, "such good friends," and that she'd come to depend on him. It was two months, on a Tuesday evening that she had off, that he brought a good bottle of wine to her shabby little apartment and got her drunk, thanks to her inability to handle alcohol. He'd kissed her but she'd pushed him violently away. "How could you do that to me?" she said, the tears already apparent. "I've never cheated on my husband."

He did the only thing he could. He apologized and fled her apartment.

It was two weeks before he called her again. He apologized once again and asked her to have lunch. She was reluctant but she finally agreed. Another month of lunches. He was the good friend and nothing more. And then at one of their two o'clock meetings her hand suddenly took his and she said, "I hate myself for even saying this—it isn't right to even think it—but I have feelings for you I shouldn't and I don't know what to do about it."

Three more lunches and they ended up in bed in her apartment. He always thought of it as teenage sex, that virile, that tireless, that purely erotic. Teenage sex but with a more knowing understanding of the various ways of coupling. Months and months of it. And for all her guilt—which he knew was real—she matched his passion every time they made love. What he enjoyed especially about it was that it wasn't just somber humping and bumping. They laughed a lot; a lot. They watched porn tapes on her DVD player, something Jane would never allow. He even convinced her to let him tape one of their sessions. There were days, numerous days, when they couldn't see each other. He said the tape would help him through those times.

Jane, understandably, wondered why they so seldom made love these days. She also understandably wondered why he was so suddenly uninterested in family life. At the dinner table he frequently changed the subject when Jane talked about her day or Carrie her time at school. There had been a time when he'd doted on hearing about their lives.

Looking back he realized that he should have taken Susan's first hints of divorcing her husband and marrying Brody more seriously. But he'd been so caught up in the sex that he sort of half-assed thought that maybe that wouldn't be a bad idea. Yes, marrying her so that he could have these simple, sweet, orgy-filled times indefinitely. Somehow it would all work out. He put it out of his mind; all he wanted were the good times.

His disaffection came when Susan started writing him letters. They'd agreed that they would never, *never* send each other e-mails. He hadn't even thought about letters until hers began arriving at his office. They forced him to take seriously her ideas about their someday marriage. They also forced him to realize that the sex was no longer enough and that Jane had begun to stir him deeply for the first time in years. And not just carnally. He was *interested* in her again as a woman.

And one more thing. Even though Susan was generally well spoken, her letters were disasters of clichés and illiteracy. *What was he, a freaking literary critic?* he thought, feeling guilty about his arrogance. But Jane had once written him love letters that had approached real poetry, or so it had seemed to him at the time. He used the office shredder to get rid of Susan's letters.

It was at this time that he created a Dr. Wohlner and poor Carrie's desperate mental problems as a shield against Susan's now *constant* plans for their marriage. That fantasy had protected him for a time but Susan's letters indicated that Carrie's problems would no longer keep talk of marriage at bay.

So now he sat in the same office where he'd first met her, wishing fervently that he never had to see her again. He loved Jane and Carrie. He was a respectable middle-class man. *Didn't driving a Volvo mean anything these days?* But he was beyond humor. Susan was desperate enough to—

To what? Grimly, he considered the possibilities. Write Jane. Tell her husband. Or—she certainly wasn't dumb—drop a note to his boss informing him that Brody had taken advantage of her and seduced her when all she'd wanted—needed—was simple advice.

The ultimate scandal. He would be fired, of course, but even worse he would be disgraced. The media would love it. And poor Carrie and Jane. My God, what they'd go through.

He tried to calm himself by thinking of how sweet Susan was. Sometimes she was almost an innocent. Her lower-class life had kept her from knowing so many things—a trait he'd found so charming in the beginning. He'd loved introducing her to more sophisticated music, movies, even a novel or two. But like the sex, her intellectual limitations had begun to pall, too. Jane got all his references and jokes and now they were back to laughing at the dinner table the way they once had.

Tomorrow would be critical. The motel room. He had to come up with a way to make Susan see that he was in no position to split from his wife.

Dammit, he had to.

"Was I all right today?"

Her need for reassurance, one more thing he'd once found endearing. "You were perfect as always, Susan. I was the one who was off. I'm sorry."

They lay next to each other on the bed where so many other adulterers had lain before them. Though the motel was respectable enough, it did have a reputation for being an upscale site for cheaters. Now it was scented with her perfume and musk. He longed for Jane's arms and aromas.

"Something's wrong, isn't it?"

She rolled over and put her head on his shoulder. Her flesh was warm from their lovemaking; her breasts pressing against him—even though he was done with her—enticing.

He knew he would give his best performance on his feet. Pacing a little, brooding. He didn't ease from bed, he sprang from it.

"We have to put her in a psychiatric hospital." He slammed his fist into his palm. "My little girl in a psych hospital." He knew that this would have been better if he'd put his clothes on first. He was afraid that walking around naked might lend his lies a certain comic undertone.

"Oh, God. I'm so sorry."

Sorry for yourself, you mean.

"But maybe they can make her better in there. That'll relieve your mind, won't it?"

"I suppose." He did a little pacing now. Then he touched his hand to his head as if an invisible axe had just cleaved it in two. Too much?

He'd spent all those long hours trying to come up with a fresh story for her—something so dramatic she'd agree that they needed to take a small break—but the Carrie card ended up being the only one he could play.

"Are you coming back to bed? We still have time." She was sitting up now, the white sheet covering her breasts, her blond hair tousled and the red lipstick in need of refreshing.

"I'm sorry, Susan. We've got one of the supervisors from the capital spending the day with us. I need to be there."

Then came the shock. In all their time together he'd only seen her angry three or four times, and it had always been something about her job. But now, springing from the bed herself, heading straight for the bra, panties and dress laid so neatly over a chair, she said, "Well, this is just great, Michael. First it's Carrie and now it's your supervisor. I don't seem to fit in anywhere anymore, do I?"

He didn't respond at first. This was where he needed to be delicate. He didn't want to infuriate her into doing anything that could destroy him.

He went to her. She'd already started crying—her and her damn crying—and he took her in his arms the way he sometimes took Carrie when she was sad. Her face was warm in the hollow of his neck. "This is a rough time for both of us, Susan. But we just have to be patient. Nothing's changed between us. That's what we have to remember."

She leaned away so she could see him. "So you still love me?"

A very nice fake, warm laugh. And his finger tracing a warm tear down her cheek. "Of course I still love you."

Her makeup was a thorough mess now. "And you're still going to get a divorce?"

"You mustn't know me very well, Susan. You can't tell how much I love you?"

Even though he hadn't answered her question, she took his face in both her hands and gave him a deep and watery kiss.

Something like pity filled him then. She'd been a wonderful lover and was more than not a very decent human being. He wished there was some way he could say this to her. Include these feelings in the final time they came together, when he said goodbye forever.

"We just need to be patient a little while longer."

Her laugh was as watery as her kiss. But the laugh had been empty; the gleaming sorrow in her eyes belied it. "You and your 'patience.' A girl could get suspicious about that, you know."

"I know. But I have to spend my time helping my daughter now. It won't be long. I'll visit the hospital and meet the staff and make sure it's a good place. It's private, not state."

"And Jane'll be with you?" Then, quickly, "Damn, I shouldn't have said that. *Of course* she'll be with you. She's your *wife*. I just get so jealous. It's insane."

He kissed her on the cheek and said, "I'd better get going. I need to kiss a little ass with the supervisor."

"I hate that. It's the same with the new restaurant manager. He thinks he's this really cool guy. Two of the girls are always flirting with him. I just can't do it." She touched his arm. Then, "Can I say something?"

"Sure."

This time the laugh was pure. "Before you leave, you'd better put your clothes on."

"Whew!"

And Jane rolled over and immediately started to tickle him. "You're hornier now than when we were going out. And I love it."

Eleven sixteen. Carrie asleep for three hours. And them making love the same number of times, three.

"Wouldn't my girlfriends be jealous if I told them? They're always complaining about not getting enough sex from their husbands. And here I'm married to a satyr."

She knew just how to tickle him so he went on laughing. "You'll make me pee." Giggling as he said it.

"Is that right, little boy?" But, taking him at his word, she stopped.

He lay looking at the lurching shadows the early spring trees spread across the bedroom wall. Home. God, it was so comfortable. His time with Susan seemed not only morally wrong now but dull. Except for the sex, he couldn't think of any aspect of that time that was even remotely memorable. He hadn't seen or heard from her for four days. Maybe she'd finally understood the message in all his stalling. That it was over over over.

He touched his head to Jane's and relaxed even more. He'd not only accommodated himself to her extra flesh, he now reveled in it. She was right. For more than a month now they had been enjoying the kind of sex they'd had when they were younger.

"That was so sweet when you put Carrie on your lap tonight. You haven't done that in so long. She looked so happy."

A tender kiss which he took to sleep with him. It had been a grinding day at work and after the lovemaking he fell into a sweet slumber . . .

He came awake abruptly and confused. *What the hell time was it and who the hell would be calling?*

And then in that terrible second just as his fingers felt the phone beneath them . . . *Susan.*

"Hello."

"It's raining and I don't have any place to go."

From behind him, sleepy: "Who is it, honey?"

Hand cupped over the phone. "Nancy from the office. Just go back to sleep, sweetie."

"Well, how bad is it?" he said to the phone.

"What're you talking about?"

"I'm sorry he bothered you, Nancy. But I'm not going to talk to him tonight. Tell him he'll have to wait until tomorrow morning at the office. And he should at least have had the nerve to call me directly."

"He started drinking tonight for the first time and accusing me of cheating on him while he was in prison. He used to get like that all the time before he beat me up. That's why I got out of there tonight. Now I don't know where to go."

"As I said, Nancy, I'm sorry he put it all on your shoulders. But there's nothing I can do about it tonight. We'll figure it out in the morning. Now you and I both need to get some sleep."

After he lay down again, Jane said, "Is everything all right?"

"One of my clients was at a loud party tonight. The police came and he hassled them a little, so they ran him in for drunk and disorderly. He used his one call to phone Nancy. She feels sorry for him. He was afraid to call me directly. I guess he wanted her to plead his case with me. His wife bailed him out and now he wants me to call him at home."

"He sounds like a sad case."

"Sure. A lot of them are, the nonviolent ones, anyway."

She rolled over and kissed him on the cheek. He loved the warmth of her flesh and the moistness of her lips. "You're a good man, honey. You really are."

It was the second Thursday morning of the month, which meant staff meeting. He trudged through it and then faced a day that involved testifying in court; visiting with two defendants in the office and one at home; and then returning the call of a social worker with whom he shared a client. She was afraid that the man's temper at work was going to cost him his second job since his release seven months ago. The wife was terrified.

By late afternoon all he wanted to think of was one of Jane's margaritas and how comfortable their relatively new leather recliner was. But he had been a bad boy and there was penance to be paid (lapsed Catholic, but still some of those old concepts applied) and that penance would come in the form of a call from Susan.

It came one half hour before she was due back at the restaurant from her break.

"I'm not sorry I called you last night."

"All right."

"I feel deserted. I used to feel that way when my dad went on one of his binges and we wouldn't see him for a week or two."

"There wasn't anything I could do."

"I don't mean just about last night. I mean everything. You're pulling away, aren't you?" But she didn't wait for him to answer. "I heard when you called her 'sweetie' last night. You thought you'd covered the phone but I heard. You sounded like you used to sound with me."

"Susan, it's pretty hard for me to talk here. At work, I mean."

"That's a lie and you know it. We used to talk about everything when I called the office. We even talked about sex."

And God had they. At times he'd been almost paralyzed with need during their conversations.

"Just tell me the truth, Michael. Just tell me it's over."

The temptation was there. To take her at her word and tell her the truth. But she wasn't handling any of this well—not that he blamed her. He liked to think of himself as fair—he remembered when his sophomore girlfriend had broken up with him, he'd wanted to die—but he couldn't be honest with her. Right now she was dangerous because of her grief; he was afraid of her, of what she could do to him. If he broke it off she would only be more of a threat.

"You know what I'm going through with Carrie."

"Oh, Carrie—Carrie this and Carrie that." Then, "I'm sorry; I should never have said that, Michael. Please forgive me."

"I know you didn't mean that. It's all right."

"It's just—I'm in a nightmare. All our plans. Our marriage—"

Crying. Of course.

"It's not over. I wish you'd believe that."

"I don't believe that, Michael. Your voice isn't even the same anymore. There's no love in it. I'm not an idiot."

"You're not an idiot, Susan, but you *are* imagining things."

"I wish I could believe that."

"You can."

Her silence seemed interminable. "I don't know what to do, Michael. I'm having all these terrible thoughts. Thoughts that aren't like me. They're really not. But I can't help myself."

"Don't do anything crazy, Susan. Promise me that."

"Anything crazy? You mean like not go back on my word and leave you? Crazy like that, Michael?"

His entire body clenched. All the revenge scenarios she might pick up on filed through his mind in 3-D and living dead color.

"Susan, you need to calm down."

"Maybe I could call your dear Dr. Wohlner and he'd calm me down."

Difficult, Brody thought, since dear Dr. Wohlner doesn't exist.

"Seeing a counselor might not be a bad idea, Susan."

"Oh, go to hell, Michael. We're done and you know it."

And then she was gone.

He sat in shock and panic for ten minutes. Just sat there. His marriage, his job, his future. My God, if he'd wanted to have an affair, why not with somebody whose husband wasn't a client? Who might have been more experienced with these things so that when they ended she wouldn't have come apart? Who wouldn't have sounded so damned threatening at the end?

Then came the brief and unrewarding process of trying to convince himself that she would, in fact, calm down. That some of her old feelings for him—she was as sentimental as Jane—would pacify her enough to see that there was no point in trying to destroy him. Their relationship, as she herself had said, was over. Retribution wasn't going to bring him back.

Jane called just before he left. "I just got home from the office after a very long day and our sweet little girl Carrie suggested that since I'm so tired and frazzled we should all go to Pizza Hut for dinner. She's doing this for my sake, you understand." Her soft laugh warmed him.

God, but he loved Jane; he loved her so much.

For the next two days Brody took a Lexapro before work each morning. He'd taken the antidepressant a year ago when the work overload had started to stress him. But as work returned to its normal flow he put the Lexapro in the bathroom medicine cabinet and forgot about it.

Now he needed it.

Every time his assistant said there was a call for him, his stomach churned. Every time he walked to his car in the parking lot he was afraid she would bloom out of nowhere and start shrieking at him in front of his coworkers. Every time he examined the mail at home he looked for a white envelope with no return address.

The telephone fears were worse at home. Relaxing was impossible. Carrie was just old enough now to have friends call her. Jane was a social person and generally received three or four calls a night.

The real terror would be another late-night phone call. Wouldn't Jane get suspicious? He rarely got work-related calls so late. And two of them?

He found sleep elusive both nights. The second night he took two Lexapro. To hell with it. If he was groggy in the morning he'd compensate for it with coffee. But not even with the increased dosage could he fall asleep. Antidepressants didn't work like an off-and-on switch. He was being stupid.

On the third day, drained but resolute, he went to work determined to focus on dealing with his clients and nothing else. Maybe the drug was finally kicking in.

She didn't call. She wasn't lurking in the parking lot. And there was no letter from her.

But at dinner Susan did appear after all.

They were having dessert—a pumpkin pie Jane had bought at Emma's Pies, the ultimate expensive yuppie (but very, very tasty) store that was one of the main culprits of her weight gain—when Jane said, "I had a strange experience at work today. Actually, at Waldo's." The café where Jane and her coworkers usually ate lunch. "I was so busy I didn't get there until almost two-thirty. Anyway, when I left the office I saw this young woman standing out front. I assumed she was waiting for somebody in the building. The only reason I noticed her was because she was so pretty. I didn't think anything about her until I got to Waldo's and she took a table directly across from me. I'm not paranoid"—here she touched his hand and smiled—"I leave that to you."

He tried to mumble something. But body and mind were a jumbled conflict of warring instincts. He wanted to say something. He wanted to puke. He wanted to scream for Jane to shut up, to not say anymore.

"Anyway, I noticed that she just ordered coffee. And then she just sat there and every few minutes she'd stare at me. I didn't have anybody to talk to and I didn't have a magazine or anything, so I suppose I stared back at her as often as she stared at me. Then after a while she just got up and started walking toward my table."

He pictured Susan. Pretty, as Jane had said. He imagined she had the cheap trench coat on and maybe her blue dress that flattered her so much and probably her black flats (she hated heels), all this with one difference—her face. What had her face revealed? Rage, sorrow, panic?

"I had this weird feeling that she was mad at me for some reason; I wanted to get up and hurry back to the office. She kept coming closer and closer and closer. Then she said, 'We need to talk.' It was as if she knew me or something. But then she stopped. That was as weird as everything else. She just stopped. And then she turned around and ran out the door."

By now he was studying Jane's face for any sign that she might be suspicious of him. Of Susan having something to do with him. But Jane was always honest. If she did suspect anything she would say so. Several years ago she'd felt he was overly friendly with a woman at the office who'd asked him, drunk and playful, to slow dance at the Christmas party. Right in front of Jane. No matter what he said—and he was being honest; the woman was certainly sumptuous but she was also a pain in the ass—she wouldn't believe him. Fortunately, the woman took another job and Jane's jealousy finally faded.

So if she distrusted him now she'd likely say so.

She was eager to go on but the phone rang. Carrie rushed to answer it. She loved being grown up and giving her memorized greeting. "The Brody residence. This is Carrie." Then, "Mom, it's Karen."

Before going to the phone, Jane did the unexpected. Gave Brody a kiss on the cheek and said, "I won't be long, hon."

His smile was ridiculously boyish.

At first he wasn't sure she was working today.

Brody got to the restaurant just after eleven o'clock when the two waitresses were serving a few customers but also setting up tables. Neither of them recognized him because he'd never been there before. He'd never wanted to distract Susan while she was working and if he was sitting there she'd be tempted to come over and talk to him.

The dining area of The Hearth was built in a semicircle in front of an enormous native stone fireplace that operated seven or eight months a year. There was a fire today but it was subdued. For all the bite of this April morning, spring was definitely coming.

Another night of bad sleep. Four cups of coffee this morning. Dread and anger in equal parts. Control was the key. If she ever got out here he'd have to be careful. Couldn't afford a scene, much as she deserved one. He played and replayed the images of her stalking Jane. Bitch.

Lots of people break up. It's hard. But they do it without going crazy.

That was the tone he needed to—

Even from a distance he could tell that she'd had the same kind of night he'd had. Her shoulders were slumped, there was no smile, she moved with awkward purpose and the ordinarily lovely gaze was dull.

At first she didn't even notice him. She spent several minutes setting up the tables in her section in her crisp white blouse and black skirt. She was late so she had to hurry.

When she finally turned his way she squinted as if he was an apparition. Fury then in the eyes and the pinching mouth as she recognized him. She started to move quickly toward him but then stopped herself. She was trying to keep herself under control as well.

They spoke in clenched, small voices that only they could hear.

"What're you doing here?"

"I think you know what."

"Do I?"

"You followed my wife yesterday."

"It's a free country."

"The legal term is 'stalking.'"

A bitter smile. The face was haggard in that moment, the measure of her struggle. "Go ahead and call the police."

"You know I can't."

"You broke every promise you made me." Slightly above a whisper this time; she glanced around anxiously. "Every promise."

He actually said it: "Lots of people break up. It's hard. But they do it without going crazy."

"I'm not one of them. I trusted you completely." Her slender hands were fists now.

He almost reached for her but caught himself in time. "Just please tell me you won't do that again. We both need to get on with our lives, Susan."

"Some life I have with John. His job offer fell through. He steals money from my purse and drinks it up."

"I'm sorry."

Then her voice was acid. "You're 'sorry,' you bastard. You're not sorry for anybody except yourself."

"Please. Susan, listen to me. You're going to destroy both of us if you keep acting like this."

"You think I care anymore what happens to me?"

She said something else but he didn't hear it. The impact of her hatred stunned him. The gentleness, the sweetness, the childlike vulnerability—none of it was left in her now. All that remained was her loathing and alienation.

She was far more unstable and dangerous to him than he'd realized until right now.

Everybody heard the slap. The force of it jarred and paralyzed him. His cheek burned and ears rang as they all watched the little soap opera. But it wasn't "little," was it?

No, it wasn't little at all.

❊ ❊ ❊

Brody had appeared on TV twice before. Once he'd been interviewed about the duties of a parole agent and the other time he'd been asked, along with a defense attorney and a judge, about the decline of recidivism in the state.

Both times Jane had clung to him, excited like a schoolgirl, bubbling comments while he was on the screen.

Jane refrained this time.

The lead story on Channel 8 Action News three days following his visit to Susan's restaurant was that a recently paroled man named John Richard Cahill had beaten his wife Susan to death in their apartment. The police confronted him seven hours later outside a tavern and he confronted them with a butcher knife.

The video portion of all this showed Cahill's mug shot and then the crime scene on the sidewalk outside the tavern where Cahill had died.

Brody came next. A heavily freckled and very young female reporter did the interview.

"This is a real tragedy. Susan Cahill had come to my office once or twice because she was worried about her husband's temper. Before he went to prison she'd called the police, but later dropped the domestic abuse complaint."

"How about Cahill himself? What was your impression of him?"

"Well, he hadn't been out very long and we didn't have that much contact. He put on a good front for me—as some of my clients do. He did get agitated at one point, though."

"What agitated him?"

Brody's eyes met the eyes of the camera. "He said there was no way anybody was ever going to put him in prison again."

"So maybe when he went after the officers with a knife—a knife against a gun—he was committing suicide."

"Yes," Brody said, "yes, it certainly seems that way."

When the story changed, Jane said, "You looked so handsome."

The melancholy smile was perfectly crafted. "I'm just sorry it had to happen."

She slid her arm through his there on the couch and said, "I just wish more people understood how hard your job is sometimes. He must really have been a monster."

Yes, Brody thought, and never more of a monster than when he'd opened up a small package sent anonymously and played the old-fashioned VHS tape inside. And seen his naked wife posing for the unseen lover operating the camera.

It had been a calculated risk but Cahill had acted just as Brody had hoped he would.

Jane's cell phone played a few bars of "Girls Just Want to Have Fun" and she picked up. "Hi, Pam." Then she giggled and said, "I know, didn't he look handsome?" Then she poked Brody and said, "See, I told you, you did."

An Afterword, of Sorts

Ed Gorman has been writing full-time since 1984 after a career in advertising. Prolific in the mystery, dark suspense and western fields, he has written more than a hundred stories and many novels. His short fiction, distinctive for its emotional depth, is a favorite of anthologists. Writing in *Ellery Queen's Mystery Magazine*, Jon Breen describes Gorman as "one of our finest short story writers regardless of genre."

Perfect Crime Books had a few questions, which Gorman agreed to answer.

Q.: The stories in this collection could all be called horror or at least menacing—without bending categories too much—but you've also written in other genres, notably western and mystery. Are there things you find you can do in a horror story that you can't in the other fields—besides making a reader uncomfortable, which seems an important part of these stories?

A.: A number of my stories are horrorific in effect without being outright horror. I'm comfortable working in this dark suspense area. Of course there are times when outright horror makes the story stronger. As for consciously trying to make the reader uncomfortable, yes there are times I do. "Cages" is certainly one of them as is—I hope anyway—"The Baby Store" [*Noir 13*, Perfect Crime]. There's a segment of society that has turned having children into a competition. There was a *Salon* article not long ago about how the entire lives of children are being laid out in advance by wealthy parents. That horrifies me. As does the prospect of creating children to order—color of eyes, looks, temperament, etc. This will happen sooner or later.

Q.: Perfect Crime published a paperback edition of your novel *Cage of Night* a while back. It shares some ideas with "The Brasher Girl." Can you tell us how these two came about?

A.: Well, "The Brasher Girl" is somewhat of an homage to Stephen King's really fine short story "Nona." I took it in my own direction, of course. A year or two later my agent asked me if I had an idea for my next novel. So I expanded "The Brasher Girl," but probably eighty per cent of the book is original. I'd been rereading Nathanael West at that time. I wanted to recreate that undertow of mystery and grief West captured in *The Day of the Locust*.

Q.: There are significant differences between the "Brasher" short story and the novel, for example the portraits of Cindy—and that bit at the end of *Cage of Night* in which the boy's father tells him his wife is a whore. Without too much in the way of spoilers, can you say anything about this?

A.: *Cage of Night* is one of those books that was just THERE when I sat down to the computer. I have to "hear" books before I can write them: define a voice or tone. I used some of the establishing plot points from "Brasher," but the "tone" was very different. The characters were different, too.

Q.: The story "Scream Queen" in this new collection should resonate with any guy who has enjoyed undressed actresses in horror films. Do you remember how this one came about?

A.: I've had incurable cancer for thirteen years. Right now it's in a version of remission. I've spent dozens of hours in chemo rooms and have gotten to know a lot of the feelings of women who have this disease. Not just the dread of death but feelings about how their body will look. I ran across an article about a scream queen who was tired of showing her naked breasts on screen. I took the story from there.

Q.: There is a kind of dismal sickness in many of your characters—the people in "Angie," "Render Unto Caesar," "En Famille." They all have a strong feeling of reality about them—as if you grew up around them. Any comment?

A.: These are my people. I grew up around them and in some respects resemble them. Of course they're exaggerated in fiction but not by all that much. Angie is real; I am the narrator in "Render Unto Caesar" (the old man is real, too); "En Famille" is my family at large filtered through Zola. These are all from the neighborhoods I grew up in. When I was nine the crazy woman two houses away wanted to punish her four-year-old boy. She stuck him in the oven and burned the left side of his face. Her nine-year-old son, my friend, grabbed her and stopped her burning him even more. To this day the younger boy is horribly scarred. Neither boy ever recovered from it.

Q.: Does your sense of the Midwest owe anything to Sherwood Anderson?

A.: I reread Anderson every few years. He nailed the Midwest of his time. So did Sinclair Lewis, though he wasn't the poet Anderson was. By the way, I really recommend the film version of Lewis's *Dodsworth*. Walter Huston is brilliant. One of the finest American films ever made.

Q.: You mention at the end of "The Brasher Girl" that you have been strongly influenced by Stephen King. What other writers have influenced you?

A.: I'm never sure how to answer this because there are so many writers who've influenced me. Here's a list, in the order of when I started reading them: Ray Bradbury, Mickey Spillane, the Gold Medal writers—John D. MacDonald, Richard Prather, Charles Williams, Lionel White, Peter Rabe, Vin Packer—Robert Bloch, Richard Matheson, Harlan Ellison, Graham Greene, F. Scott Fitzgerald, Ernest Hemingway, Ross Macdonald, Ed McBain, Zola. Those would be the basic writers, but many, many more have certainly affected my work.

Q.: Given the popularity of urban horror, readers might be interested in whether some of your novels fit that category. Or are you considering something?

A.: There is some extraordinary work is being done in that field. I would like to do work in that genre someday.

Q.: Your mysteries, westerns and horror tales have all been well-received. Is there anything you've tried to write but can't bring off—a mainstream novel that sits in a drawer? A book of religious revelations?

A.: I'm smiling at your mention of "religious revelations." One of my all-time favorite episodes of *The Simpsons* is when the Rapture comes and everybody is drawn up to heaven *except* Homer. That's enough of revelation for me. As for a mainstream novel . . . back in the '70s Charles Scribner & Sons ran a short story contest (this was the Scribners of Joseph Conrad, Hemingway, Fitzgerald, Thomas Wolfe, not the commercial house of today), and I won one of the slots. An editor called and said there was a novel in my story and why didn't I give it a go. I'd been selling stories to very lowdown literary magazines and even lower-down men's magazines and starting and finishing mystery novels and never getting anywhere. I thought maybe I had a mainstream novel in me after all. I worked on it six months but gave up. I was bored out of my mind. I am a genre writer.

Short story collections from www.PerfectCrimeBooks.com

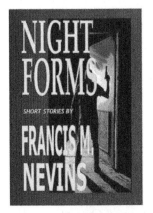

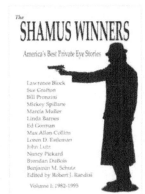

NIGHT FORMS
Francis M. Nevins
378 pages $16.95
ISBN: 978-1-935797-00-5

THE SHAMUS WINNERS
Volumes I & II $14.95 each
Vol I ISBN: 978-0-9825157-4-7
Vol II ISBN: 978-0-9825157-6-1
"Must-have items." James Reasoner

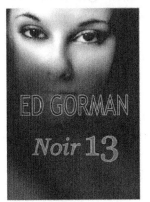

NOIR 13
Ed Gorman
250 pages $14.95
ISBN: 978-0-9825157-5-4
"Strong collection." Publishers Weekly

THE HOLLYWOOD OP
Terence Faherty
246 pages $14.95
ISBN: 978-1-935797-08-1
"Writes this era like he was there."
Crime Spree

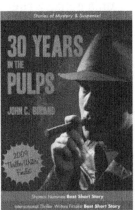

THE GUILT EDGE
Robert J. Randisi
232 pages $13.95
ISBN: 978-0-9825157-3-0
"One of the best." Michael Connelly

30 YEARS IN THE PULPS
John C. Boland
346 pages $14.95
ISBN: 978-0-9825157-2-3
"Style, substance, versatility."
Ellery Queen's

Available in Trade Paperback and Kindle editions.
Visit our website: www.PerfectCrimeBooks.com.

CPSIA information can be obtained at www.ICGtesting.com
Printed in the USA
LVOW03s1515170414

382146LV00007B/291/P